A BILLIONAIRE'S PROMISE

THE CALLOWAYS
BOOK TWO

LAURA RILEY

Copyright © 2024 Laura Williams
All rights reserved.

ISBN: 9798332934520

Cover Artist: Steamy Designs
Photographer: Wander Aguiar
Model: Phillipe Belanger
Editor: RJ Locksley
Formatter: Champagne Book Design

Published by
Laura Williams
www.authorlaurariley.com
Sign up to my newsletter and never miss a release.

No part of this publication may be reproduced, stored in a retrieval system, copied, shared, or transmitted in any form or by any means without the prior written permission of the author. The only exception is brief quotations to be used in book reviews. Please don't steal e-books.

This novel is entirely a work of fiction. All places and locations are used fictitiously. The characters are figments of the author's imagination, and any resemblance to real people is purely a coincidence.

This book is written by an English author, and all spellings are British English.

For Louise Hallett, for being my beta reader all the way through my chapters, and for your amazing feedback.

A BILLIONAIRE'S PROMISE

THE CALLOWAYS
BOOK TWO

ONE

Millie

"Rise and shine, sleepyhead," I say, and open the blinds. Sunlight spills into the room, reflecting from the porcelain-tiled floor.

My roommate Hayley groans. "Tomorrow, I promise." Her words are muffled as she buries her head into the pillow.

I laugh while pulling on my navy hoodie and matching bottoms. "If I had a pound for every time you said that…"

Hayley waves me off in an 'I know, I've heard it all before' gesture.

I secure my hair into a low ponytail and head for the door. I grab the bottle of water I left out last night and squeeze it into my pocket.

"Hey, Mills," Hayley calls after me.

I know what she's going to say. I return to the bay window and twist the cord on the blinds. Her small frame is once again cloaked in darkness, and I'm pretty sure she's snoring by the time I leave our hotel room and head for the beach for my six a.m. run.

From the outside, it's easy to confuse the hotel for a large house, but that is part of its charm. A home away from home is what I like to call it, and it really is. Standing at three storeys high, Stanton and Mills is quintessentially quaint. The exterior of the building is white with cobalt-blue bricks surrounding the lead-paned windows. What makes the hotel extra special is my great-grandfather was one of the construction workers who laid the very first bricks.

I bite down my smile and jog down the concrete steps that lead to the beach. The aroma of salt and sand dunes engulfs me as I jog toward the shoreline. With the sun on my face and the ocean as my never-ending backdrop, I start my morning as I would any other. Except today isn't like any other—today is *the* day I single-handedly run Stanton and Mills Hotel for the first time.

Today is big, bigger than big. It's huge, because I, Mildred Edith Mills, will finally have the opportunity to prove not only to myself, but everyone, including Malcolm, my uncle, that I have what it takes to run the most successful hotel in town. The *only* hotel in town. And once Malcolm sees first-hand that I have what it takes, my hope is that he will finally agree to me buying his share. Yes, this is going to be a good day, I just know it.

I pull my earbuds from my pocket and, after pressing them into my ears, scroll through my playlist on my Apple Watch. The crash of the waves harmonises with the classical song and the cry of seagulls as they soar overhead. Life really doesn't get any better.

I'm starting my run when I notice Mr Porter heading in my direction. He waves with one hand, while the other holds a long retractable lead attached to the collar of George, his golden retriever. Mr Porter owns Sprinkles, the beachfront ice cream shop. The old man never fails to wear his Jolly Roger-embroidered T-shirt and cleverly designed cone-shaped hat. Tufts of fluffy white hair appear beneath the rim. His head literally looks like an upside-down vanilla ice cream cone.

I'm about to step aside for Mr Porter, but he stops

unexpectedly at the water's edge. I pause the song I'm listening to and jog on the spot as he unhooks George's lead.

"How's your father?" he asks, and hurls a tennis ball out to sea. Green felt skims over the turquoise waves before the ball finally comes to rest. Not a moment later, George is bounding in after it.

"You know my dad," I say. "Busy with *Genie*."

Genie is the name of my father's fishing boat. He and my brothers practically live out at sea. *Genie* and another family's boat named *Grimsby* are responsible for catching all the fish we eat here on the island.

Mr Porter rubs his protruding belly. "That's what I like to hear. Audrey and I have family staying with us this weekend, so plan to place a big order."

"Thank you, Mr Porter, my family and I appreciate your support."

"And I appreciate the fine fish your family bring to my table."

After a long night at sea, my father docks the boat at the harbour, and he and my brothers hand-deliver the fish to *Genie's* Catch of the Day: Mum and Dad's fishmongers. It's there my mother prepares the fish and lays them out on the iced display counter ready to be purchased.

Mr Porter doesn't ask any more questions, and instead smiles out of politeness. I take it our conversation is over. I sidestep him just as George bounds back onto the beach. Watery missiles shoot in all directions as he shakes out his coat.

"I hear young Daniel returns on Monday," Mr Porter calls after me.

"That's right," I say and try to keep my tone even. Daniel and I have been best friends since we were at school. For as far back as I remember we were inseparable. We would have been together now if it wasn't for him leaving the island a year ago to attend Birmingham's top catering college. Our dream is that when

I own the hotel, he will run the restaurant and serve Michelin-quality food to the guests.

Mr Porter gives me a knowing smile. "You kids make sure to behave yourselves."

At the age of eighty-five, he refers to everyone below thirty as 'kids'. In another three years I may actually qualify as an adult in his eyes.

Mr Porter returns his attention to George and their game of fetch. I seize this moment to get away and start my morning run.

There are a lot of perks about living in a small town on our own little island. It's like living on our own private slice of heaven. But the downside is that there is no privacy—everyone knows everyone's business, and it's not uncommon to find out something about a family member from the local gossip.

I head north to where the lighthouse stands in the far distance. I run where moments ago the sea caressed the shore. Here the sand is firm, damp, but not wet. I get the occasional spray from the ocean against my ankles and calves, but that doesn't prompt me to change my path—no, it's all part of the magic.

On my way back to the hotel I bump into Mary Adams, the town's librarian, along with Reverend Mortimer. They of course stop me for small talk and ask after my father. My old man really is a big deal to the locals.

It's after eight when I make it back to my hotel room. The blinds are open and natural light spills into the small open-plan living area. To my right is our kitchenette. A few feet away is our wall-mounted TV and our cream two-seater sofa, which is where Hayley is sitting. She is already dressed for work in her black Stanton and Mills tunic and trousers. She catches my gaze and smiles while running the hair straighteners through her brown bob. "Did you enjoy your run?"

"Very much. Did you enjoy your lie-in?" I retort and make a point to lean back and peer through the open door of our shared bedroom.

She pouts. "I'd hardly call seven thirty a lie-in."

I ignore her comment, my attention fixed on her bed. The Egyptian cotton sheets lie in a crumpled mess in the middle of the mattress. "And you call yourself head of housekeeping."

Hayley's cheeks glow red. Like me, she takes great pride in her work, and our shared hotel room is always pristine. "I'll make my bed after I've done my hair. You know how it gets when I don't straighten it right away."

I'll never understand why she doesn't embrace her natural curls. "Okay, I'm going to get showered," I say, untying the arms of my hoodie from around my waist.

"I'll have our breakfast waiting for you when you're done." She lowers her straighteners onto the nest of tables to her right, picks up the hotel phone and presses the number one for reception. She coils the phone lead around her index finger as she awaits an answer.

I don't hang around. I have under an hour to get showered and ready to start my shift, and I cannot be a minute late for the most important day of my life.

After a team briefing with the housekeepers and garden staff, I get to work. I stand behind the desk in the lobby and oversee the running of the hotel while taking new bookings. It feels so nice not having my uncle breathing down my neck checking everything I do.

Tanya is working at reception with me, and while she greets our new arrivals, I take calls and pencil new bookings into the diary. As soon as I put the phone receiver down, it begins ringing again. Normal bookings are a doddle, but our wedding packages take a little more time to sort. Once they're booked in, we have a wedding coordinator at hand to tend to their needs.

"Millie," Tanya says.

I lift my index finger, signalling her to wait. I return my attention to the diary and the customer at the end of the phone. "That date is available. I'll need a ten percent deposit today to secure your booking." I type her details into the card machine, which is especially slow when the phone is in use.

"The payment has gone through," I tell her as a receipt is being fed from the machine. I tear it off and staple it beside her booking in the diary. "Please make sure to pay the remaining balance thirty days before your stay. We look forward to seeing you in December."

I wait for her to cut the call and place the receiver on the desk in front of me to stop anyone else from getting through. I turn around and offer Tanya my full attention. "Yes?"

Tanya Robinson-Parker has been working alongside me for the past eleven years. We went to school together, though she is a few years older than I am. She feels more like a second sister than a work colleague, and I'm sure she feels the same way about me. She fidgets with her long ebony braid, her emerald eyes flashing between me and the handsome stranger who stands at the opposite side of the desk.

My breath catches in my throat as I take him in. His eyes are the first thing that have my attention, a blue so light they're almost grey. His face is a mix of sharp edges, from the set of his jaw to his cheekbones. But it isn't just how he looks that has my attention, it's the confident way that he holds himself.

I clear my throat. "Can I help you?"

He runs his fingers through his hair, which is a mix of brown and sun-kissed blond highlights. I can't help but look to his hand for a wedding band—a guy this good-looking has to be off the market. Apart from a chunky ring on his middle finger, all others are bare.

"I'm Gage Calloway." His voice is deep and demanding. He extends his hand, though my gaze has moved up and is focused on his full lips.

"I'm Gage Calloway," he repeats, his tone more clipped. Light blue eyes that I was getting lost in moments ago narrow.

I nod, because what else am I meant to do? Oh, right, his hand. I slip my hand into his. His grip is firm and purposeful as he shakes.

"I heard you the first time. You're Gage Calloway." I don't see the need to prolong physical contact with this man, so pull my hand from his.

"Yes. Second oldest son of Duncan Calloway…?" His words trail off, as if I should have a light bulb moment and instantly know who his father is. Gage tilts his head as if trying to suss me out. I figure he's waiting for me to fill the silence, so I do just that.

"And I'm Millie Mills, daughter of Edith and Jonathan." I look at Tanya and the phone. Neither one has moved a single inch from the last time I looked. I'm about to ask her to start taking bookings when Gage speaks.

"Your name is Millie Mills?" There's a hint of something in his voice. Humour?

"Are you making fun of me?"

"On the contrary." He presses his lips together, amusement dancing on his face. Amusement that is starting to irritate me. So I decide on a different approach.

I stand tall. "I'm Mildred Edith Mills, acting manager and part shareholder of Stanton and Mills Hotel."

Gage flashes me a devilish grin. "I'm Gage Archer Calloway, owner of Calloway Hotels, and as of last night, I too am part shareholder of Stanton and Mills. It's nice to finally meet you… partner."

TWO

Gage

Forty-five miles from Penzance, Aura Isle is a small island just off the south coast of England, population nine hundred and eighty-nine. I'm pretty sure I can get nine hundred and eighty-eight of those people to like me, but I have a sneaking suspicion the last one may take a little more work.

Millie doesn't say a word, and I smile inwardly, knowing I have her attention. I nod my head toward the glass door leading to the front patio area, where the taxi is parked.

"My case is outside. Have a porter take it up to the penthouse suite." I glance around. The lobby looks like it fell out of the 1960's. Black and white porcelain tiles line the floor and continue up some of the walls, and those walls that don't follow the chessboard theme have been decorated with a dark red paper. Overall, the hotel is clean, spotless in fact, but is in serious need of modernising.

"We don't have a penthouse suite," the receptionist offers, her hand over the mouthpiece of the phone.

I flash a glance at her name tag. Tanya. The first thing I notice about Tanya is her eyes, vibrant and green. Her hair is pinned back in some kind of fancy braid, which falls over the shoulder of her white blouse.

"It's nice to see someone working around here," I say, more to snap Millie out of her trance and prompt her to sort my room. I don't like to be kept waiting, and, sighing, drum my fingers on the mahogany desk. One second, two… three. I pinch the bridge of my nose and close my eyes. This is going to be one hell of a long day.

"We have a honeymoon suite vacant. Room 211," Tanya offers.

Honeymoon suite? I can't help but laugh and picture what the papers back home will say. *Gage Calloway, Cornwall's most prolific bachelor and ladies' man, staying in romantic getaway's finest honeymoon suite!*

"Not in this lifetime," I retort. "What else have you got available?"

I lean forward and try to see the laptop screen behind the reception area. I'm shocked when there isn't a laptop, a desktop, or even a tablet. Instead, there are piles of neatly stacked papers, a shit ton of stationery, and a monster book. The pages barely close due to the wads of Post-it notes poking out and the receipts stapled to every page.

"We have a family room available."

There she goes again, using words I hate. 'Honeymoon' and 'family', my worst nightmares. I don't know why people do it to themselves. I rub my forehead, feeling that this is taking longer than necessary. "I just want a single room."

Tanya spins on her heel, opens a glass-fronted wall cupboard and unhooks a brass key. A large wooden tag hangs off the metal ring with the number 201 displayed. She slides the key in my direction, and I wait a beat before taking it. "No room card?"

"Nope, just good, old-fashioned keys."

'Old-fashioned' is an understatement.

I glance at Millie—Mildred, whatever her name is. She's pleasant to look at, with a full face, shapely lips and a dusting of freckles covering her nose and cheeks. Her mousy brown hair has been secured into a neat bun that along with her subtly applied make-up and black blazer make her look the part of a businesswoman.

I clear my throat to get her attention, but her gaze is fixed. Her dark brown eyes stare past me, and I'm curious to know what she's looking at. She hasn't said one word since I introduced myself as her business partner. Either she is overcome with joy or is in a state of shock. I suspect it's the latter, as her eyes are wide and her mouth opens and shuts like a kipper.

Which reminds me. "I hear your old man's a fisherman."

Finally, her gaze locks on mine. "This is a joke."

I let out a throaty laugh. "You'll have to take it up with Mr Porter. He told me your old man works out at sea."

She shakes her head exasperatedly. "How do you know Mr Porter?"

"I took a quick tour of the island this morning and introduced myself to the locals. I must say, Mr Porter's salted caramel ice cream is the best I've tasted."

Millie waves my last comment off. "Introduced yourself as what?"

"The co-owner of this place, of course."

"This is a misunderstanding, it has to be. You see, my uncle—"

"Yes, I did see your uncle," I interrupt. "Last night in London, in fact. He joined me and my brothers for a few games of poker. He thought he was onto a winner and bet his share of the hotel on a hand of cards."

"I don't believe you," she spits out and turns her attention to Tanya. "Can you hold the fort until I return?"

Tanya nods. "Of course."

Millie makes her way around the reception desk, and when she stops in front of me, I ask, "Where are you going?"

She laughs, but it isn't with humour. "We are going to my room." She grips my arm, her fingers lacing around the stark white cotton of my shirt. Without a word she attempts to… what? Move me away from the desk? I find the very idea funny as hell, because I'm going nowhere.

I pull my arm from her hold. "I'm more of a second-date kind of guy, but thanks for the offer."

Her cheeks glow red. "I wasn't propositioning you."

I look from her to Tanya. "It kinda sounded like you were."

Tanya nods in agreement, then, as if thinking better of it, quickly shakes her head.

"My phone is in my room. I want to speak to my uncle and call you out on your bullsh—" Millie stops herself from carrying on.

"Shit?" I offer. "You can swear. It won't offend me, or affect our working relationship."

Millie's nostrils flare. "Will you just come with me to my room?"

I take a step back and lift my hands. "Please, stop begging, it's embarrassing."

The phone rings, and guests begin to queue at the reception desk.

"How about you go speak to your uncle while I stay with Tanya? It looks as though she could do with the help." I offer a small smile and, unfastening the buttons at my wrists, I roll up the sleeves of my shirt.

I can see the anger simmering in Millie's stare. Her breaths are slow and controlled as she smiles through gritted teeth. "I'll be right back."

"Miss you already." That comment earns me a death stare, and, biting down a smile, I make my way behind the reception desk.

An hour passes, and in that time I sign people in and hand out keys. Tanya on the other hand has been answering the phone. I watch her take bookings in that pitiful excuse for a diary and decide the first thing I'm going to do is buy the reception staff a laptop.

One hour becomes two, and my calves are beginning to ache. I'm not used to standing in one place for long periods of time. I'm usually sitting at my desk busy with conference calls or visiting my many hotels. I'm relieved when Millie appears at the bottom of the stairs.

"I'll be seeing you, Tanya," I say and make my way around reception. Millie meets me halfway in the lobby, and we stop inches apart. She doesn't look as confident or as put together as she did earlier. Her cheeks are flushed and her eyes bloodshot.

"Are you okay?" I ask out of genuine concern. "Have you spoken to your uncle?"

"I have," Millie confirms.

"And…?" I prompt.

"He said he's staying in London for the foreseeable."

I nod. "I can't say I blame him, it's not as though he needs to hurry back."

If Millie is annoyed by my comment, she's doing well to hide it. "Have lunch with me?" she asks, though her question isn't a question, it's more of a command.

"First you ask me to your room, and now lunch. My, my, Mildred Edith Mills, aren't you the dark horse. I'm curious though, is this our first date?"

She shoots me a death stare, and without another word heads towards a set of double doors, which lead to the in-house restaurant.

Like the lobby, the restaurant is dated. Dark red carpet, matching wallpaper. The only redeeming feature is the large floor-to-ceiling glass windows that offer an uninterrupted view of the ocean. With that as a view, it's easy to overlook the godawful décor.

Waiting staff mill around, but they're really not needed seeing as lunch has been laid out buffet-style and drinks are available on tap for guests to refill.

Millie heads for a corner table. I follow, and we sit. The chairs are clunky, and yet the table wobbles when I place my elbows down.

I open my mouth to speak when Millie leans in. "Gage Calloway, son of Duncan, brother of Malachi, Lucian and Farrah. Your net worth is somewhere in the billions. You own hotels in nearly every English town. You have it all."

"You've been busy googling me," I say.

"Yes, the internet is full of information. And I want to know exactly who I'm dealing with. You run hotels, this is a hotel, I get it. But tell me, Mr Big Shot, what is someone like you doing wasting your time on a place like this?"

I lean forward, so close that our elbows touch. She surprises me when she doesn't back away.

"Call it a passion project," I say, and, leaning back into the chair, fold my arms.

"A… passion… project?" Millie says, waiting long seconds between each word.

"Yes. I've been given the Calloway hotel chain by my father, a business that is thriving. All I need to do is make sure everything continues ticking over, but this place"—I motion with my hands—"this is a project I can really sink my teeth into."

"Project?"

"Right. I'm in two minds as what to do. To improve the place will take a lot of work. I have a group of builders back home who would gladly help, from decorating to structural. I would also kit the place out with top-of-the-range technology. We also need to look at employees." I motion to the waiting staff. "Other than looking pretty, the waitresses aren't doing anything. There are no porters in the lobby when needed, so rather than fire people, we could simply reallocate them within the company."

Millie quirks a brow. "Company?"

"Yes. When the hotel is up to scratch, we will rebrand it as a Calloway hotel. The name alone will bring a lot more clientele through the door. The hotel will need more rooms. We could extend or knock the place down and start again. There's nothing like starting with a blank canvas…"

"Knock the place down?" Millie can't hide the horror in her tone. But I'm here to reassure her this is all in the name of business.

"The island is stunning. Mildred, you are sitting on a potential gold mine. I had a look through the booking diary and I forecast your yearly profit to be around fifty thousand. How would you feel if I added another zero to your yearly takings? Fuck it, I like to be ambitious. What about two zeros?"

Millie is doing that thing again of opening and closing her mouth while staring into space. I watch her for long seconds and realise she isn't trying to impersonate a fish, but instead is counting to herself.

"I'll be back." I get to my feet and head for the buffet. Plates, serviettes, and cutlery are laid out on a table. I grab two plates and two serviettes and join the queue.

There are three buffet displays, the first heavily featuring fish, the second a range of sandwiches and salads, the third a mix of fruits, jellies and desserts. In true buffet style, I load my plate with a bit of everything and do the same with Millie's. When our plates are full, I return to our table, then head back to grab our cutlery and drinks. I'm disappointed there are only soft drinks on tap, and in passing I ask one of the waitresses to bring over a bottle of Jack.

Millie's gaze is on me, and it appears she has finally stopped counting.

"Tuck in," I say, and motion to her knife and fork. I see this lunch as a kind of peace offering. The last thing I want is for us to get off on the wrong foot.

Millie reaches for the plate of food and takes a ham sandwich. She holds it to her lips and then pauses.

"I'll buy you out," she says, and takes a small bite.

"You couldn't afford to, and even if you could, the answer is no." I pop a sushi roll into my mouth. The flavours of the raw fish explode onto my tongue. As ugly as the hotel is, there is no denying the quality of the food is above and beyond.

"This is amazing. My compliments to the chef," I say and pop another roll into my mouth.

"That fish is five hours old and straight off my father's fishing boat this morning." Pure pride shines in Millie's stare.

"I'd love to meet him," I say, picturing me shaking his hand, if not for anything else but this amazing food.

"Yeah, that's not going to happen. I think you're confused as to what this is." Millie points between us and then gets to her feet. "Lunch wasn't for us to get to know each other. It was my chance to find out what you want, and now I know it'll be easier to get rid of you."

I laugh. "Get rid of me? Darling, I'm going nowhere."

She places her hands either side of her plate and leans forward. "You see, that's where you're wrong. I've lived on this island all my life, and I know there is absolutely no way the locals are going to accept some high-flying big shot coming here and changing everything."

I take a gulp of my drink. "What are you going to do, have them run me off the island with their pitchforks?"

"Exactly. So I wouldn't get too comfortable in Room 201, because you won't be staying."

"Is that right?" I challenge.

"It is."

I take the napkin and place it over my plate. "Let the games begin."

THREE

Millie

"What am I going to do?" I say, and sink down onto the double bed.

Hayley lowers her bottle of cleaning spray onto the bedside table and joins me. "Do you want my honest opinion?"

I glower at Hayley. "If you're going to side with Gage, then no."

Hayley sighs. "I agree he shouldn't walk in and take over. But seriously, Mills, the place is in desperate need of a makeover."

"I know," I mumble, and tug on a loose piece of thread on the duvet.

"So why don't you sit down with Gage and have a proper conversation?"

"We did that already."

Hayley places her hand over mine. "No. He did all the

talking. You need to tell him what you want and see what you can agree on."

"What I want? What I want is for Gage Calloway to get on the ferry, return to London and forget he ever set foot on this island. Then I can get back to my life and forget he ever existed."

Hayley shakes her head and grabs her bottle of cleaning spray. "I have to get back to work."

I place my elbows on my thighs and rest my chin in my hands. "I need to figure out how to make him leave…" I let my words trail off.

"Why not work with him rather than against him?"

I narrow my eyes. "Work with someone who wants to knock the hotel down? Hayley, whose side are you on?"

Hayley's expression hardens. "I don't know why you wanted to speak to me. If you want someone to agree with everything you say, you need to speak to one of the less senior members of staff."

"Hayley…"

"No, Millie." Hayley gets to her feet. "I have worked here six days a week for the past fifteen years. For the past two years I've been asking for new vacuums. Oh, and let's not forget about the bed linen."

"There's nothing wrong with the bed linen," I insist, and hurry after Hayley, who is seconds away from leaving the room. "And last time I checked, the vacuums work just fine, and as my uncle always said, if it isn't broke, don't fix it."

Hayley freezes inches from the door, her fingers wrapped around the handle. She turns just enough to make eye contact with me. "The same uncle who'd glue torn sections of wallpaper back down and hide worn carpet with plant pots? Don't tell me you're turning into him."

"That's not fair," I say, but deep down know she's right. I hated how my uncle ran the hotel, but I said nothing. It was a means to an end if it meant one day he'd sell me his share, and then I'd revamp the place and run Stanton and Mills my way.

Hayley crosses her arms over her chest. "You wanted my opinion, Millie? My opinion is you need to speak to Gage."

The door opens and clicks shut, leaving me alone with my thoughts. Hayley is wrong about Gage. There is no point speaking to him because my mind is made up. But she's right about one thing. I lift off the bed just enough to pull my phone from my trouser pocket.

All those years of saving to buy my uncle out have been for nothing. One good thing that has come out of this is all the free cash I have in my bank account, cash I intend on spending.

The sound of my alarm does nothing to motivate me the following morning. Two snoozes later, I am up and blindly pulling on my hoodie and joggers. Like my mood, the room is dark, and I can't be bothered to wake Hayley to try to persuade her to join me for an early morning run.

I will feel happier when I get to the beach, I tell myself. Because there is truly no better sight to wake up to.

Once outside the hotel I jog down the concrete steps. Instinct has me reaching into my pocket for my bottle of water.

"Damn it," I curse under my breath. My pocket is flat and empty, because that's right, I didn't leave a bottle of water out last night. Last night I made a point of working late, mainly to keep tabs on Gage. If he wasn't in his room, I wanted to know where he was and whom he was talking to. But apart from him passing reception after our lunch, I didn't see him again all day.

Trying to shake the thought of that awful man out of my mind, I glance out at the horizon. The sky is beautiful, a mix of light pinks with powder blue. The sea is on its way in today, creeping its way up the shore. Given the time, I won't be able to run as far as I normally do, but that doesn't matter. To have the breeze blowing through my hair is cathartic. Listening to the waves, the seagulls, and my classical playlist is all I need to start my day with a positive mindset. Despite having a cocky know-it-all billionaire trying to worm his way into my business.

I take to a light jog and select the playlist on my Apple Watch. Sunlight reflects off the screen, which is blank, because obviously I forgot to charge it last night. Tears are starting to well in my eyes. What else is going to go wrong? I was looking forward to this weekend for so many reasons. It was finally my time to shine, and Daniel is coming home Monday. Everything was supposed to be perfect, and instead everything has gone from bad to worse.

Blinking away my tears, I pick up my pace, because I will not let Gage Calloway beat me.

Time and reality slip away as I continue down the beach. The burn of lactic acid in my calves only spurs me to run faster and run harder. Beachfront shops with their awnings merge into a rainbow of colour, and people pass by in a flash. I can't do small talk, not today, so try my best not to acknowledge anyone. My focus is trained on the lighthouse that stands proud in the distance, a small dot that gets a little bigger the further I run.

Daniel would join me every morning. We'd each have an earbud in and listen to the same song. It was magical, because for that precious hour nothing else existed, nothing else mattered. It was just us and the ocean. We always said one day we'd play hooky from work and while away the hours at the lighthouse. We were going to have a picnic, sunbathe, and swim in the sea. But that day never came, because like me, Daniel is a workaholic, and hooky was just not an option for either of us. But with him in Birmingham, and me miles away living on the Aura Isle, my priorities have shifted. When he returns, I will make our dream a reality, and we will make it to the lighthouse.

"Millie!"

I slow to a jog. Mr Porter is walking George. My smile instantly drops when I see Gage walking alongside them. Dressed in a pair of black jogging bottoms and a grey T-shirt, Gage appears to also be out for a morning run. His hair is darker and his forehead glistens. The grey material of his T-shirt has faded damp patches, a telltale sign that he has finished his workout and is on his way back to the hotel. I can't help noticing how the thin cotton strains against his chest and biceps, displaying the prominent muscles beneath.

Mr Porter smiles wide. "Gage was just talking about you."

"Oh, I'm sure he had lots to say." I side-eye Gage, who looks like a big kid holding a large ice cream cone in his hand.

"He did." Mr Porter pats George on the head. "Come on, boy, it's getting late. Our ice creams won't sell themselves."

Late? "What time is it?"

Gage glances down at his watch. "It's twenty to nine."

Panic hits me in a wave and, trying to blot everything out, I take long and controlled breaths. I'm in a calm place when a hand flashes in front of my face.

"Are you counting to ten so you don't punch me?" Gage laughs. "You can if it'll make you feel better."

"Don't tempt me," I bite out, and stuff my balled fists into my pockets. I spin on my heel and jog toward the hotel, which is further away than I expected.

"You may want to pick up the pace if you plan on making it to work on time," Gage says, jogging in step along side me.

I pass him an incredulous stare. "You shouldn't run and eat at the same time. You'll get a stitch."

Gage takes a long and slow lick of his ice cream. As infuriating as he is, I can't help but smile. Gage smiles back. *Crap.*

I shake my head and frown at the ice cream cone. "How old are you, twelve?"

"I'm thirty-six." He winks, and I can feel my ears pinking. "If you want to know my age, you only have to ask."

I pick up my pace. "I don't. I don't want to know anything about you."

"That's a pity, because I want to know everything there is to know about you." Gage matches my pace with ease. "But there's no rush. And anyway, I have a ton of work to be getting on with today, so will spend much of it in my room."

I breathe a little easier knowing that Gage won't be around. And as the saying goes, out of sight, out of mind.

"I'll find out everything I need to know about you when we have dinner with your parents later."

I gasp, almost tripping over. "What?"

Gage picks up his pace and runs ahead. As fast as I run, I can't keep up, not even close. "See you at seven!" are the words I'm left with as he speeds off.

It's exactly nine when I make it back to the hotel. Tanya is checking an elderly couple in when I arrive. She catches my gaze and smiles.

"I'll be as quick as I can," I pant and hurry past.

I'm about to run up the stairs when Rex Mitchell enters. Standing at almost seven foot tall and dressed in his red postman uniform, he's kind of hard to miss.

"Ah, Millie." He waves, a stack of envelopes sandwiched between his fingers.

"Rex." I close the space between us and take the envelopes. I'm about to take them to Tanya when Rex calls after me.

"You have a delivery too. A big one by the looks of it."

Excitement bubbles in my stomach. I know immediately what has come.

"I just need you to sign," Rex says, and holds out his phone for a digital signature.

I sign just as Mervin and Cooper—also wearing their red

postman uniforms—carry in large boxes stacked one on top of another. I jump and clap my hands together.

"Put them over there." I signal to the corner of the lobby.

I waste no time pulling my key from my pocket and ripping open the tape. I tear open the first cardboard flap, expecting to see bed linen and top-of-the-range vacuum cleaners inside, but freeze at what I uncover.

FOUR

Gage

The knocking pulls my attention from the laptop screen and conference call.

"I didn't order room service," I call, hoping that'll be the end of it, but the knocking only gets louder.

"Can you just open the door?"

Hearing Millie's voice, I sigh and return my attention to the laptop. Simon and Gregory Lancaster are the heads of my marketing team. I have spoken with them in depth about the island hotel, and they have a lot of ideas.

"Keep up the good work," I say. "We'll touch base again tomorrow."

They nod and exit the call. The knocking continues, and, groaning, I slide off the bed and loosen my silk tie from around my neck. I make my way across the room and open the door. "Mildred, hi, what a pleasant surprise."

But there is nothing pleasant about her being here. She

doesn't greet me, and instead charges past, a cardboard box wedged under her arm.

"I'm great, thanks for asking, how are you?" I say to the empty hallway and close the door, shutting us both inside.

"What's this?" she asks accusingly, placing the box on the edge of the bed.

Surely this is a trick question? I take a few steps forward and peer inside. Poking out under a mass of packaging is a box. "It's a laptop," I say dryly.

Millie scoops out a handful of polystyrene foam and tosses it at me. "I know what it is. What I want to know is why a laptop and half a dozen tablets have arrived today."

I pluck a piece of polystyrene out of my hair. "A hotel can't run without technology."

"We've managed just fine up until now." She folds her arms in front of her chest. "No. I won't allow it."

"Is that so?" I can't help but laugh. "Tell me, because I'm curious. How do you intend on stopping me?"

She opens her mouth to speak when I place my index finger over her lips.

"I'm sure our staff will thank me. I've made everyone's life a hell of a lot easier." I let my words sink in before carrying on. "How about a vote? If the staff are in favour of staying in the nineteen sixties, then I will return it all."

Millie steps back, and my finger loses claim on her lips. "Did you know I ordered new vacuums and bed linen last night? I couldn't wait to show Hayley. They arrived this morning as well, but…" Her words trail off.

"But what?" I say and make a point of looking at my watch.

"How can I compete?" Her gaze meets mine, and I shrug.

"You can't, so stop trying. Work with me, rather than against me, and life will be a lot easier. The sooner you do, the sooner I'll leave."

Silence.

"Will that be all?"

"Why can't you just go back to London?" she mutters.

I adjust my tie. "I could, but I'm in the mood for a change of scenery."

She throws her arms in the air. "My God, you're so annoying."

"Well, aren't we a pair?"

We're at loggerheads. She will not back down, and neither will I. I can't help wonder if this is how things are going to be with Millie and me from here on out. Is she going to remain a goddamn thorn in my side?

She breathes deeply, as though composing herself. "You'll have to set up the laptops and the tablets and show us how to use them."

"Us?" I keep my expression neutral, but can't help feeling a sense of victory. "My, how fickle you are."

Millie glowers at me. "I can't use the diary if Tanya is using the laptop. There'll be too many double bookings. Aside from that, I figure the sooner you get what you want, the sooner you'll leave."

I nod. Despite how much I'm enjoying getting under Millie's skin, there's a lot of work waiting back home for me. The sooner she implements my changes the sooner I can leave. Win-win for everyone.

I have an important conference call in the next five minutes. "I'm busy for the next hour, but I will be down shortly."

Millie flashes a glance at my laptop on the duvet and the half-empty bottle of Jack that lies alongside it. "Do you always drink when you work?"

"Actually, no. I like to have a bottle at hand ready for when I finish. Jack Daniels and I go way back. We happen to be good friends." That comment earns me an eye roll, but I couldn't care less. I nod toward the door. "Now, if you don't mind…"

"Is this right, Mr Calloway?" Nadia asks, her voice unnaturally high. I don't think it's a coincidence that her breasts are pressing into my arm as she leans into me to get a better view of the tablet.

Since ending my conference calls, I've spent much of the afternoon in a small room behind reception training staff members on the new equipment. The apps I've installed aren't technical, and yet some people have seemed to grasp them quicker than others.

"Not quite," I say, and click off the housekeeping app.

Nadia bats her lashes at me as she gazes up. "Maybe I need some extra support."

My gaze bypasses her doe eyes and travels down to her cleavage. The top two buttons of her blouse are open, giving me the perfect view of her pink lacy bra beneath. Nadia is definitely the type of girl I'd take to bed. She has long blonde hair, big blue eyes, and a great figure. She reminds me a lot of my sister-in-law Chelsea and her sister Amber—both stunning, and unfortunately both spoken for.

"That can be arranged," I say, and subtly adjust the waistband of my trousers.

"Tonight?" Nadia suggests.

Before I have a chance to answer, Nadia hooks her index finger around the collar of her blouse and, working her finger down to her cleavage, slowly refastens the buttons. "My break's over." She takes the tablet from out of my hold, and, clicking on the app, signs into the staff portal. She signs herself in and selects room ninety-five.

She looks up at me innocently. "What can I say? In the right hands, I'm a very fast learner. So I guess we'll have to find something else to do with our time this evening."

I cock a brow. "I'm sorry to disappoint you, but I've already made plans."

"Which you're going to cancel." Nadia turns on her heel, my gaze following her tight little ass every step of the way until she's out of the door.

As she leaves, Millie enters, and all indecent thoughts disappear from my mind.

I smile. Millie doesn't. She is so damn hard to read. Unlike other women I've met, Millie is completely unaffected by my presence. Her skirt isn't hiked up, nor are the buttons of her blouse open, which oddly makes me wonder what lies beneath. *What are you hiding beneath all that fabric, Mildred Mills?*

She clears her throat. "When you've finished looking at my breasts"—my eyes snap up—"you have fifteen minutes to show me how to use the booking software on the laptop."

She enters the room, and, closing the door behind her, makes her way to the laptop on the desk beside me. There are no niceties; she doesn't say 'excuse me' so she can take the swivel chair. Instead, she pulls it from beneath the desk, resulting in the hard back crashing into my groin. I'd be lying if I said I didn't see stars.

"Jesus fucking Christ," I holler, and, folding in on myself, grab my throbbing cock.

Without a backward glance Millie takes a seat. I don't hear an apology, not one 'are you okay'. Just uninterrupted silence with the sporadic tapping of her fingers on the keyboard.

When the throbbing has subsided, I stand straight. Millie's fingers glide over the keyboard with ease, and to my surprise, she has completed several practice bookings.

She meets my gaze and smiles. "What can I say? In the right hands, I'm a fast learner."

I don't miss how she used the exact words Nadia did and can't help wonder how much of our conversation she overheard. Millie hits the enter key and kicks off the floor. The wheels spin and the swivel chair jolts back, but I'm ready for her this time. I grab the back, spin the chair around so that she's facing me and hold her still.

"I don't get you, Mildred Mills," I admit.

"There's nothing to get," she says, while slowly getting to her feet. I don't back away as she gets up. We stand toe to toe and nose to nose as I lean down to match her height. There is so much tension between us, tension I can't place. She hates me for absolutely no reason, and deep down I love it.

Millie leans in, so close that her cheek brushes against my cheek and her warm breath beats against my ear. "I really appreciate you taking time out of your busy evening to give Nadia some one-on-one attention." For the first time I get emotion from her. Sarcasm.

I back up a little so our faces are only inches apart. I look from her eyes to her full lips and back. "I told Nadia that I have plans."

"Which no doubt you'll cancel. It's just a pity your evening is fully booked. Guess you won't have time to have dinner with my parents."

That's where she's wrong.

"Now, if you don't mind," she continues, "my break is over and you're standing in my way."

I could move back and let her pass, but I'm enjoying our exchange way too much. "Quite the predicament you're in."

Her expression remains stoic. "Move."

She attempts to shoulder past, but I block her. Her eyes narrow as she looks up. "I said move."

"You forgot to say please," I tease.

Her teeth clench together. "Please."

"I'm sure you can do better than that. I mean, for fuck's sake, you're working front of house. The last thing guests want to see is your sour expression. Now, why don't you try that again? But this time, say it like you mean it. You could even smile."

Millie rolls her eyes, and then with the fakest smile I've ever seen she says, "Please."

I can't stop the eruption of laughter. This girl, this woman is too much.

I jump as two hands shove me. They catch me off guard and I stumble back just enough for Millie to slip away. She's almost out of the door when I call after her. "Don't worry, I'll rearrange Nadia's training for another evening."

Millie snorts. "I'm sure her 'training'"—she air-quotes—"is very important and can't be missed."

"Very important," I agree. "But it can wait. I'll meet you in the lobby at six thirty and we'll walk to your parents' house together."

She lets out a harsh breath. "Great. Can't wait."

I rub my palms together. *Neither can I.*

FIVE

Millie

After a long day at work, I jump into the shower. I spend long minutes under the spray. I should get dry, get dressed, and get ready, but try as I might, I can't will myself to move.

The bathroom door opens. A cloud of steam escapes into the lounge as Hayley steps onto the tiled floor. "Hon, you've been ages. Either you get out, or I'm coming in," she says, and whips off her robe.

Sighing, I step out of the shower and grab the towel that I draped over the basin. I head to our shared bedroom and slip into my robe, then lay out a pair of jeans and a pale blue T-shirt and matching cardigan for dinner this evening.

The TV is already playing when I enter the lounge. Hayley has left our favourite Netflix series on, and I watch the rest of the episode while drying my hair. No sooner have I put the dryer down than Hayley picks it up and begins blasting her short bob. She tries but fails to brush out her natural spirals, though they begin losing shape and definition with every stroke of the brush and soon her hair resembles a large ball of frizz.

"Straighteners, Millie." She points.

I reach to the nest of tables to my right and pass them to her. It's unusual that we are both doing our hair at this time of the day. Come to think about it, Hayley never showers after work unless she is going out. I study my friend. "What's his name?"

"What?" Hayley asks, all doe-eyed and innocent.

"You know what," I say, and playfully nudge her.

"I'd rather not say yet." Hayley's cheeks are beet red as she runs the straighteners through her hair. "You know what the locals are like for gossiping."

"Only too well." It wasn't so long ago that rumours spread about me and Daniel. Everyone was convinced we were an item, even my own parents. With a higher percentage of the elderly and retired living on the island, weddings are kind of a big deal here. As soon as a local girl has a ring on her finger, she'll be asked constantly whether she is pregnant. There is an island promise that when the population reaches a thousand we'll throw a beach party, but with more deaths than births, I don't see that happening any time soon.

Hayley's hair crackles as she runs the straighteners through the back, which is obviously still damp. "I've been seeing him for a while, but tonight is our first official date," she admits.

I clap my hands together. "I'm so excited for you. Tell me, does he work at the hotel? Or does he work at one of the beachfront shops? Please tell me he isn't a guest." Staff hooking up with guests happens a lot, despite being against hotel policy.

"No, he isn't a guest."

I breathe a sigh of relief because I didn't want to have to give Hayley a verbal warning. "When did he ask you out?"

Hayley's lips twitch in a way that tells me she's trying not to smile.

"What is it?" I ask.

Hayley unplugs the straighteners and places them back on the nest of tables to cool. "Just that…" Her words trail off.

"What?" I ask again, though I'm unable to stop myself from smiling.

We get to our feet at the same time, and Hayley tucks a wayward strand of hair behind her ear. "Just that in that second you reminded me of Mary Adams."

Oh, my God, she's right. My smile drops immediately. Mary Adams is the town's biggest gossip, or 'hen', as we like to call her. As the town's only librarian, she lives as a spinster and has dedicated her life to butting her beak into everyone else's business.

"Millie, I'm sorry. I didn't mean…" Hayley squeezes my arm in a friendly gesture.

"It's fine," I say. "It's none of my business. You have fun tonight."

"And you," Hayley says with a wink. "I want to know everything that happens with Gage when you get home later."

I stay rooted to the spot as Hayley hurries past me and into the bedroom to change. It dawns on me that as unconscious as it may be, we both have a little bit of Mary Adams in us. Every day living here is the same. Nothing ever changes, so when it does, curiosity naturally takes over. I wonder, in years to come when Hayley and I become the next generation, will we be known as the island gossips, the local hens?

God, I hope not.

We leave our hotel room at the same time. Hayley looks beautiful, wearing a skin-tight Hawaiian-themed dress. Her make-up is flawless and her hair so silky smooth that it shines. She is dressed to impress, whereas me? I'm dressed for a typical evening with my parents. I haven't bothered with make-up, except for a dollop of bronzer Hayley pressed onto my cheeks. My hair is styled in the usual way, which is scraped off my face and secured into a bun. Unlike Hayley, I have no one to impress.

We make our way down the stairs to the hotel lobby. I'm not

surprised to see Gage standing at the bottom of the stairs. His hand is on the banister and he is facing away from us. He is wearing a stark white shirt and dark jeans. The combo of smart casual seems to be Gage's signature look. My heartbeat picks up pace the closer we get, and not because of Gage—no, because I'm nervous as hell about how this evening at my parents' is going to go.

I'm a few steps from the bottom when, as if on instinct, Gage turns. My heart slams into my chest as I take him in.

His hair has been sleeked back, his skin a little darker, seemingly from his morning run. But what has my attention are his eyes. Those damn eyes are on me and me alone. He looks… my God, he looks nice.

He holds out his hand for me to take. Of course, me being me, I trip over my own feet, and instead of gracefully accepting his hand, I fall straight into him.

Smooth, Millie, real smooth.

My face slams into his solid chest and my fingers fist his silk tie. He smells so good, so masculine. As I look up, Gage looks down. I have to remind myself that this is Gage Calloway, the same man who owns half of my hotel. He may be good-looking—though good-looking is an understatement tonight—but he is a snake through and through.

"I'll be seeing you later," Hayley says. I turn just in time to see her pass the reception desk and leave through the lobby door.

I glance back up at Gage, fully aware that we have been standing far too close for far too long. His hands are clasped around the small of my back, where they must have rested in his attempt to steady my fall. Alarm bells are ringing in my head, and yet I can't get myself to move.

Gage leans in, and for a second, I'm curious about what he's going to say. "We could always continue this in my room, if you'd prefer."

I let out a bitter laugh. "I don't even like you."

"You may tell yourself that, but your body disagrees. And

anyway, two people don't need to like each other to indulge in each other's company. Emotions are overrated."

The thought has me pushing off Gage and putting as much space between him and me as possible. I make a point of walking ahead, and pass the reception on my way to leave.

Monica and Nadia are standing behind the desk. Monica is covering the evening shift, and Nadia? I have no idea what she is doing here seeing as her shift finished an hour ago. I doubt she's doing overtime. More like she's waiting to catch sight of a certain billionaire.

I don't wait for Gage, instead walk as fast as I can in hopes of losing him. I'm halfway out of the door when I catch his reflection in the glass panel. He's looking at Nadia. I can't make out the expression on her face, but am able to make out her stance, which is rigid, her hand on her hip. I figure she saw the moment we shared when I tripped and landed on him. If I didn't know better, I'd say she was jealous, though she really needn't be. There is no way in this lifetime I would give Gage the time of day.

I stop just in time to see Gage shrug. "What can I say? Women literally fall at my feet."

I cringe and exit the hotel. The evening breeze is cool, cool enough that I'm considering heading back to my room to grab my lightweight coat. But going back into the hotel would mean more time, and dragging out an evening that I want over as quickly as possible.

I head down the concrete steps and onto the beach. I don't turn, but know Gage is following close behind. The breeze is cooler as I make my way to where the sea laps the shore, and within a few steps I am hugging my chest to stay warm. I jump when an arm wraps around my shoulders and I'm pulled into Gage's body.

"No, thank you," I say, and duck out of his hold. I begin shivering.

"Stop being so damn stubborn, woman." Again, his arm

snakes around me and he pulls me close to him. His body is warm, and, pressed against his chest, I stop shaking.

I glance out at sea and catch sight of our reflection. To someone who didn't know, we would look like love's young dream, but that is far from the truth. I hate Gage Calloway, hotel owner and billionaire. But walking together along the beach he is just Gage, and I guess that 'just Gage' is tolerable.

"I'd offer you my jacket if I had one," he says, walking alongside me, our steps in sync. We walk like us spending time together is perfectly normal when it isn't. Far from it.

"Okay, thanks, but that's enough." I pull out of his hold for a second time. This time he lets me go.

What am I doing with Gage? Why am I entertaining this idea of him meeting my parents? I should have cancelled, except when I tried my mother wouldn't hear another word. It seems Mr Calloway, the hotshot billionaire, has become something of a celebrity on the island.

Gage bends down, plucks a pebble from the sand and attempts to skim it out to sea.

"Oh, my God, that was awful," I say, and stop walking.

Gage folds his arms in front of his chest. "Oh, yeah? Then show me how it's done."

I find the perfect pebble and pick it up. "The trick is, you have to find one that is completely flat." I show him the stone, and, flicking my wrist, skim it out to sea. It bounces three times before being taken by the waves.

The corner of Gage's mouth quirks up as though I've set him a challenge. A challenge he has accepted. We stand on the water's edge, skimming pebbles out to sea. Try as he might, Gage just can't do it.

"It's all in the wrist action," I say, and again manage three bounces with my pebble.

"Is that right?" Gage cocks a brow.

I shake my head and dust off my hands, which are coated

in a layer of sand. I decide it's best we leave pebble throwing for now and get this evening out of the way.

"Did I say something wrong?" Gage asks, and appears to my right.

"It's just, why have you got such a dirty mind?"

"Dirty mind? Do you care to elaborate?"

"Everything has a sexual reference with you."

Gage side-eyes me. "I made no reference to anything being sexual. Perhaps, Mildred Edith Mills, you're the one with the dirty mind."

I can feel my ears pinking. "It wasn't what you said, it was…" I stop speaking, for once not knowing what to say. But there is one thing I wanted to ask Gage, and figure now is as good a time as any.

I pull a folded piece of paper from the back pocket of my jeans. "Here," I say, and hold out my hand for Gage to take. He doesn't, and instead leaves me hanging, my arm hovering in the air.

"It's a cheque." I make a final attempt to hand it to him.

"Yes, I see that." Gage turns his attention to the sea and the crashing waves.

"I'll give you all of my life savings in exchange for your share of the hotel."

The breeze picks up random strands of his hair, which he rakes back into place with his fingers.

"Will you at least look at the amount?" I can hear the plea in my voice, and still he won't look at me or acknowledge the money I'm offering. "Gage." I reach for his arm, his biceps solid and tense.

"Sorry, no," Gage says. "I refuse to get your hopes up." I release his arm as he stuffs his hands into the pockets of his jeans. "I told you before, I'm not interested. I have more money than I know what to do with. Why would I want more?"

My shoulders slump, and I nod in a kind of acceptance that this is my life.

"I have so many ideas for the island hotel. I plan to have all the rooms decorated before the rebrand. My marketing team are working on the launch as we speak."

"No freaking way," I spit out. There is no way he is turning Stanton and Mills into some fancy-nancy magazine-looking hotel. "This is my hotel. If anyone is going to redecorate, it's going to be me."

"Correction, Stanton and Mills is *our* hotel." Gage's expression sobers. "Tell me, Mildred, where are you going to find the funds to redecorate if you buy me out?"

I open my mouth, but what can I say in reply? Nothing, that's what. I'm so angry I feel like I'm going to explode, whereas Gage looks so relaxed and put together.

"I'm genuinely confused, Mildred. Don't you want to improve the hotel?"

He's missing the point completely. "You just don't get it, do you? You don't get what Stanton and Mills is all about." Gage opens his mouth, but I don't give him a second to answer. "Stanton and Mills is a home away from home. Not some high-flying, high-faluting show home!" I pant, my words taking a lot out of me.

Gage waits patiently for my breathing to return to normal. Then he looks skyward. "I don't have time for this."

I bite back a smile. Does this mean he's finally leaving?

He rubs the back of his neck. "You're going to make any changes to Stanton and Mills difficult, aren't you?"

I lift my chin. "I surely am."

He looks at me for long seconds, like I'm a puzzle he just can't figure out. "Come to London with me."

"What?" My brows shoot up, his words catching me off guard. "Why would I want to go anywhere with you? How about you go and I'll stay here?"

Gage wraps an arm around my waist, my body flush with his as his hand rests over my left ass cheek. I should push him away, hit him, yell at him, but instead I'm standing poker straight and saying nothing. It takes me a second to realise what he's doing, and it isn't grabbing a feel. His hand slips from my trouser pocket and he pulls out the cheque. The paper flaps in the breeze as he holds it between us.

"Come to London with me for three days. Come and see my hotels first-hand, let me show you what Stanton and Mills can become. If you genuinely aren't satisfied, then I'll take this cheque and walk away. You'll never see me again. Do we have a deal?"

SIX

Gage

Millie's dark eyes are wide, as though my words have stunned her into some kind of trance. A tiny dusting of freckles spans her cheeks and nose. One freckle in particular sits on her left cheek and looks to be the perfect heart shape, though I can't be sure without stepping closer, and we're dangerously close as it is.

There's something I like about this girl, something I can't quite put my finger on. She is a closed book, yet I find her so easy to read. Her stubbornness is infuriating yet captivating. She isn't conventionally attractive yet has an allure that surpasses beauty. She is utterly riveting, yet a complete enigma.

An enigma who is yet to answer my question. The waves continue to crash against the shore as my patience begins to wear thin.

"Mildred?" I snap my fingers in front of her eyes and she blinks.

"Why do I need to go to London with you when I can just look at the hotels online?"

"Seeing a picture isn't the same as really seeing it. You can't see how the hotel is run from an image, nor can you feel the ambience. No, to really get a feel for the Calloway hotels you first need to step inside one."

"I… er…" Millie opens her mouth to say something before closing it again. She runs her hand along her arm several times before speaking. "It's just I've worked at Stanton and Mills seven days a week since I was fifteen. I've never taken a day off. If I did, who is going to run the place while I'm away? And who is going to oversee the staff?"

Her admission shocks me. "A successful hotel runs itself. You are the owner, not a babysitter, nor are you an employee. It isn't your job to stand at reception day in and day out. That's what you employ receptionists to do."

From the way her face contorts I can see my comment has royally pissed her off. She places her hands on her hips. "I am the face of Stanton and Mills. People expect to see me."

"No, they don't. Seeing you in person adds nothing to their holiday experience. You are a nameless face they'll forget the second they return home." As true as my words are, I can see they are not helping to persuade her, so I decide a different approach. "I'm returning to London tomorrow afternoon. If you are not on the ferry with me, then the offer is off the table."

Her eyes are wide with panic. "Tomorrow! That doesn't give me a lot of time."

"On the contrary. You have all evening to make the necessary arrangements and pack your things."

"Pack my things? You're so confident I'm going to join you."

"I know you will. That is, if the hotel means as much to you as you claim it does."

"Stanton and Mills means everything," she says with confidence, and yet she isn't taking me up on my offer. I know what

I'm asking of her is a lot—the girl has never set foot off the island. But life is all about change, and those who can't move with the times get left in the past. "Daniel, my best friend, is returning to the island on Monday. I can't leave before he gets home."

"We'll send him a postcard." That comment earns me a death stare, so I decide to ease up. "I don't need your answer now," I say and nod in the direction where the harbour and her parents' home is located. "Come on. As the guest of honour, I'd hate to be late for dinner."

We walk to her parents' home in silence. Her pace quickens with each step and I imagine her head is filled with a million different scenarios. She takes the lead, and I fall into step a few feet behind.

As expected, the town is quiet for the time of day. A few people are milling around, but most are jumping into their cars and heading home for the evening. Open signs that hang in shop doors flip to closed. Shutters are pulled down and streetlights begin to flicker. An eerie calm hangs over the small town as we make our way down the cobbled path to *Genie*'s Catch of the Day.

The shop is painted white with a large caricature fish on the side. It sits in a prime location a few metres from the harbour where their fishing boat *Genie* is moored. Like the shop, the boat is painted white, with an identical yet smaller caricature picture of the fish painted onto the hull. I can't help but admire their execution of branding.

The doors to the fishmongers are open and the strong scent of fish hangs in the air as we approach. We wait in the doorway as the last few customers are being served. I love the old-fashioned way Millie's mum wraps the fish in newspaper and secures it with a length of string.

She looks up just as she finishes serving the last customer. "Ah. Gage, Millie. I would come hug you, but, you know, fish guts and all." She rubs her hands down the front of her yellow and blue striped apron.

Millie holds her hands up and jumps back, stepping on my toes in the process. "As much as I love you, Mum, stay away."

Edith chuckles to herself and begins covering the produce. "Your father's expecting you. Why don't you make your way upstairs while I clean up and shut the shop."

Millie's mum is a petite lady, with short brown hair that is mostly covered by a white mesh hat and hairnet. Apart from their dark eyes, Millie and her mother share no obvious resemblance.

"Sure." Millie wastes no time. She shoulders past me, and once in the fresh air she takes deep gasps, the kind I'd expect when someone has been holding their breath.

"Something wrong?" I ask.

She holds her index finger up for a beat before answering. "Everything's fine."

Without another word she makes her way to the side door and lets herself in. Deep voices echo all around us as we walk up a narrow flight of stairs. We enter the flat through a door into an open-plan lounge and kitchen. The scent of a hearty home-cooked meal fills the small space.

"Millie," a gruff voice calls. I don't have time to look around properly before I, along with Millie, am pulled into a tight hug. With a face full of hair, I lean back and briefly make eye contact with Jonathan, Millie's father. He's a unit of a man, taller than me, and wider than me and Millie put together. His round face is dominated by a thick coppery beard and an overgrown moustache.

"Good to see you again, son." Jonathan claps me on the back.

"You too, sir." I'm relieved when he loosens his grip on me and loops his thumbs into the shoulder straps of his dungarees.

Hugging is not something I am used to, especially when it comes to the same sex. I can't remember a time in my life when my own father or brothers pulled me into a hug.

No sooner am I released than I'm pulled into another suffocating bear hug.

"Good to see you, Gage. I'm Bruce." Millie's brother ruffles my hair before releasing me. Like his father, Bruce is a unit. He is tall, not as wide, but equally as hairy as his old man. Bruce wears a pair of dungarees with a classic grey button-down beneath.

Bruce releases me and grabs his sister into a bear hug.

"I'm Austin," a slimmer, less hairy man says. Like his father and brother, Austin also pulls me into a tight hug.

I relax when I'm finally released. What the hell is wrong with these people? Millie is nothing like them, and if anything I'd say she's standoffish. I can't help wonder if she was adopted. I look to Millie, expecting her to be as stiff as a board, but am surprised to see her hugging her family with equal enthusiasm. Millie is no different to her family—she isn't standoffish at all, she's just aloof with me.

"We've missed you, sis." Bruce says, and, with one arm around Millie and the other around me, attempts to lead us into the lounge.

I raise my hand, signalling I'm good, and pull from his hold. Millie doesn't. She lets him guide her toward an oak dining table positioned to the far right.

"I only saw you the other day," she laughs. "Hey, where's Travis?"

"He went out on a date," Austin says.

"He did, eh?" Millie ponders her brother's words for a beat before she takes a seat at the dining table where a board game waits.

Austin sits to Millie's right and Bruce to her left. I stand in the doorway like a forgotten piece of furniture. It was stupid, my coming here this evening. These people are perfect strangers. Sure, I was expecting them to welcome me into their home, but I wasn't expecting to be welcomed with three sets of open arms. I shift from foot to foot and look at the door as a way of escape. I feel the most uncomfortable I've ever felt in my life and want nothing more than to leave.

"Come, sit." Bruce pulls out a chair for me.

I stand tall and, dusting my shirt down, head toward the chair.

"Have you played Monopoly before?" Bruce asks as he counts out the colourful notes.

Millie stifles a laugh. "Gage doesn't need to, he plays the game in real life. The last thing he needs is to be given the power to buy any more hotels."

Her tone is sharp, yet playful. If she is setting me a challenge, then I accept.

"I'm familiar with the game," I say, and reach for the game pieces. But Millie gets to them first and hands me the small silver ship.

She smiles sweetly. "Look at how similar the ship looks to the ferry you arrived here on. And will soon be leaving on."

I take it from her and place it on 'go'. "Prepare to lose."

Being the youngest, Millie rolls first, followed by Austin, Bruce, and finally myself. Pots and pans clink together as her father busies himself in the kitchen with our dinner. We're off to a good start, and properties on the board are being snapped up.

Millie's mum arrives, says a quick hello, and excuses herself while she gets changed.

"So, you're the new co-owner of the hotel?" Bruce asks, and, cursing under his breath, moves his piece—the hat—to jail.

"That's right," I say, taking the die and rolling a seven. I move the ship seven spaces and smile wide. "Would you look at that? Mayfair."

I hand Austin, the acting banker, my printed money, and in return he hands me the card.

"Please tell us you're going to buy our Millie out so she can come work here with Mum," Austin says.

"Not in your lifetime." Millie rolls two doubles. The first she lands on a station, which she buys. The second roll takes her to Park Lane.

Damn. The property I needed to complete my dark blue set and own the two best spaces on the board.

"I want to buy it," she announces.

"Can you afford to?" Austin asks, his gaze on the small amount of money she has left. "Because if not, it'll have to go to auction."

Millie gives Austin her last note in exchange for the card. The irony of us both owning fifty percent of the same set isn't lost on me.

"Austin made a good point," I say, and Millie looks up. "Why don't I buy your share of Stanton and Mills, and you work here with your family?"

"No." Millie doesn't elaborate and sits silently for a beat before taking her turn. After rolling she moves the little Scottie dog around the board, and, passing 'go', she collects two hundred pounds.

"She hates fish," Bruce blurts out. The table jolts, and Bruce's face contorts. It wouldn't take a genius to figure out that Millie has kicked him.

"It's a secret," Austin says. "If you tell anyone, we may have to kill you." His tone is light-hearted, though his expression is deadly serious. "It isn't good for business. Wouldn't be right if folk round here knew that the only daughter of the town's fisherman hated fish."

My brows shoot up as I think of all the amazing seafood dishes I've had over the years. "How can anyone hate fish?" I laugh, and it's genuine. I'm feeling less stiff and less tense than I did when I arrived.

"I don't hate them," Millie butts in. "I just don't like the smell or the taste."

Time passes and the game reaches its end. Dinner becomes more of an afterthought as Jonathan and Edith stand around the table and watch us play.

"I'm out," Bruce announces after paying me the last of his

money for landing on Bond Street, which of course has its customary hotel.

"Just you and Millie left," Austin says. He was the first to be out, after some rotten luck with the chance cards. After landing on three of my properties in a row, he had no other choice than to declare himself bankrupt.

As the game stands, I own numerous properties and hotels on yellow and green. Millie owns all of the stations and hotels on light blue and red. One wrong roll of the die will see one of us out of the game. I roll a nine, and Millie watches as I move the ship to one of my own squares.

I casually lean back in my seat. "Your turn."

She takes long seconds shaking the dice in her hands before she rolls. The dice roll right off the table. Jonathan locates them and shouts out the number five, which lands her right on Piccadilly.

"What rotten luck." I pick up my yellow card and check the amount of rent she owes me, then look at her money—or lack of. I sigh and drum my fingers on the oak table. "Oh, dear." I try but fail to keep my expression neutral.

Millie's eyes narrow. "Bite me."

"Millie." Her comment earns her a tap on the arm from her mother.

Seeing as she can't pay me the money for the rent, I decide to give her another option. "Give me Park Lane, and consider your debt wiped." I've won anyway. I just want to own the best set of properties on the board before we call it a night.

Millie picks up the card and holds it to her chest. "Never. I would rather go bankrupt than give you what I own."

The playful edge in her tone is gone, and I know she is no longer referring to the game.

I'm about to speak when Millie's father clears his throat. "And that concludes the game of Monopoly."

Austin begins clearing the board and pieces away as Edith

and Jonathan see to dinner. Conversations play out around me, but my gaze is trained on Millie's parents. Edith grabs a set of sage-green oven gloves and takes a crock dish from the oven. Jonathan makes his way to the opposite side of the kitchen and grabs the plates and cutlery. They meet in the middle of the kitchen island, like two magnets being pulled together. Jonathan wraps his arm around his wife's shoulders and, pulling her close, kisses her on the head.

They are the image of happiness. The happiness I wish my mother had encountered while she was alive. The happiness she deserved. My father put on a good show of pretending he loved her, but the truth is it wasn't enough to keep him from straying into the arms of other women. The hunger I felt moments ago turns to something else, a throbbing pain that begins in the pit of my stomach and makes its way to my heart.

I reach for the stem of my wine glass and drink it down in one. With everyone's attention on someone else, I grab Austin's glass and drink that too. Alcohol has always been good for numbing the pain and taking away memories I refuse to remember.

Laughter erupts around the table, and I look up just as Austin is imitating a fish at the end of Bruce's invisible line. Bruce reels him in, and, flapping his arms, Austin throws himself onto the floor. I side-eye Millie, whose cheeks are red as she laughs, tears streaming down her face.

"I get it, I get it," she howls, waving her brothers to stop.

Jonathan steps over Austin and places a serving dish in the centre of the table. He lifts the lid, causing steam to rise from a golden-brown beef stew. Chunky carrots and pieces of broccoli bob on top. The scent of gravy and garlic explodes around us. I figure that is what has Austin jumping up from the floor and back in his chair.

Edith brings over a bottle of red wine and refills glasses while Jonathan slops a serving of stew into everyone's bowls. Elbows knock into elbows and voices grow louder as everyone competes to be heard over the ruckus. Dinner in the Mills home is disorganised chaos. I usually eat in total silence and scroll through emails on my phone. Looking around, I notice there isn't a single device out, and, to my surprise, they all seem to be enjoying one another's company.

"Is your dinner okay?" Edith asks. I haven't touched my food, not as much as a single bite.

"It's wonderful," I lie, taking the fork and bringing a piece of beef to my lips.

"So, Gage, tell me about your parents," Edith begins.

I pin her with a pointed stare. "There isn't too much to tell, really. My mother died when I was nineteen, and my father is an arrogant arsehole."

Edith's mouth drops open, and conversations around the table quieten down. I never have been one to mince my words or get into a long conversation that I could easily summarise with a sentence or two. Millie's eyes are on me, questioning, yet she says nothing. I nod my head toward the centre of the table. "Please, would someone pass me the salt?"

Conversations continue around me, I, however, eat in silence. It's not a surprise that no one knows what to say to me. Once I've finished eating, I dab the corners of my mouth with a cotton napkin and stand from the table. "Thank you for your company, and this fine food."

"Hold on, son, I'll see you out." Jonathan gets to his feet also, and after clapping a hand on my back walks me toward the door. I don't think I will ever get used to his use of the word 'son' or his need for physical contact.

As much as I've loved the break from my normal life, I am looking forward to returning home. Which reminds me.

Jonathan opens the door for me, but before I go, I peer at Millie. "My ferry leaves at three o'clock."

SEVEN

Millie

I watch each hour pass on the digital clock beside my bed. Eleven o'clock, midnight, one. It's two a.m. when the bedroom door creaks open and Hayley tiptoes in. With the blanket swaddled around my head, I lie in the darkness and watch her silhouette as she slips out of her dress and gets into bed. Her movements are stealthy as she tries her hardest not to wake me. She plumps her pillow once, twice, three times before lying down.

"I don't know what to do," I announce.

Hayley jumps and sits bolt upright. "Oh, my God. You gave me a heart attack." She slaps her palm to her chest, which I'm sure is for dramatic effect. "How long have you been awake?"

I look at the red numbers on the digital clock face, which seem to be taunting me. "Since ten."

"You could have told me you were awake."

I shrug. "Could have, but didn't." There's a playful edge to my tone, but inwardly I'm freaking out. I've done nothing but lie awake and think about Gage's offer of joining him in London. With time slipping away, I still haven't come to a decision.

"I need advice." I sit up and flick on the small bedside lamp. My gaze homes in on Hayley, or more specifically her neck. I rub my eyes and squint. "Is that a hickey?"

"Of course not." Hayley tries but fails to conceal the red blotch with her hair. She quickly realises her attempts are in vain and resorts to pulling the blanket all the way up to her chin.

"That's great, but you can't do that tomorrow when you're on shift."

Hayley rolls her eyes. "That's what make-up is for. Now, enough about me, what did you want to ask?"

I sigh. "Gage wants me to go to London with him. In just over twelve hours."

Hayley is quiet as I tell her all about Gage's insane proposal.

"I can't go, I just can't," I insist. "I have far too much to do here."

There's a mischievous glint in Hayley's eyes, and I already know that I'm not going to like what she has to say. I shake my head and turn off the bedside lamp. "I'm sorry. Forget I said anything." I spin around in bed and pull the blanket over my face, trying to hide from reality.

Light filters in through the fibres. Hayley has turned the bedroom light on. I scrunch the blanket between my fingers and lower it down. The room slowly comes into focus as the mattress dips. Hayley slides in next to me and nudges my butt with her knee, signalling me to move up, which I do.

"You wanted my advice, so here it is. You should go."

I should have known this would be how she'd react, forever the chancer. "But what about this place?"

"It'll be fine. Think of it like this: either you'll be blown away by the Calloway hotels, and Gage will fix up Stanton and Mills, or you'll be completely underwhelmed and he'll sell you his share. Either way, it's a win-win."

I sit silently and ponder her words. Hayley and my family seem to be in agreement that I should go with Gage. They have a point, but it would mean leaving all I love and all I know. Here I'm somebody—I have a purpose, a life, a job. London is big, bigger than big. It's huge, with a population of over nine million. How will I stand out in a place so populated?

"Oh, I was meaning to ask." Hayley leans in close. "How did dinner go with your parents and Gage?"

"You know my parents. They love everyone, and Gage seems to be the shiny new toy on the island." I pause and pass Hayley a sideward glance. "My brother Travis was absent tonight. You wouldn't happen to know where he got to, would you?"

The blush on Hayley's face says it all.

"Oh, my God," I blurt out, and once again find my attention drawn to her hickey.

"I love him," Hayley admits, and throws her arms around me. "I think he's the one. And who knows, maybe we could be sisters one day."

Although I hug my roomie, I can't help feel a sudden pang of dread. My brother has made a name for himself as the island's womaniser, and I'm sure there isn't a girl on the island who hasn't dated him at some point. I thought Hayley knew better than to get involved with him.

Hayley pulls away. "I say now is as good a time as any to pack your case."

"Pack? But I haven't said I'm going."

Hayley gets out of bed, and, walking across the small room to her wardrobe, pulls out her suitcase. "You're going. I want some time with Travis, and with you out of my hair, I can invite him back here."

The very idea of her entertaining my brother in this room has my skin crawling. "Have you forgotten the strict policy we have in place that no men are allowed in staff bedrooms?"

"I don't need the bedroom. We have the shower, and not forgetting the settee."

That image will give me nightmares for as long as I live, I'm sure.

"Come on, Mills. Three days is nothing. I mean, seriously, what's the worst that can happen?"

After pulling an all-nighter with Hayley, and packing a suitcase—despite the fact I haven't said I'm going anywhere—I go for my six a.m. run. The sky is particularly dull this morning, and grey clouds hang overhead. There's a dampness to the air. I'm expecting rain any moment.

While running I keep checking the time on my Apple Watch. This time tomorrow Daniel will be home. I can't wait to see him and hear all about his time in Birmingham. I booked the morning off work so that I could meet him straight from the ferry. I have our morning all planned out and a picnic packed in readiness. Whatever the weather, I am determined to have our picnic at the lighthouse.

That's another reason for me to stay here on the island. I can't leave when Daniel is due to return, it just wouldn't be right. We have so much to catch up on.

I hear my name called over the classical song I'm listening to and pull out my left earbud. "Good morning, Mr Porter."

He is making his way up the beach, in the direction of his ice cream shop. George's blond coat is sodden and weighed down with sand. Looks like they beat me here this morning.

Mr Porter stops walking, which tells me that I'm due one of his long conversations. I pull out both earbuds and jog on the spot.

"I saw young Gage earlier. He said you're joining him in London," Mr Porter begins. I run my palm over my eyes and shake my head. I'm annoyed, but part of me is trying not to laugh because Gage is turning into the local hen.

"It's a good job, seeing as Daniel is staying in Birmingham," Mr Porter continues. "Maybe you can meet up."

The smile plastered on my face drops instantly. "What?"

Mr Porter frowns, an expression that could be read as, 'How didn't you know?'

I shake my head. I'm sure he's mistaken. Positive, in fact. Daniel and I usually talk every day, with the exception of the past few weeks because he has been super busy with final exams and coursework. But even so, Daniel would have told me something so big.

"Where did you hear that?" I ask more out of curiosity. I want to know where the incorrect gossip is coming from.

Mr Porter unhooks George's lead—and signals for the dog to go home, which he does—then returns his attention to me. "Mary Adams."

I laugh. I should have known.

"She spoke to Daniel's mother last night, and I guess you could say she heard straight from the horse's mouth."

I open my mouth to say something, but the something that was on the tip of my tongue has gone.

"I best get back." Mr Porter signals to his ice cream shop, a sandy-coloured building with a red and blue striped awning. Like my parents, he lives in the small apartment above his shop. "You kids be sure to stay safe in London," are the words that trail over his shoulder as he leaves.

I stand still at the water's edge and look out to sea, which appears rougher than normal. The breeze has picked up, causing short strands of my hair to blow in my face. Ignoring the sudden change in weather, I pull my phone from my pocket and scroll down my list of contacts for Daniel's number. I hit the call button, and he answers on the sixth ring.

"Yo, Mills, what's up?"

"So, I heard the funniest thing today." I crouch down and pick up a misshapen pebble.

"Oh, yeah?"

"Yeah." I flick my wrist, skimming the pebble into the sea. I manage two bounces before it's taken by a crashing wave. "Apparently you're staying in Birmingham." I laugh, waiting for Daniel to laugh too, but he doesn't.

Silence from his end is all that follows, long uncomfortable seconds of silence. The wind whistles, making it harder for the seagulls to soar overhead.

"Daniel?" I ask.

"I was going to tell you," he finally replies. "I'd planned to call you weeks ago, but… I just couldn't find the words."

"You weren't busy with exams at all, were you? You were avoiding me. You're a coward, Daniel. A coward!" I sniff, trying to fight the tears. Growing up, Daniel was never good with confrontation. Silence was his answer to everything, with everybody, except for me. But in this instance, I've been well and truly given the silent treatment.

"I'm sorry, Millie. I've been offered work experience in a five-star restaurant. It's too good of an opportunity to pass up on. If they like me it could lead to a full-time position."

His words hit me like a tsunami as I stand on the water's edge. The sea laps against the shore, occasionally wetting my trainers, but I don't move. I can't move. Daniel continues to talk, and I stay rooted to the spot, trying to take in everything he is saying.

"I'm sorry, Millie," Daniel says, for the third, maybe fourth time, and yet the words aren't sinking in.

"But Stanton and Mills, the hotel, it's our dream," I say in a last-ditch attempt, hoping he'll see sense and come home.

The line goes quiet for a beat, and I lift the phone away from my face to check our call hasn't been disconnected. It hasn't. "Daniel?"

He blows out, and finally answers. "The hotel has always been *your* dream, not mine."

"But you wanted to work here with me," I grit out.

"I did," Daniel agrees. "But things change. People change."

I shake my head, still not believing the words I'm hearing. I look in the direction of where the lighthouse stands proud in the faraway distance, the place we were going to enjoy a picnic. Will that happen now? "But the island is your home."

"It is, but I want more from life."

Silence.

It's as though someone grabbed for the sound remote and switched the volume right down. The seagulls no longer cry out overhead, the sea no longer crashes against the shore, and the chattering voices of people as they pass melt into nothingness. All I can hear is my heart, which booms like a drum in my ears.

"I want more," he repeats.

I can't stop the tears that roll down my cheeks. It feels as though I'm losing—or rather, I've lost—my best friend.

"Say something, Millie, you're making me nervous."

I sniff and wipe my eyes. "I don't know what to say," I admit, while my mind plays out the life I saw for us. Me and my best friend working side by side, making the hotel the best it could be. I planned to make him head chef. I picture our morning runs on the beach listening to my classical playlist on the earbuds, the laughs we would have had during our breaks. My imaginings are replaced by the cruel reality that he may never come back, and I will always run alone.

"My mum tells me you're coming to London for a few days. It's only a train ride away from Birmingham. Maybe we could meet up," Daniel says, bringing my mind back to the now.

Despite the hurt I feel, it would be good to see him. It feels as though the universe is telling me to go to London, yet still something deep down is preventing me from taking the leap.

A single spot of rain falls on my face, followed by another, and then another. Within seconds a heavy downpour of rain falls around me, causing ripples on the sea.

"Millie, are you still there?" Daniel questions.

I blink rapidly to shield my eyes from the rain. "I don't know whether I'm coming to London," I finally answer. "I only have a few hours to make what could be the most important decision of my life, and still, I don't know what to do."

EIGHT

Gage

"Do you have to leave? We didn't get the chance to get to know each other." Nadia is perched at the end of my bed, watching all doe-eyed as I pack my case. It hasn't gone unnoticed that she's hiked her skirt up a few extra inches, and her shirt buttons are only partially fastened, giving me the perfect view of her red lace bra.

"I do," I say.

Nadia is quiet as I fold the last of my silk ties and zip up my case. I pull the case from the bed and without a backward glance head for the door.

"Take me with you," she calls after me.

I freeze, one hand on my case, the other on the door handle. I try not to laugh as I turn and face the young woman who still sits on my bed. She pulls at her ponytail and lets her long blonde hair cascade down her back. I have always been partial to blondes, and thoughts of fisting her hair between my fingers flash through my mind.

"Take me with you," she repeats.

"As what? The hired help?" Although I'm not laughing, there is humour in my tone.

"Your assistant, silly. There's something kind of kinky about an office fling with your PA." Nadia stands up and makes her way toward me. She rolls her hips with each step in an attempt to be seductive. When all the space has been erased between us, she prises my hand from my suitcase and wraps my arm around her back. My hand rests on her ass, but I don't move it.

I sigh, and silently curse women for being so bloody complicated. I haven't slept with this girl and already she is making demands.

I lean close, so close that her breasts are pressed against my chest. She shudders as my lips find the shell of her ear.

"No," is my one-word response. I offer no explanation because why the hell would I? This girl is falling for the idea of us. Unfortunately for her, I don't entertain fantasy or romance, or women for that matter. My life is far too busy for such ridiculous notions.

"Please? Take me off the island." She glides the back of her fingers up and down my cheek. I capture her wrist to stop her.

"No," I say, and lean back so I have a full view of her face. Her blue eyes are full of hope, full of this crazy fantasy. She looks from my eyes to our hands and our now-entwined fingers.

"If you gave me a chance I could show you just how committed I can be to my work. We could be good together, I just know it."

She is no longer referring to us in the professional sense. I need to nip this delusion in the bud before it has chance to grow roots.

"In your dreams, maybe. I don't need another PA, and I don't need some random woman tagging along with me." I shake my head, because it's more than that. "I don't want a woman in my life."

Her expression sobers. "So tell me, Gage Calloway, what *do* you want?"

Her lower lip trembles and she is clearly fighting the tears. There is no point prolonging her pain, so I answer the best way I know how, and that's with complete honesty.

"What I want is casual sex with different women who fit in with my day-to-day life." I pause so there's no chance of confusion. I want her to not only hear my words but take them in. "I don't do relationships. Don't do strings. Don't do feelings."

A tear falls from the corner of her eye, but still her stare remains fixed on me. "Who hurt you so badly to make you so cold?"

My God, this right here is worse than her practically begging me to take her away. She sees me as a project, something broken in need of fixing. This I will not allow. Out with the nice Gage. Insert asshole version. This version of me keeps women at bay—it keeps them from wanting more.

"Look, honey, my rule is simple: fuck them once and move on. If you're that desperate, bend your tight little arse over that bed and I'll give you the most memorable fuck of your life. But know this, I will forget you the moment we are done." I lean in close. "I won't remember your name or your face. You know why? Because you women are all the same. Forgettable."

The tears in her eyes are gone and are replaced by something else. Anger. I can't say I'm shocked when she throws her arm back and slaps me across the face. Because yes, I deserved it.

"Asshole," she spits out, and, shouldering past me, lets herself out. The door slams shut behind her, and before I leave I catch sight of my reflection in the wall-mounted mirror, the red handprint throbbing on my left cheek. I smile at my reflection, because alone is where I see myself. Alone is where no one can get too close, no one can hurt me. Alone is the only time I'm truly happy.

I leave Room 201 and fumble the brass key into the lock. The first thing I'm going to do is have the doors electronically fitted with key cards. I look first left and then right, and with no porter in sight, I have no choice other than to wheel my own case down to the lobby.

I take the lift to the ground floor and am surprised at how busy the lobby is. A group of approximately twenty people crowd around the small reception desk. I'm not at all surprised to see Millie at work. She is dressed in her customary black blazer, her mousy hair pinned back into a bun. It amazes me that with little make-up, and despite her annoying-as-hell personality, she still manages to look at least half-decent. Though half-decent is a major disservice.

She catches my gaze and I wave. Her eyes narrow and her face twists into a scowl. *It's so nice to see I've made a lasting impression on the girl.* I flash a glance at my watch. One twenty-three. It's fair to assume she isn't joining me in London. A tiny part of me is disappointed because in a way, me letting Millie buy me out was the easier option. Millie, much like the hotel, seems like too much effort. But there's a part of me that enjoys riling this woman up, and it's that part of me that is determined not to make this easy for her.

Not only that, I want to be able to say that I've built something up from nothing. I'm sick of living in my father's shadow. This hotel was my chance to show what I am capable of.

I wait until the reception clears, and guests pass by with their suitcases and head toward the lift. The brass keys jangle against the chunky wooden number plaques as they pass.

"You really do need to consider hiring a few porters," I say, and lean my elbow on the mahogany reception desk.

She nods once, and plasters on the most unnatural smile I think I've ever seen. "I hope you've enjoyed your stay. But please, don't hurry back."

I smile big. "Oh, Mildred. Sweet, naive little Mildred. Don't think for one second you're getting rid of me that easily. I leave in under two hours. If your uptight little ass isn't beside me on the ferry, then next time our paths cross I will have a bulldozer and a team of builders with me. Do I make myself clear?"

"You wouldn't dare," she challenges.

I raise a brow. "Wouldn't I?"

She flashes a glance at my left cheek. "I don't suppose you want a handprint on the other side to match?"

My eyes narrow. "Is that a threat, Mildred?"

"No, it's a promise—that if you aren't out of my hotel in the next thirty seconds I will slap you silly."

Her words are as threatening as a gust of wind. "Righto." I can't help but laugh before my expression sobers. "Here's a promise of my own. I promise to fix this hotel up and make it ten times more profitable than it is now."

"Over my dead body," Millie spits out.

I tap my chin several times as if in thought. "Hiring a hitman is a little excessive, don't you think? No, I want you very much alive and with a front-row seat."

The corner of Millie's eye twitches in irritation. The way she rocks back and forth suggests that she is trying her hardest not to explode.

"I see my work here is done." I wink at Tanya, who blushes, and proceed to drag my suitcase toward the door to leave. "I'll be seeing you again very soon," I call over my shoulder.

I arrive at the port an hour early and spend that time sitting on a bench catching up with emails, conference calls and checking in with my family.

I cut the call to my brother Malachi as an incoming call from my sister comes in. I pick up right away. "Farrah, how are you?"

"How am I? How do you think I am? It's my big day tomorrow, and Father tells me you're in another country!"

"In another country? I'm on a small island off Penzance."

My laughter is drowned out by the sound of chattering voices as people begin to queue to board. "Farrah, I have to go."

"Go where? Are you coming home?"

With my phone sandwiched between my shoulder and my ear, I crouch down to grab my case. "Yes, so stop wo—"

My phone falls to the ground as I'm shoved. I stumble several steps backwards as my back collides with the wall. It takes a few moments before my brain has a chance to register what has just happened.

"What the fuck, dude!" I yell as angry grey eyes stare into mine. His breath is harsh against my cheek as he leans in close.

"You've made your point, Travis," Millie says as she attempts to pull this brute from me, but he doesn't back up. This guy is taller than me and wider than me, but Travis—if that's his name—doesn't intimidate me. I have never been one to shy away from a fight.

"Get off me, Millie." He shrugs away her attempt to separate us.

Travis and I stand, our faces inches apart, both breathing heavily. He is what I'd describe as rough and ready. His dark hair, like his beard, is feral. There's a silvery scar slicing through his right eyebrow, which carries on over his eyelid and down his cheek. I flash a glance at arms that are coated in full-sleeve tattoos, muscles and veins protruding from beneath the sleeves of his black t-shirt.

"You want to dance? I won't be the one to throw the first punch, but I guarantee I'll throw the last," I grit out between clenched teeth.

"I said that's enough." Millie, now dressed in a pair of denim jeans and a pink cardigan, forces her way between us. With her as a distraction, I take a second to look around me. Onlookers watch on, and a stocky bald policeman is heading our way. A policeman who could easily stop me from boarding the ferry today.

"What's going on here?" he hollers.

"Nothing, Bill," Travis says, and takes a step away from me. "I was just saying goodbye to my new friend."

Bill eyes me sceptically.

"What he said," I say, and hold up my hands to emphasise that there's nothing to see here. Bill doesn't look convinced. He nods, but his feet remain rooted to the spot, as if ready to step in if a fight breaks out.

I lower my gaze to Millie. "Next time you may want to leave your Rottweiler at home."

The large grey suitcase to her right doesn't go unnoticed as she shuffles from foot to foot. She looks to Travis and back to me. "Travis is my—"

"I'm her big brother," Travis butts in. "Millie told me you bullied her into going to London. Now I'm telling you, if you so much as lay a finger on her, or hurt her in any way, I'm coming for you."

I can't help but laugh. "Is that right?"

Travis leans forward, once again entering my space. "It is. I've worked out at sea all of my life, and I know where to dump a body to ensure it'll never be found."

Is this clown threatening me? He bloody is. The tension is so tight between us that I can feel it close to snapping. I should back down, I should try to defuse the situation, but where would the fun be in that?

I look down my nose at Travis as though he were no more than a speck of dust on my Armani suit. "Well, life has provided me with the luxury that I need not get my hands dirty. I only need to make one phone call to have you permanently silenced."

Travis opens his mouth to speak when a hand flashes between us. "That's enough time to say your goodbyes." Bill claps me on the back and motions to the ferry. "I believe it's time to board."

"I believe you're right." I narrow my eyes at Travis before bending down to retrieve my phone. Farrah is still talking on the other end. I'm not sure how much she heard, but quickly cut the call.

"Come, Mildred." I grab the handle of my suitcase and, without a backward glance, head for the sloped ramp leading to the top deck.

My heart is racing with adrenaline and it takes every ounce of self-control to keep walking. My father's words play over and over in my mind. 'Think of your reputation, son. You are the face of Calloway Hotels, therefore you cannot afford negative publicity of any kind.' Which has me thinking. I am going to be spending several days with Millie. I have never been seen publicly with a woman on more than one occasion—well, not since Daphne. I can only imagine the stories the press will fabricate.

Maybe inviting Millie to come to London with me wasn't such a good idea after all. But I'm too stubborn to back down now. Millie joins me on the ferry and I wrap an arm around her waist.

"I'm glad you came to your senses," I say, and before she has a chance to pull out of my hold I turn back and offer her brother a 'fuck you' wave.

NINE

Millie

Before heading to Penzance, the ferry makes several stops at the Isles of Scilly, our neighbouring islands. We pick several tourists up from St Mary's and drop others off at St Martin's. I spend much of the ferry ride sitting alone on a bench. A couple who stayed at the hotel sit opposite, their young daughter playing on an iPad.

I smile at the couple. They don't smile back, and instead look away like they don't recognise me. Like I haven't greeted them with a 'good morning' every day for the past two weeks. Like I didn't take the time to get their room upgraded so they could have a sea view. Gage's words replay in my mind, that I am just a face people will forget as soon as they leave. I shake his words from my mind. Of course they recognise me. They have a child, they're just preoccupied being parents.

With my earbuds in I sit and listen to my classical playlist. Gage sits beside me for a while, and several times tries but fails to strike up a conversation. Every time he speaks I turn up the volume on my earbuds a little more. He finally takes the hint when my song is playing loud enough for him to hear. He soon scurries off to who cares where, though I guess I'll have the misfortune of his company soon enough.

My phone vibrates in my hand, and I glance at the screen.

> Travis: I mean it, Millie, if he lays so much as a finger on you, I'll kill him and wear his bollocks as earmuffs.

I laugh at the imagery. With me being the baby of the family, my big brothers have always had my back, Austin and Bruce in more of the 'kill people with kindness' kind of way. Travis is quite the opposite and doesn't hesitate to talk with his fists.

> Me: I assure you that touching me is the last thing on his mind.

> Travis: I'm a guy, and guys know guys.

I start writing out my reply, telling him how ridiculous he's being, but press delete instead of send. Travis is like a dog with a bone; it's sometimes best to agree or change the subject.

> Me. Love you, bro. I'll let you know when I'm in London.

I push my phone into the pocket of my jeans and look out to sea. The island, my home, is getting smaller and smaller with each passing second.

The lighthouse stands proud. I smile, but it's a sad smile because all I know, all I've ever known will soon be a tiny speck in the faraway distance and I don't know how I feel about that. I have never set foot off my homeland, and why would I? Everything is there—my family, my friends, my job and my life. Hayley said it was time that I spread my wings, but why would a bird fly away when it has everything it wants, everything it could ever need right there at its feet?

I jump as an earbud is pulled out and my song becomes

noticeably quieter, the music drowned out by the sound of the crashing waves against the ferry and the people talking.

"Hey, give it back," I scold as Gage sits to my right and pushes the earbud into his ear. He holds his arm out as a barrier to stop me from getting closer and then, reclining back, closes his eyes. Sharing earbuds and listening to the same song is something I would do with Daniel. It seems intimate somehow, like letting someone listen to music that speaks to my soul is giving them a small piece of me. A piece I'll happily share with Daniel, but not Gage.

"I said give it back," I say, and reach up, just as Gage hands over the earbud.

"With pleasure. My God, Mildred, you have shocking taste in music."

"I'm sorry?" His insult hits me like a slap across the face.

"In most cases I would say there is really no need to apologise, but this is a clear exception."

My eyebrows shoot up. "Tell me, Mr Fancy-Pants Big Shot, what music do you like?"

He shrugs. "Anything that is half decent. I like a bit of soul, indie, reggae, opera…"

"Opera? How old are you, ninety?"

His expression is unchanged. If what I have said has offended him, he manages to hide it well. He looks at me thoughtfully for a second. "You know, you really shouldn't elevate your eyebrows so unnaturally. The expression is not flattering in the slightest, and it makes it hard to distinguish whether you're in a state of shock or in pain. Aside from that, you're only encouraging wrinkles."

Unbelievable.

I press my earbud into my ear and turn my back toward him for the remainder of the journey. I keep my attention on my island and watch as it becomes smaller and smaller. Soon the island is no more than a speck, the lighthouse no more than a memory, and I feel the most anxious I have ever felt.

It takes just over an hour to make it to the port in Penzance. Penzance, apparently one of England's most popular seaside resorts, though on first glance I am underwhelmed.

My shoulders slump as I stand on deck and peer down. The beautiful turquoise waters, powder-blue sky and lush green landscape I left behind have been replaced by an overcast sky, murky blue-grey waters, and land that is overtaken with buildings. The first thing I notice about this part of England from this quick glimpse is just how fast-paced and overpopulated it is. At home I'm used to seeing two, three people max walking side by side along the quaint cobblestone paths. Here in Penzance all I see is crowds, crowds everywhere. Instinct has me stepping back onto the ferry, wishing I could be teleported home.

"Here, allow me." Gage takes the handles of both of our cases. The wheels squeak as he pulls them along behind him and toward the ramp leading down. Passengers from the ferry begin to move forward and I'm cajoled along with them.

The salty essence of the sea is mixed with the scent of fish. It's a smell that reminds me of home, though distorted by whiffs of perfume, tobacco, and food stalls set up on the street.

"Come on, Mildred," Gage says, but his words are drowned out by everything happening around me. People are everywhere, scurrying around like ants. Busy little ants. Voices and the tap-tapping of shoes against the concrete ground merge into a monotonous hum. Cars zoom by on the busy road, horns honk, children scream, and workmen power heavy machinery on a cordoned-off building site across the street. I close my eyes and try to block out all the ruckus, but it's no use, because for the first time in my life I can't hear the ocean over all the noise. How has life here got so busy that they've been able to drown out the sound of nature's most natural melody?

I catch up with Gage, and we make our way away from the

port. He stops on the street corner and begins to type out a message on his phone. People weave past us and in and out of small knick-knack shops. Families head to and fro from the beach, children skipping merrily with bucket and spades in hand. There are a variety of dog breeds being walked by their owners, but by the way the dogs pull I question who is really walking who.

It's all too much, too many people, too much going on around me. I feel claustrophobic all of a sudden and unable to breathe. The world begins to spin with everything closing in around me. I don't know what to do to steady myself, so grab Gage's hand.

He laughs and begins wriggling free of my hold. "Was this your plan all along? Get me alone all to yourself and seduce me? Because if it was…"

"Shut up, shut up, shut up." My words come out as a chant as my body and hands shake.

"Shit, Mildred, are you okay?" His words echo.

"Please, stop talking. Just hold onto me until this crazy world stops spinning."

"Okay, Mildred." He doesn't shoot me with a sarcastic comment or make any snide remarks. To Gage's credit, he actually does as I asked. We stand perfectly still, hand in hand. It's as though we're standing in the eye of a storm, in total calm as everything spins in chaos around us.

It takes a little time for my heart to stop racing, a little longer for my hands to finally stop shaking, and finally I'm able to breathe.

"Are you okay now?" Gage asks, and gives my hand a soft tug.

I swallow the dry lump that's been lodged in my throat and nod.

"Excellent." Gage pulls his hand from mine.

I feel stupid, more than stupid. I've completely embarrassed myself in front of the one man I didn't want to give an ounce of ammunition. I may as well have handed him a loaded gun. I know he will use this against me, I just know it.

"Do you want to sit down?" He looks genuinely concerned. "You could listen to some more of that terrible music of yours."

I narrow my eyes at him, but don't feel an ounce of anger. It strikes me that we have established an odd sort of love-hate relationship. I hate him, and as crazy as it sounds, I love it.

"Has anyone ever told you you're a jerk?" I wonder aloud, surprised by my forthrightness.

Gage smiles wickedly. "All the time."

I frown, and it hits me that Gage actually likes it when people don't like him. He does little to change the fact, and if anything he enjoys the back and forth. As a self-proclaimed people pleaser, the thought of purposely pissing people off seems totally foreign to me.

We stare at each other for long seconds, neither saying a word. It's as though we're coming to some kind of unspoken truce, though what that truce is, I have no idea. Our eye contact is broken when Gage's phone starts to ring. He looks down and accepts the call. Without a word he begins looking along the long line of cars parallel-parked on the opposite side of the road.

"I see you," he says, and cuts the call. He pushes his phone into his trouser pocket and takes the handles of our suitcases. "Mildred, come."

We make our way to a set of pedestrian traffic lights. He presses the button and we wait for the lights to change so we can cross.

"Why do you keep calling me Mildred?" I ask, more out of curiosity than anything else.

He shrugs, his attention fixed on the road. "Because it's your name."

"It is, but you know everyone calls me Millie."

Gage turns his head and offers me his full attention. "Mildred is formal. Millie is a pet name, something you'd give to a puppy. Yes, I'm aware friends and family call you Millie, but seeing as I am neither, it only seems right for me to call you Mildred."

My mouth falls open. I'm about to respond when the traffic lights beep and the green man appears, signalling for us to cross. I follow a few steps behind Gage, replaying his words in my mind. Gage has a point—we aren't friends, and never will be. At least there's no risk of any lines getting blurred. We both know exactly where we stand.

I have three days to get through, and if the Calloway hotels are anything like what I've seen of the south of England so far, then I'll buy Gage out and Stanton and Mills will finally be mine.

We make it to the pavement on the opposite side of the road. Gage doesn't wait for me, and if anything, his pace only quickens.

"Where are we going?" I call, but the second the words leave my lips I see it.

Of course Mr Big Shot has an Aston Martin, and his own personal driver to go with said car. The driver is an elderly man with wispy white hair, dressed in a black suit.

Gage stops and opens the back passenger side door. "My lady."

"How much longer?" I ask, sliding along the leather seat.

"To London from here without traffic?" Gage wonders aloud, his attention on his driver.

"It's a five-and-a-half-hour drive, sir," the old man pipes up.

"Thanks, Charles," Gage says and returns his attention to me.

"Is this day ever going to end?" I sigh, and, squeezing my eyes shut, cover them with the palms of my hands. "I'm tired and I'm starting to feel hungry. All I want is a quick snack before crashing in a big comfy bed."

"Lucky for you, it's only an hour to where my private jet is located. And as for food, we can pick something up on the way."

"Private jet?" I swallow the lump in my throat. I suddenly don't feel hungry anymore. He didn't say anything about flying. I've never been on a plane, and I don't know how I feel about being so high up in the air. I lift up in the seat and glance out of the rear window. There is a sign for a B&B only feet away, and a hotel not far from that. "Can't we stay here? Or in a Calloway hotel that isn't a million miles away?" Gage raises his brow, and I shake my head. "Okay, maybe a bit of an exaggeration. But what's so good about London anyway?"

"What's so good about London?" He sounds genuinely offended. "Sweetheart, London is our country's capital, you can't come to England and not visit its beating heart. London is home to our royal family, Kensington Palace, Westminster Abbey, St. Paul's Cathedral, and not forgetting my personal favourite, the Royal Opera House. The list goes on."

"But I'm here to see your hotels, not sightsee."

"Please, correct me if I'm wrong, but you have never set foot off the island."

I sit tall. "That's correct."

"Then I see it as not only my duty, but a public service to show you what you've been missing."

I can honestly say that no part of me wants to waste my time looking at buildings I could see just as well, if not better, from the search engine on my phone.

Gage smiles, or at least I think he does. He is quick to cover his mouth with the back of his hand and yawn. "Aside from dragging your virgin-traveller ass around with me, I have a few prior engagements taking place in London that I can't miss."

Gage doesn't continue the conversation. Instead, he closes the back passenger side door and, to my surprise, he hauls our cases into the boot of the car—a job I thought his driver Charles would do.

Gage makes his way around the vehicle, and he and Charles sit in the front. Charles starts up the engine and begins to punch an address into the inbuilt satnav.

I lean forward and place my arms on the back of Gage's seat. "Is London as busy as it is here in Penzance?"

"Busier." Gage leans forward in his seat and pulls down the sun visor. Our gazes meet through the small mirror. "London is like nothing you have ever experienced in your life. The city alone receives hundreds of thousands of tourists each year. During the peak of the season the streets are teeming with people, street performers and market stalls. If you think Penzance is busy, trust me when I say you've seen nothing yet."

I sink back in my seat, my heartbeat beginning to pick up pace. The unease I felt moments ago warps into fear. I've spent all my life surrounded by people, but never too many at any one time. Small gatherings I can handle, but huge crowds and streets so packed that I'll be squished like a sardine has my anxiety rising. I have never had a fear of drowning until now, but it isn't the water I fear, it's the sea of faces.

The car inches forward, and in no time we are pulling out of the parking space and onto the main road. I should look forward, because this is what the trip is all about, but I don't, I can't. All I can do is look back, in the direction of the port and the small ferry we arrived on. Back to where the ocean lies, and to where my island resides.

"Goodbye for now," I say in a whisper.

TEN

Gage

It's almost eight o'clock by the time we get to the Calloway Hotel in Knightsbridge. Charles stops the car outside the front, and Millie and I hop out.

The hotel is glorious, if I do say so myself. The white brick exterior stands five storeys high and large spiral pillars stand proud either side of the revolving door.

"What do you think?" I ask Millie. I'm expecting her to be mouth agape, totally in awe.

"Yeah, great. Can we just get signed in so I can get some sleep?" Millie's tone isn't one of excitement, and her stance isn't one of anticipation. I can't help but feel a pang of disappointment as we make our way inside.

The lobby is immense, with Calacatta marble flooring, lavish gold wall tiles and large crystal chandeliers hanging down from the high domed ceiling. Its focal point is a highly polished half-moon marble reception desk. A fleet of staff are busying themselves behind the half-moon, some stationed at the phones while others sign people in.

"Good evening, Mr Calloway." I am greeted by a maid, who holds two fluted glasses of champagne on a silver tray. "Can I offer you a complimentary drink?"

I take the glasses. I offer one to Millie, but, heavy-eyed, she declines. Great, more for me.

"Have the remainder of the bottle waiting on my bedside," I tell the maid, and after drinking both champagne flutes I place the empty glasses back on the tray.

"Of course, Mr Calloway." The maid scurries off.

We are signed in right away and a blonde receptionist passes me a key card. A porter has already loaded our cases into a trolley by the time I turn around.

I can't help but pass Millie a side glance. "And this, Mildred, is how a hotel should run."

Millie flaps her arm in a pitiful attempt to wave me off. She wasn't kidding when she said she was tired. The girl's beyond exhausted. I was sure she'd go to sleep on the way here, but she surprised me. She said something about talking in her sleep, and she didn't want to say something embarrassing that I would later use against her. For this reason alone, I kept constant tabs on her. Millie is the most reserved yet stubborn woman I think I've ever met, so the idea of her talking utter bullshit in her sleep intrigued me. Would she actually loosen up when she wasn't conscious?

We ride the lift all the way to the top floor and to penthouse one. I swipe my card in front of the card reader and open the door.

Millie is quiet as I show the porter where I want the cases to be left. Without a word she flops down on the sofa.

Penthouse one is the largest and most extravagant room in the hotel, and at over fifteen thousand pounds a night it is only the super-rich, celebrities and royalty who can afford to stay here. Despite the fact this room is mostly empty, I didn't want to take any chances, so booked it out a year in advance in preparation for Farrah's big day. What I hadn't prepared for was a plus-one to be joining me. A plus-one who will have to stay in one of the spare bedrooms, seeing as the hotel is fully booked.

With my case in the master suite, and Millie's in bedroom two, I walk the porter to the door. He leaves with a big tip and an even bigger smile.

I haven't told Millie we will be sharing a suite for the three days we're in London. Before I tell her the good news, I head to the minibar and grab myself a bottle of Jack. I need some liquid courage before the fireworks go off, said fireworks being the little spitfire who's sitting on the sofa.

I crack open the lid and take a gulp. Much better. I place the bottle back in the minibar and head over to where she's sitting. I walk up behind her and place my hands on the cushion either side of her head. The sofa is surrounded by floor-to-ceiling windows, giving Millie the perfect view of the city. A city that in only a few short hours will be lit up by thousands of tiny lights.

I take a slow, yet deep breath in. "The hotel is fully booked." I pause, waiting for her to explode, or fill in the gaps. When she does neither, I continue. "So, because of that we'll have to share the penthouse suite. Don't worry though, because you have your own room and bathroom. We'll hardly see each other."

Nothing but silence comes back. I smile triumphantly. She took the news better than I thought she would.

"Mildred?" I ask, when I notice her breathing is heavier than normal. I round the sofa. Her eyes are partially open, but she isn't awake.

"Mildred," I whisper, and give her arm a nudge.

She grunts, but continues to sleep. Her hair hangs loose around her face, and each time she blows out it causes a small tendril to take flight before coming back to rest over her mouth.

I stand and watch her for long seconds. Not in a creepy stalker kind of way, but more intrigued. She's kind of cute when she's asleep. The fact she isn't talking or glowering at me is a huge plus. I lean forward and brush the small lock of hair behind her ear. Apart from currently resembling Regan from *The Exorcist* with her creepy all-white eyes, Millie is very attractive in a 'girl next door' kind of way. My gaze lowers to her little pink cardigan. The top buttons are open, giving me a glimpse of her cleavage.

My dick twitches in my pants, and I jolt back. Admiring Millie's beauty is one thing, but getting an erection over her is something entirely different.

Although I've put space between myself and the sleeping pain in the ass, I still can't help but watch her. Girls I sleep with are all the same—blonde hair, blue eyes, pumped-up lips and breasts—and I like it that way because they're forgettable. Is it wrong that I want to fuck a girl I'll remember for once, a girl who is different from all the others?

I shake the thought from my mind. I have never mixed business and pleasure, and I don't intend on starting now.

I crouch down and slide one hand under Millie's thighs and another around her back. Without a word I pull her into me and lift her from the sofa. Her head flops to the side, and her hair is directly under my nose. I take a deep breath of her scent as I walk her to the second bedroom and lay her on top of the rich satin bed linen. She plumps up her pillow and, turning onto her right side, curls up like a cat.

"Goodnight, Mildred," I say, and turn off the lights.

It's seven thirty the following morning when I have the displeasure of Millie's company. To say Millie isn't happy to discover me in her hotel room this morning is the understatement of the century. What starts off as 'my God, you scared the crap out of me' soon escalates to 'get the hell out of my room', and to her then losing her shit. I don't deal with irrational women, so simply ignore her until she runs out of steam.

She's a live wire, I'll give her that. For the past fifteen minutes she has been pacing back and forth verbally bashing me while I sit and catch up on yesterday's news.

"No, no, and hell no! I don't care what the reason is, I refuse."

I recline on the sofa in the open-plan living area and turn the page of the newspaper I'm reading.

Millie stops pacing and stands with a hand on her hip. "Are you even listening?"

I sigh and give Millie my full attention. By the look of her, she isn't long out of the shower. She is wearing a brilliant white Calloway Hotel-branded robe. Her hair is scraped back in a towel, also branded with the logo of the Calloway Hotel. There's a small puddle beginning to form at her feet and fading footprint impressions on the floor lead from her bedroom to her. I figure the air con is starting to take effect on her as she begins dithering.

"I want you out," she says through chattering teeth.

"No," I answer simply.

"No?"

"That's right, no. This is my penthouse suite, I'm going nowhere." I do a sweeping action with my hand. "I mean, come on, Mildred, look at how much space we have, we're hardly on top of each other."

The penthouse has three king-sized suites, all of which are en suite, two luxury bathrooms with large jacuzzis, a living area, a study, two terraces overlooking London, its own kitchen and dining area, and not to mention its own state-of-the-art gym. Each room is fitted with luxury features such as Ralph Lauren opal glass sconces, art décor and antique vanities. Surely with so many rooms and so much space Millie will stop complaining.

But judging by her expression I'd say that was wishful thinking. Millie balls her hands into fists. "Being in the same country as you is too close, let alone the same suite."

I laugh. "That is something you will have to get used to over the coming days."

Her expression hardens, but she says nothing.

"Have you quite finished?" I say, and return my focus to the business section of the paper.

"I've not even begun." She reaches forward and swats at the paper. "I can't believe you have the audacity to read when I'm trying to talk to you."

"Are we going to attempt to have a civilised conversation?"

Her scowl is immediate. "This isn't what I agreed to."

I lean forward and take my mug of tea from the glass table. I take a sip and am grateful for the generous splash of whiskey I poured in. "What can I say? Things change."

Tiny droplets of water trickle from the towel wrapped around her hair and continue on down her face. If her anger could be felt, I'm sure each droplet would turn to steam.

"I want to go home," she says, her voice breaking.

I nod toward the door. "I will arrange transport. A five-hour car journey should be enough time for you to calm down."

"My God, Gage! You're insufferable."

"Why is that?" I stand, and within seconds have closed any distance between us.

"Because you're a cocky rich jerk." She makes a point of jabbing me with her index finger with every word.

"And you're an annoying pain in the ass."

"Potato, potahto," she fires back, clearly running out of things to say.

We lock gazes for long seconds, though the anger that shines back in hers begins to weaken and is very soon replaced by tears. "Take me home, please. Just take me home."

She lowers her head so I don't see her cry, but it's too late. I blow out and, reaching for her chin, lift her face up so she's forced to meet my stare.

"It's my baby sister's twentieth birthday today. My brothers and I arranged a surprise celebration over a year ago. I love my sister dearly, and I will not miss her big day for anything or anyone. Do I make myself clear?"

Millie wriggles from my hold and wipes her cheeks.

"How about I stay in my bedroom?" I suggest. The knocking at the door causes us to break eye contact. "Ah, that'll be our breakfast. I hope you're hungry."

"You ordered breakfast?" Millie says, a ghost of a smile touching her lips.

She's hungry, of course she is. I am too, given the time we spent travelling yesterday. "Of course I ordered breakfast. I am a gentleman after all."

"Debatable," she scoffs, but her eyes come alive at what I can only imagine to be the thought of food. "What did you order?"

"Oh, you know, mussels, oysters, caviar…"

Her expression sours. "Fish for breakfast? Gross, who does that?"

"Plenty of people," I point out.

I know she hates seafood, and for that reason I may have ordered an off-menu assortment of fish just to piss her off. But I'm not a complete jerk, I also ordered everything from the breakfast menu so she'd have a choice.

I see this little trip to London as my chance to get to know her properly. I want to know what makes her tick. I also want to know how I can thaw out her ice-cold heart. Having Millie as an enemy is counterproductive. What I need is her onside. What I need is her as a friend.

There's another knock, only this time louder. I nod toward the door in an 'aren't you going to get it?' type action.

Millie's feet stay rooted to the floor. "After you."

We make our way through the living area, and Millie opens the door. Though we aren't greeted by a member of staff delivering our breakfast.

"Farrah," I say. "What an unexpected surprise." I look past my sister and make eye contact with the man standing to her right. I take a step back so they can enter the room.

"And who is this?" Farrah asks, staring at Millie.

"I'm sorry, how rude of me. This is Mildred. Mildred, this is my sister, Farrah, and her bodyguard, Dante."

Millie takes a step forward. "Please, call me Millie."

A huge smile explodes on my sister's face as she looks from me to Millie. "Oh, my God, Gage. This must be your girlfriend," Farrah squeaks. Black hair is everywhere as my baby sister literally launches herself at Millie. "Just what I wanted for my birthday, another sister!"

ELEVEN

Millie

I'm hit with the strong scent of lavender as Farrah launches herself at me. I turn to look at Gage, or at least I would if I could see through the mass of hair.

"She isn't my girlfriend," Gage says, peeling his sister from me.

Farrah releases me and looks me up and down. There's a knowing look in her eyes, which I can only assume is from the fact I am wearing a robe, and it is very obvious from the towel I have around my head that I have come from the shower.

"Would anyone like a cup of tea?" Gage asks, breaking the awkward silence.

"No, thank you," I mumble, and stuff my hands into the flannel pockets of the robe.

"Yes, please, but only leave the bag in for a minute," Farrah says, and, passing me, shows herself to the sitting area.

"In other words, you want hot milk?" Gage calls after her, and heads for the kitchen, while I and Dante join Farrah. She is sitting on the sofa, and, smiling, taps the empty space next to her for me to sit.

I rock on my heels, looking between Farrah and my bedroom. I feel so uncomfortable, but will feel better when I'm at least dressed appropriately.

"I'm going to get changed," I say, excusing myself.

Farrah nods and turns her attention to her bodyguard. "Dante, come sit."

My eyes widen and I can't help but stare. The guy's seriously hot. His skin, like his hair, is a golden brown. A trim beard and moustache frame his face, but what has me staring are his eyes, eyes that are guarded, eyes that look as though they hide many secrets. I'd guess him to be around the same age as myself, but there's something in the way he stares that tells me he's lived many lifetimes.

"I'm fine standing," he says, his tone noncommittal.

I return my attention to Farrah. She holds Dante's gaze for a second before gazing down at her manicured nails. "Suit yourself."

I point over my shoulder. "I'll be right back," I say, and head for my room.

Gage and Farrah are mid-conversation when I reenter the lounge. I half listen as he fills her in as to our arrangement. It appears that in my absence the hotel staff arranged our breakfast on the long glass table in front of the sofa. Luckily for me the fruit has been placed away from the seafood.

Who eats caviar for breakfast anyway? Gage Calloway, that's who!

I sit beside Farrah and try not to gag as I reach for a banana.

"What I don't understand is why you'd put all this effort into a random hotel in the middle of nowhere," Farrah says.

Gage plucks an oyster from the iced platter and swirls it

around the shell. He tips his head back and swallows it whole before speaking. "Why not."

"It just doesn't make sense. Unless there's more to it." Farrah keeps looking at me and smiling, like her mind is adding two and two together and coming up with five hundred.

I peel back the banana skin and let out a laugh. "Trust me when I say there is nothing more to it."

Farrah's shoulders drop. "I see."

The disappointment is so clear in her voice that I almost feel guilty. But then I remember the reason for her disappointment is because I'm not head over heels in love with her jerk of a brother, and my guilt dissolves.

Long black lashes frame her emerald-green eyes. My God, Gage's sister is beautiful, the kind of beautiful that is intimidating. I wouldn't exactly say that I fell out of the ugly tree, but I know I'm not gifted in the looks department, whereas Farrah really is something else. Long raven hair hangs around her face and falls in soft waves down her back. Her eyes are long and catlike, her nose small with a slight upturn, and her lips are beautifully shaped and full. Lips that only now I notice are moving. She's talking, but I haven't heard a single word.

"Say yes, say yes," she chants. She claps her hands together, and I jump, almost dropping my banana.

"Say yes to what?" I side-eye Gage, who is spooning caviar from a small ceramic bowl.

"To joining me this morning for a spa day," Farrah squeaks. "We have unlimited access to the pool, sauna and steam room, and I have a ton of treatments booked in with the beauty therapist. Chelsea, my sister-in-law, is coming too. She and my brother Lucian are due to arrive any moment."

"Mildred and I have plans today."

"Hush, Gage. I was asking Millie."

I try not to grimace. A spa day is my worst nightmare. The thought of being semi-naked while having some random person all up in my personal space is spiking my anxiety. "No, thank you. It's really not my thing."

Farrah's excitement deflates like a balloon.

"As I was saying," Gage interjects, "Mildred and I have a busy morning all planned out. I'm sure you will have a nice time with Chelsea." Gage gets to his feet, I figure to see Farrah out.

Farrah stands, and without being prompted heads toward the door. She pauses and looks from me to Gage. "Will you at least join us for a coffee after?"

"I will have to decline." Gage glances at his watch. "I have some late morning conference calls that I can't miss."

Farrah's gaze lands on me. "What about you?"

I smile, although she's put me on the spot. I can't deny that I want to get to know Gage's sister a little better, and maybe she has some entertaining and highly embarrassing stories about her brother. "Sure, I'd love to."

Gage sees Farrah and Dante out and makes his way back into the living area. With his right arm outstretched he fastens his cufflink, which I notice is a golden four-leaf clover, encrusted with emerald-green diamantes. "When you've finished with breakfast, we'll begin your guided tour of the hotel." Gage switches arms and fastens the cufflink on his left wrist.

I place the banana skin on the glass table and get to my feet. "I've finished."

Gage eyes me sceptically. "Are you sure? Because you've hardly touched the food. The whole point of you coming to London is to see and experience everything a Calloway hotel has to offer. And that includes the cuisine."

I let out a sarcastic laugh and twirl my index finger around a short strand of hair that hangs loose over my face. "You're right, Gage. Maybe I'd have been willing to try more of what the hotel has to offer if *someone* hadn't ordered a bucketload of seafood."

Gage's eyes crease at the corners, and he offers me an open-mouthed smile. "Point taken."

Although I'm frowning, I can't help notice what a nice smile Gage has. How straight and white his teeth are. Of course they are—I bet he had the best dental care money could buy.

"Right, let's get the show on the road. Time is money, and although I have plenty of money, I'm afraid time is something I am always short of."

I follow Gage out of the hotel room. En route he grabs his suit jacket from the back of a chair and pulls his arms through the sleeves as we walk the short distance to the lift. With one hand placed on the small of my back, he presses the button with the down-pointing arrow. The doors ping open, and together we step inside.

"First stop, the lobby," Gage says, and hits the button for the ground floor. The whole while the lift travels down, Gage's palm rests against the small of my back. I'm not sure whether he is aware he's touching me, but if he is, he does nothing to change the fact, and oddly enough, neither do I.

In no time at all the small space is filled with the scent that is Gage, and holy hell, does he smell good. I side-eye Gage as he stands beside me. He looks the same, but different somehow. He's ditched his usual smart casual look of a shirt and jeans and instead is wearing a perfectly tailored suit jacket and trousers. But that's not it. It's everything about him—the way he stands, the way he holds himself. He radiates authority and oozes sex appeal. It's just a shame his personality leaves a lot to be desired.

The lift comes to a stop, and the doors open. To say I'm blown away by the grandeur of everything around me is an understatement. I know I saw the lobby yesterday, but I was half asleep. I'm fully awake now and have both eyes wide open. Everything in the hotel is white and sparkles, like an expensive gemstone that has been laid out intentionally for all to see. And that's the point: Gage wants everyone to see just how amazing his hotel is. How the hell can Stanton and Mills compete in its current state? My body immediately tenses at the thought. Gage isn't going to want to simply redecorate, he will want my hotel demolished so he can start again, and that I will not allow.

I force a smile on my face for the start of the tour. After getting me reacquainted with the lobby and introduced to several staff members, Gage directs us toward one of the in-house restaurants.

With his fingers curled around the handle he rocks on his heels once, twice, before turning his attention to me. "Actually, you'll experience this room up close and personal later when you join me for Farrah's birthday dinner. My brother Malachi is flying in especially for the occasion."

I hold up my hand. "You didn't say anything about joining you for a family meal."

Gage releases the handle and stuffs his hands into the pockets of his trousers. "You're right, I didn't, so I'm telling you now."

I fold my arms in front of my chest. "You're telling me?" My voice rises an octave, causing guests passing-by to glance in our direction.

Gage squares his shoulders. "No, Mildred. I'm *asking* if you'd be my plus-one to my baby sister's birthday."

Farrah seemed lovely; how can I refuse? But I won't let Gage think I'm agreeing so easily. The last thing I want is for this man to think I'm easily pushed around. What may be something as insignificant as a meal today could be a demolition order for Stanton and Mills tomorrow. "Did I hear a 'please'?"

Gage forces a smile. "Please."

His eyes, those gorgeous light blue eyes, search mine as he awaits my answer. Feeling hot all of a sudden, I lower my gaze. "Fine," I mumble.

I jump as Gage claps me on the back. "Excellent. I will have a dress laid out on your bed for the evening."

My gaze shoots up. "I brought my own clothes, thank you."

Without a word, Gage looks me up and down. I feel completely naked under the intensity of his stare. I look professional today and am wearing what I'd wear for a day at Stanton and Mills, which is a white blouse, black skirt and blazer.

"Okay." Gage flashes a glance at his watch and turns on his heel. "Mildred, come."

"Where are we going?" I call after him as his pace picks up.

"To the spa."

TWELVE

Millie

"Are you sure you don't want to come in? The water's fine," Farrah calls from the jacuzzi.

I wave her off. "No, honestly, I'm good."

I'm standing on the hot, humid poolside. I try to ignore the fact I'm melting and focus on Gage and everything going on around me.

The hydrotherapy pool and surrounding area is stunning, with slate stone-effect walls and mood lighting that changes colour every fifteen minutes, from cool blue to seductive red. The area is empty, with the exception of Farrah and Chelsea. It would appear the spa has been booked out solely for them.

"Are you sure?" A woman Gage introduced as Chelsea, his sister-in-law, slides into the jacuzzi beside Farrah. They giggle as foamy bubbles explode around them, and I can only assume the jets have been turned on.

"As sure as I can be," I say, and pull off my jacket, draping the heavy material over my forearm.

Like Farrah, Chelsea is stunning. Both women are slim and petite, but whereas Farrah is wearing a two-piece, Chelsea, who I guess to be in her mid-twenties, is mostly covered up by a high-legged black swimming costume. Chelsea smiles at me before securing her blonde hair into a low-hanging messy bun. Without another word she leans her head back on the leather headrest and closes her eyes.

I notice a silvery scar on Chelsea's forehead, like my brother Travis' scar. I don't feel comfortable enough to ask her how she got it, but curiosity has me staring.

I lean into Gage. "How did—"

"Horse riding accident," he answers quietly, without me having to finish the question.

"Come, let me show you around the spa and treatment rooms," Gage says, and I follow him out of the pool area. We amble through a network of corridors, with doors leading off into a range of biothermal rooms. There are saunas, crystal steam rooms, a salt cave, a caldarium, and to my horror there is even a room filled with snow. I narrow my eyes and read the door plaque.

"The igloo?" I gasp. "What is relaxing about being cold?"

"It is referred to as the 'fire and ice' experience," Gage explains. "It's believed that switching between hot and cold temperatures has a range of health benefits, such as boosting the body's immunity, metabolism, and fat-burning."

I wave him off. "I think I'd rather hold on to my fat than freeze my ass off in there."

Gage laughs. I do too. He continues with the tour.

"We're here," Gage announces. He stops in front of a large glass door. It must work on a sensor, as it begins to open by itself. Gage holds out an arm and gestures for me to go first.

I rock forward and back several times, because something is changing between me and Gage and I don't like it. This is the man who is determined to take away my hotel, and I can't allow myself to get on friendly terms with him. I mirror his gesture, silently saying 'after you, I insist', my way of politely flipping him the bird. Gage shakes his head, and without a word takes the lead. I follow him inside.

My mouth falls open. "Wow," is the only word I can muster. It's as though we have been transported to an underground cave. The room is dimly lit, and artificial stalactites hang from a low domed ceiling. Water trickles down from the jagged sandstone walls. Soothing music is playing all around us, but where it's coming from I have no idea.

"Mr Calloway." A female receptionist stands bolt upright. I was so engrossed that I overlooked her, but it's easy to see why. The stone desk she is standing behind blends in.

"I'd like to show Mildred around one of the treatment rooms."

"Certainly, right this way," the receptionist says, and rounds the desk. She stands close enough that I'm able to read her name badge: Amanda Newton. Gage takes a few steps forward, whereas I stand still, my feet rooted to the floor. He must sense I'm not following, and turns. He pinches the bridge of his nose and looks at me as if to say, 'I'm not getting any younger.' Still, I'm not prompted to move.

"Mildred?" He flashes a glance at his watch.

"I'm sorry. It's just I've never seen a room like this before." I'm finally able to muster words.

"Impressive, isn't it?" A voice startles me from behind. I turn and am met by Chelsea. She is standing beside Farrah. Both women are dressed in matching Calloway-branded robes. They must be finished in the jacuzzi and have come for their beauty treatments. Here I am, literally standing in their way.

"Your treatment room and therapist are ready," Amanda says. She clasps her hands together behind her back and waits.

Chelsea acknowledges Amanda with a nod before returning her attention to me. "My brother in-law, Rick Rafferty, and his construction company are responsible for the interior of the spa."

"No freakin' way." The words fall from my mouth before I have a chance to stop them. But I don't care how pre-teen I sound, I am absolutely captivated. "He is seriously talented."

"He is," Chelsea agrees, pride evident in her eyes.

"You know, there is a hidden cave on the island, a cave only the locals know about," I say, my gaze roaming the intricate craftsmanship. "It's kind of our little secret. A piece of the island we won't share with outsiders."

"That's really cool," Farrah says.

"It is," I agree, and for a few magical seconds it feels like I've been transported back there. Back to my island, and back home.

Gage clears his throat, and I'm jolted back to reality. "As lovely as your little trip down memory lane was, must I remind you that time isn't my friend?"

"Like the majority of people on the planet, I'm sure," I muse, not able to contain the smile that spreads across my face. Whereas Chelsea stifles a laugh, Farrah's face is straight, her eyes are wide and her gaze bounces between us. Something tells me she's unsure how her brother is going to react.

"Excuse me?" Gage raises a brow. It would seem that he doesn't find my comment the least bit funny. His expression remains cold, though I feel the heat of his gaze burning right to my core.

He holds eye contact for long seconds before looking expectantly at Amanda. She picks up on this and says, "How about I show you to treatment room one? It is made up ready for Mrs and Miss Calloway."

"Lead the way," Gage says.

"I don't think I will ever get used to being called Mrs Calloway," Chelsea says as we are led to a room.

Amanda opens a heavy wooden door, and one by one we step inside. As I expected, the treatment room resembles a cave, yet a dull red light falls down the walls in what can only be described as a slow-flowing wave. It kind of resembles lava, and this room our own personalised volcano. Two beauty beds have been laid out side by side in readiness, and a range of products have been arranged on a stone side unit.

"Your therapist will be with you shortly," Amanda says, backing out of the room. "When you're ready, get undressed and into the beds."

It's now I notice a tiny pair of disposable underwear on each of the beds and sense that's our cue to leave. Farrah turns to Gage with a look in her eyes that says, 'Why are you still here?'

Gage runs his fingers through his hair. "Come, Mildred."

I don't need asking twice, I'm out of the door before Gage is.

"We'll be finished at one, Millie," Farrah calls after me. "Meet us at Valentino's, it's a small coffee shop a few streets away."

I put my foot forward to stop the door from closing. "A few streets away?" Inside the hotel I can just about get my bearings, but outside may as well be a maze. It's not as though Gage can walk me, he's made it clear he will be tied up with conference calls. "I don't really know my way around London," I admit.

"Why don't you meet us by the poolside loungers when we've finished our treatments," Chelsea suggests. "We'll get ready and leave together."

I release the breath I was holding. "Perfect, I'll see you then."

I remove the foot I was using to hold the door open. In the time it closes, Farrah drops her robe to the floor. Dressed in her yellow bikini, Farrah turns her back on Chelsea and lifts her hair up, silently asking her to unfasten her halter-neck top. Without hesitation Chelsea reaches forward to oblige. The door to the treatment room closes.

It's clear to see that Chelsea and Farrah have a strong bond—they're bound to, seeing as Chelsea is married to Farrah's brother and they share a daughter, Farrah's niece. I on the other hand am virtually a stranger. I feel like the nerdy girl at school being welcomed by the popular kids. Although the gesture is nice—more than nice—our worlds couldn't be further apart. We have zero common ground, and it worries me that after the initial intro, we will have absolutely nothing to talk about. I'm starting to regret my decision to join them later.

"Come, Mildred," Gage says, snapping me out of my trance, where I was staring longingly at the wooden door. *Not weird at all!*

I spin on my heel and we make our way out of the spa.

When it's time for Gage to make his conference calls, he walks me back to the spa area so I can meet up with Farrah and Chelsea. They are fully dressed and reclining on the poolside loungers when I re-enter the spa. They are both wearing cute summer dresses, whereas I am still wearing my blazer and black skirt. I instantly regret not going to my room to change.

"Millie," Farrah calls, and does a come-hither motion with her hand. I take a few steps forward and perch on the lounger next to hers. She reaches down and retrieves her handbag from the floor. "Before we go, I would really love your opinion on what colour eyeshadow I should wear." Farrah whips out a cosmetic bag.

Chelsea wags her finger. "You know you're not meant to apply make-up right after a facial."

Farrah shrugs. "I know, but Dante is waiting outside…" Her words trail off.

I bite back a smile. Has Farrah Calloway got a crush on her bodyguard? I'm tempted to ask, but know it isn't my place.

She unzips her bag and pulls out a slim bottle of foundation. She squeezes a dollop onto the back of her hand and with a make-up sponge begins to apply it to her face. She uses the tiny mirror attached to the inside of her make-up bag to check over her appearance before pulling out an eyeshadow palette. She flips open the lid and looks at me expectantly. "Which colour should I use?"

I pause and look over the many shades. I try to picture

what shade would best suit her—maybe complement the hue of her eyes, or the turquoise dress she's wearing. But it's no good. "Honestly, I don't have a clue. I only wear eyeshadow on special occasions, and I usually just pick the first colour that catches my attention."

Chelsea and Farrah exchange glances before turning to me.

"You know, Chelsea and I are really into make-up. Chelsea is a qualified make-up artist, salon owner and entrepreneur." Farrah looks at Chelsea expectantly.

"And Farrah is learning how to apply make-up professionally," Chelsea adds.

"That's great," I say. "Then Chelsea will be the best person to ask about eyeshadow."

"Maybe, but I wanted your opinion," Farrah says. I point to a light green, as it's the first colour that catches my attention, and after applying a subtle hint to the lids of her eyes Farrah snaps the eyeshadow palette closed.

"Chelsea and I plan to launch our own cosmetics brand one day," Farrah says, her expression filled with excitement and possibility.

I shuffle on the lounger. "That sounds great."

I don't know where they're going with this conversation. Are they trying to shine a light on how different we are? Because if that's the case, they needn't bother. I don't need a make-up tutorial to know that.

"It's just we Calloway women know our way around a cosmetics bag, is all, and we'd love to teach you," Farrah says. She leans closer toward me so our knees are touching.

I laugh. "Is this some kind of initiation into the Calloway clan? Because if it is, please don't waste your time. I am not going to become the next Calloway lady any time this century."

"I don't believe that for one second," Farrah says. She drops her foundation bottle into her make-up bag and fishes out a lip gloss tube.

"I'm telling you the truth." I lift my arms up for emphasis. "Gage is nothing to me. We can barely tolerate each other."

Farrah shakes her head. "I've seen the way my brother looks at you. And besides that, Gage hasn't shared a hotel room with another woman since Daphne."

"Daphne?" I question. "Who's she?"

Farrah looks at me as though I've grown a second head. "Gage's ex-wife."

My brows shoot up. "Wait, you're telling me Gage was married?"

I recall seeing something about a breakup when I googled Gage, but I didn't realise they were married. At the time I was searching his name, his love life was the last thing on my mind, so I skimmed the article and instead searched for information about his businesses and his family.

But now? Now I'm curious, more than curious. Gage was married? To whom? What was she like? How long ago were they together?

"Tell me more," I say, trying to sound blasé, but can feel myself leaning closer.

"I can't believe he hasn't told you." Farrah flashes a glance to Chelsea before returning her attention to me. "We had no idea, and only found out about it from a magazine article. By that time the marriage had been annulled. I've never seen Gage as hurt as he was then."

"About that coffee," Chelsea interrupts.

But I ignore her and instead keep my gaze trained on Farrah. "What happened?"

Farrah opens her mouth just as Chelsea appears behind her and places a hand on her shoulder. "I think these are questions Millie should be asking Gage, don't you agree? Now, about that coffee…"

THIRTEEN

Gage

While Millie spends the afternoon with my sister and sister-in-law, I busy myself taking conference calls. I'm about to turn my phone off for the day when the name of one of my assistant managers flashes on the screen. I swipe to accept and click the call to loudspeaker.

"Richard," I say.

"Mr Calloway. I hope you're well. The reason for my call is that we have evidence that confirms Robert Whitehall has been changing bookings and laundering money into an offshore account."

My brows rise. To say I'm shocked is an understatement. Robert Whitehall is a highly sought-after manager based in the Midlands. He's been with the company for years and is currently up for the position of area manager. I run my fingers over my brow. This is one headache I could have done without this weekend. In normal circumstances I would drop everything and go to the hotel in question, but with Farrah's birthday dinner later

I simply don't have the time. "Please email me everything you have."

"Already sent, sir."

With Richard on speaker, I click on my mail. Sure enough, I have been sent a PDF and several voice recordings. I flick through the PDF, and although the evidence is incriminating, it's not enough. Especially should Mr Whitehall decide to be stupid and take me to a tribunal for unfair dismissal.

"Thank you. I will have an internal investigation carried out before I decide what to do."

This has never happened before. Not on my watch, or my father's when he ran the Calloway hotels. It's for this reason I want everyone's discretion. I cannot afford for the press to get hold of the story.

"And if he is fired, who will take the position of manager?" Richard asks.

I'm sure Richard would love me to hand it to him, but the truth is that he just isn't ready. The guy is twenty and barely out of university. Sure, he has the qualifications, but he doesn't yet have the experience.

"An internal investigation could take weeks, so let's cross that bridge when we get to it," I say and cut the call.

After getting changed into something more comfortable, I head for the home gym. I take a seat on the bench of the multi-gym and ease in with several arm repetitions before upping the weight plate another ten kilos.

After working out I have a shower, get dressed in a T-shirt and jeans and spend the remainder of my morning in peace reading the property section of the newspaper. I scan the listings and notice a substantial plot of land in Staffordshire is for sale. Currently the land is home to a derelict paper mill factory. The land would be perfect to build a hotel, but the location isn't. It's mostly residential, with a primary school not far away. I forward a photo to my brother, Malachi, who owns Calloway Housebuilders.

The door to the penthouse opens, telling me that Little Miss Thorn In My Side has returned. I wait a second for the customary 'honey, I'm home', but can't say I'm shocked to hear nothing except for the clicking of her heels against the marble floor tiles. I can sense her standing feet away. Seeing as she can't be bothered to greet me, I can't be bothered to look up from the paper.

"I thought you said you would stay in your room." Her tone is laced with accusation, like she's caught me out. I just know Millie will be standing with a hand on her hip. I flash a glance in her direction, and I'm right on the money. "Do you make a habit of breaking promises?"

"Not especially," I say and turn the page of the newspaper.

She has progressed to two hands placed on her hips. She must be royally pissed off, and I love it. "Maybe it's your memory. It's got to be all the alcohol you consume, killing off brain cells." She eyes the half-empty bottle of Jack on the glass table in front of where I'm sitting.

"Maybe." I cross one leg over the other. "So, about dinner."

I flash a glance at my watch. We have four hours to kill before Farrah's birthday celebrations. I need to make sure Millie has something to wear that doesn't consist of one of the godawful cardigans she seems to love so much.

"Dinner?" She laughs. "Do you want to be wearing your food?"

"Why? Do you plan on smothering it on me?" I cock a brow. "That's kind of kinky."

"I was thinking more like an egg to the head," she fires back, but if I'm not mistaken, she's smiling. It's clear she is enjoying our little exchange just as much as I am. Millie, being Millie, won't want to advertise the fact, so spins around and heads toward her room. But I don't want her to leave. Not yet. I'm having too much fun.

I jump up from where I'm sitting and hurry after her. "Tell me honestly you don't enjoy our conversations."

"I'd rather have teeth pulled." She tries but fails to sound angry.

"Really?" I can't help but laugh. "I don't think toothless would be a good look for you." I take her shoulder and spin her round. We are standing face to face, our gazes locked—or I'm assuming they are, I can't be sure since her hair is loose and hangs wildly in front of her face.

I was too busy reading my paper and riling her up to notice she's wearing her hair down. It is usually scraped back quite severely. I'm sure with how tight she wears it that she is attempting a natural brow lift. I brush her hair behind her ear, then really look at her. Her mousy brown locks caress her shoulders and fall a few inches below.

"Is that all?" she says, and steps back, putting distance between us.

"No." I take a step forward. "Need I remind you that you said you'd accompany me to Farrah's birthday meal?"

"And I will. Did anyone ever tell you that you're a certifiable space invader?"

I frown, my mind instantly filled with colourful aliens. "As in the arcade game?"

"No." She pushes me back. "I meant a literal space invader."

"Right." I laugh, itching to close the distance between us. "Are you sure you don't need a dress for the meal?"

"I'm sure. Just because I live on an island doesn't mean I don't have nice clothes," she says, and holds out her arms exasperatedly. "Now is that all?"

Is that all? I haven't even begun. "No," I answer simply.

Millie's eyes widen. "What else could you possibly want?"

What do I want? Her question is very broad. I make a point of tapping my chin several times as if in thought. "Another few billion in the bank, the most successful hotel chain in the country, and after that world domination."

Millie rolls her eyes. It's apparent that her patience is starting to wear thin. "Seeing as I can't personally help you with any of those, I'm going to my room for a lie down." Her hair fans out as she turns around.

"But what I want from you…" I say loud enough to spark her interest, which I can see I've done, as she hasn't taken a single step forward.

"What could you possibly want from me?"

I allow my gaze to rove over her body, from the back of her head on all the way down to her toes. I stop momentarily at her ass. I lean forward till my lips find the shell of her ear. "I want to get to know you, Mildred Mills."

I inhale deeply and take in her floral scent, mixed with the essence of coffee. My breaths glide over her as she stands perfectly still. It's as though someone has hit the pause button on us, and for some reason I can't explain, I don't want this moment to end.

"I'm going for that lie down," Millie finally says, and without a backward glance heads straight for her room. The door clicks shut behind her.

It's seven p.m. when I find myself standing outside Millie's bedroom door. I was standing on the same spot at six p.m. when I gave her an hour's notice.

I clear my throat, curl my fingers into a fist and knock. "Mildred, it's time."

Silence.

Feeling warm all of a sudden, I give my silk tie a tug before unfastening the top button at the collar. "Mildred," I repeat, only this time louder. I'm met with more silence. I glance at the door handle and consider letting myself in, but that would be a complete violation of her privacy. What if she's undressed?

The thought has my mind picturing Millie in various states of nakedness. A vision that has me squeezing my fists together a little tighter, because now is definitely not the time to think those kinds of thoughts. For one, it's my little sister's birthday meal, and for another, the navy trousers I am wearing have been tailored to fit me like a glove. Any unwanted bulges will be hard to hide. I open my suit jacket and pull a small silver flask from the inside breast pocket. I eye the reflective casing like I'm looking at an old friend.

"You'll never let me down, will you, Jack?" I unscrew the lid and take a large gulp. I replace the lid, then knock on the door for the second time. "Mildred, I swear to God if you're sleeping I'll be carrying your ass down in your pyjamas." I grab for the handle, my mind at war with itself as to the reasons why I shouldn't let myself in, when the handle lowers by itself. I release the cool brass just as the door opens and Millie steps out.

My eyes go wide as I take her in. "My God, Mildred, you look…" My words trail off as I'm stunned by the girl standing before me.

"Different, I know. You don't scrub up so bad yourself." Her eyes are on me, and it's as though we are seeing each other for the first time. I've never seen Millie made up, and I like what I see. She looks the same, but different somehow, and I can't peel my eyes from her.

Much to my delight, she is wearing her hair down and styled in loose spirals. Her make-up, although not heavily applied, amplifies her dark brown eyes, high cheekbones and shapely lips. I'm pleased to see that she isn't hiding behind a frumpy old-lady cardigan and is instead wearing a teal gown that hugs her every curve.

Millie coughs, but it's more to get my attention. "When you've finished checking out my cleavage, I believe we have somewhere to be."

I raise my index finger, signalling for her to wait. "One more minute," I say, and with no shame continue to blatantly stare at her breasts.

"Gage, I'm serious." I jump as she swats my arm with the back of her hand, then crosses her arms in front of her chest. "I haven't worn this dress since Tanya's wedding five years ago. I felt uncomfortable then, and even more so now. Can we just hurry up and go so I can sit down?"

Is she serious right now? She looks utterly breathtaking, and all she wants to do is hide behind a table.

"Hmm, this does pose a serious problem," I say, and tap my chin in thought.

"What?" Millie asks, seemingly a little flustered.

I rotate my index finger mid-air several times, signalling for her to spin around.

"What's wrong?" She turns a complete three-sixty.

I shake my head. "It's just… how are you going to sit down with that giant stick you have wedged up your arse?"

Millie's eyebrows shoot up. "Excuse me?"

"You heard. Loosen the fuck up." My words clearly shock her. I'm sure she's a second away from slapping me, and I wouldn't blame her. But instead of backing away I step closer. "And another thing," I say, getting all up in her space.

Millie stands her ground. "What now?"

"You look pretty."

Her cheeks glow red and she attempts to look away, but I don't let her. I capture her chin between my thumb and index finger, holding her face in place. "Correction. You look utterly ravishing."

She shakes her head, and I lose my claim on her. "I really don't." Her words are shaky, and she looks everywhere else apart from at me.

"Damn it, woman, will you just accept the compliment?"

"I'm sorry, I'm just not used to them."

Her words shock me. How can anyone who's seen Millie not tell her how utterly captivating she is? A classic beauty she is not, but with or without make-up, this girl, this woman is something else.

"And besides," she adds, "you have an ulterior motive."

I feel somewhat insulted. "I'm not trying to get you into bed, if that's what you're insinuating."

"I was talking about my hotel."

Of course she was. I can't deny that the thought of sleeping with Millie hasn't crossed my mind, but Millie and I having sex is off the table—in fact, it was never there to begin with. And yet all I'm picturing is removing that teal silk dress from her, one delectable inch at a time.

"Can we go now?" Shouldering past me, she heads for the living area.

"Just a minute," I call, and adjust the waistband of my trousers.

I catch up with Millie, and, with my hand placed on the small of her back, I walk with her to the lift. I press the button, and when the doors ping open, we step inside.

The lift feels smaller and warmer than it has done before. I'm considering removing my jacket when Millie steps away, causing my hand to fall to my side. I step forward and again place my hand on the small of her back. She shuffles awkwardly. "Gage, stop."

I rake my fingers through my hair, needing something to do with my hand. "Let me guess, this is when you call me a space invader again?"

"No." Millie's words are barely audible.

"Don't you like being touched?" I ask.

She doesn't speak for a second, and instead stares at me, almost trancelike.

"Earth to Mildred." I click my fingers in front of her face. She snaps out of her trance, her gaze locking onto mine.

"No," is her reply.

I stuff my hands into my trouser pockets, making a mental note not to touch her again. Though in all honesty, it was something I'd done subconsciously. For some reason totally foreign to me, it just felt right having contact with her.

"It's not that. I like being touched." Millie's cheeks are beet red, and she looks down, seemingly unable to hold my stare. "Just not by you. I mean come on, Gage, we don't even like each other."

"Are you sure about that?"

Millie is silent, a silence that speaks louder than any words. She parts her lips to speak, but closes them just as quickly.

"Just as I thought. You can't answer because in truth you don't know how you feel about me, do you?"

She swallows loudly. "I don't like you, Gage Calloway."

"Who are you trying to convince?" I question. "How about you say that again, but this time look at me?"

During our conversation I have been getting gradually closer to Millie, while in turn she has been moving further away. Her back meets with the corner of the lift, and for the first time, she has nowhere to go. I gently tug one of her spiral curls until the curl is poker-straight, then on its release I watch as it springs back into the perfect spiral.

Her breaths are shallower now, and with her gaze locked on mine she bites on her lower lip. "Gage—"

"Yes, Mildred?"

She watches me intently as I lean my face toward hers. She doesn't turn away, nor does she flinch when my breaths caress her cheek.

"I'm going to kiss you now," I say, and close any distance between us. My lips brush softly against hers. She doesn't part her lips in response, but doesn't pull away either. Our bodies are flush. We're so close that it should feel wrong, but it doesn't. It's like we're trying one another for the first time, a small sample before deciding whether we want more. And I do. I want more of this, more of her. I part my lips just as the lift doors ping open.

Instinctively I turn around, giving Millie just enough time and space to shimmy away.

Guests from the lobby begin to filter in, leaving us no choice but to exit the lift. We don't speak as we head for the restaurant. I side-eye Millie, and she side-eyes me right back before looking away. It's as though we are playing a warped game of cat and mouse, and I do like the chase. We stop walking when we reach the set of double doors.

"About what happened in the lift," I begin, but Millie cuts me off.

"Nothing happened. I've told you already, Gage, I don't like you." She's still playing the denial card.

"So you keep saying." I motion with my hand toward the door. "Shall we?"

She takes a deep breath in, then, closing her eyes, blows out. She repeats this several times before nodding. I take the brass handle and pull the door open.

"After you," I say.

"No, no. Please, after you." Millie's crossing and uncrossing her arms. It's as though she can't settle.

"Not nervous, are we?" I capture her hand and hold her arm in place.

Her eyes narrow immediately. "Of course not."

"Because I could hold your hand if you were, you know, for moral support…"

"I think not." She pulls out of my hold and does a shooing action with her hands. I can't help but laugh.

"And for the record," I say, and look her up and down one final time, "I don't like you either."

She glowers at me, and I glower right back. It doesn't take long for her frown to be washed away by indifference.

Voices ricochet off the walls as we enter. The voices that can be heard above the rest are those of my brother Malachi and my father.

There is a large circular table positioned in the centre of the room. I spot Farrah immediately, seeing as there is an obscenely sized balloon with the number twenty secured to the back of her seat. Next to Farrah is Chelsea, my brother Lucian, Malachi, my father and his girlfriend, Julie. I spot the empty seats that have been reserved for us, and we make our way over.

"Gage, Millie," Farrah squeaks. Conversations around the table stop immediately, and all eyes land on us.

FOURTEEN

Millie

My heart is beating so hard in my chest that it booms like a drum in my ears.

Everywhere I turn, he's there, from his scent that lingers in every room he's been in, to his touch that feels as though it has been branded onto my skin. And when we aren't together he's a constant companion in my mind.

Being this close to Gage has my mind in a spin. He's toying with every single emotion of mine. Anger, annoyance and loathing dance with joy, intrigue and lust. On the outside I'm letting annoyance take the lead, but on the inside I feel like a jumbled mess.

He is too much, yet somehow is not enough. I can't escape him, though part of me doesn't want to. Pushing my emotions aside, I force myself to focus on the here and now.

I'm in awe of the restaurant. The décor, although bold, is tastefully done. Intricately carved stone pillars line duck egg-coloured walls. Crystal chandeliers hang from a domed glass ceiling, their light emitted from dozens of candles. At full capacity I imagine this room would easily accommodate five hundred people, but for this evening the floor space has been cleared of tables and chairs, with the exception of one. One beautifully dressed circular table with a fancy white tablecloth and duck egg runner. A bonsai tree takes centre stage on the table, with a smaller floral piece surrounding it.

As much as it pains me to admit, Gage wasn't wrong about the interior design. To say his hotel is impressive is an understatement. I guess it wouldn't be a terrible idea to spruce up Stanton and Mills. Whereas the Calloway Hotel screams luxury, I want Stanton and Mills to look modern yet still keep its 'home away from home' feel. With Gage and I wanting opposing things, someone will have to bend, but that someone won't be me.

I skim the sea of faces. There are half a dozen people sitting around the table, and all eyes are on us. Apart from Farrah and Chelsea, no one is smiling. As well as not smiling, no one is speaking, not so much as a word. It's quiet, so quiet I'm sure we'd easily hear a pin drop. I feel very small and on show all of a sudden, and without thinking tug on the sleeve of Gage's suit jacket, I guess more to remind him that I'm still here.

Gage's stance changes immediately, and, picking up on my cue, he clears his throat. "Everyone, meet Mildred Mills, my business partner at Stanton and Mills Hotel."

With his hand on the small of my back, he walks us around the table and toward two empty seats. The silence seems to follow us every step of the way. Gage pulls out a chair for me beside Chelsea, and it isn't until we sit down that people continue with their conversations.

Without knowing where to look, I keep my gaze trained in front of me, where a champagne flute has been filled. A bright red raspberry floats in the sparkly gold liquid, bobbing as fizzy bubbles pop around it. An array of cutlery has been laid out around a bone-white china tea plate. There must be four forks and as many knives. I haven't even got to the spoons.

I jump as a hand lands on my lap, and Gage leans in to me. "Don't worry about the cutlery. Just follow my lead."

Am I that transparent? Or is Gage secretly able to read my mind? I'm about to ask when he nods at the man sitting beside Chelsea. "Lucian," Gage says.

Lucian, who I learned is Gage's younger brother and Chelsea's husband, nods back. "Tell me, old boy, how's life treating you?" His striking green eyes meet mine, and I stop breathing for a beat. My God, Lucian Calloway is gorgeous, with a bronzed complexion, strong chiselled jaw and full lips. He smiles at me and I smile right back, but am quick to return my attention to the man sitting at my side.

Gage's gaze remains on Lucian, his eyes creasing at the corners. "Good, as always." Gage reaches for his flute of champagne, pauses, then turns his attention to me. "I'm sorry, how rude of me. Allow me to introduce you to everyone." He lifts his hand to his chin and subtly points. "My brothers, Malachi and Lucian."

My gaze hovers on Lucian before landing on Malachi. Like his brothers, Malachi is attractive—broad, dark and handsome—but what has my attention are his eyes. They are the darkest brown I have ever seen, so dark it's as though they cast shadows over everything they touch. But it isn't just that, there's something else. Whereas Lucian's and Gage's eyes hold a warmth, Malachi's do not. His stare is so cold it sends an icy chill down my spine. He doesn't smile, not because he's incapable, but it's as though smiling would be too much of an inconvenience. Instead, he merely offers a curt nod.

"My father, Duncan Calloway, and his partner, Julie," Gage says, and then pauses, as if giving us a chance to get acquainted.

Duncan is the typical old guy, with stark white hair and wrinkled skin. I smile when I notice the shoulder braces peeking out from beneath his suit jacket because it reminds me of my late grandfather. Which has me thinking that Duncan has a kindly grandfather look about him. Although there is nothing kind about the way he is looking at me.

Shifting in my seat, I glance at Julie, who smiles big. "We're really pleased to meet you, Mildred. Aren't we, dear?"

She reaches under the table, and whatever she does causes Duncan to jump. He grunts before adding, "Very pleased." He looks past me and asks, "Chelsea, sweetheart, when is my darling granddaughter making an appearance?"

As well as Lucian's arm draped around her, Chelsea is wearing a midnight-blue gown and her blonde hair has been pinned back in a clip. Chelsea smiles at the old man before flashing a glance at her diamond-encrusted watch. "I expect she'll be awake any moment. The nanny knows to bring her down as soon as she makes a sound."

"I get cuddles first," Farrah interrupts. The balloon that has been secured to the back of her chair bobs as she bounces up and down. As immature as some of her actions are, tonight she looks so much older than her twenty years. Her gold dress hugs her curves, twinkling in the light from above. Her long black hair falls in loose spirals around her face, with small sections being braided and pinned back. She looks beautiful.

"Well, that's everyone." Gage concludes by reaching for his flute of champagne and knocking it back—raspberry included—in one large gulp. He raises his hand to get a waiter's attention, then gestures to his glass for a refill.

"You really should watch how much you drink," I mutter.

Gage side-eyes me, his gaze so intense that I'd be lying if I didn't admit that my heart did a little pitter-patter. "For your information, I do watch my drink, very closely in fact." He gestures toward the waiter, who brings a bottle of champagne over, before continuing. "I watch as it's being poured out of the bottle and into the glass."

I reach under the table and discreetly slap his thigh. "Not

funny," I say, but can't help the smile that creeps its way onto my face.

Gage leans in to me, his lips inches from my ear. "It's nice to know you care."

His warm breath caresses my neck, causing a shiver to skate the length of my spine. I quickly shake my head. "I don't care, it's just seeing as we're to be working together, you… you really need a clear head. Not only that…"

I stop talking when Gage's hand finds mine under the table. He links our fingers together and places our joined hands on his thigh.

"What are you doing?" I say, only loud enough for Gage to hear.

He leans in to me and smiles. "I'm holding your hand."

"Why?" is all I am able to muster.

Gage offers a half shrug. "Because you're nervous."

"Am not."

"You are too. Your rambling is a clear giveaway." I'm about to protest when he reaches up with his free hand and places his finger over my lips. "And because I want to," Gage continues.

I feel hot and clammy all of a sudden, from my head all the way to my toes. Not wanting Gage to know how he's affecting me, I attempt to pull my hand free, but his grip only tightens.

"Let go," I whisper-shout.

"As you wish," he says, and just like that his hand is gone and, turning his back on me, he picks up a conversation with Malachi.

I immediately regret my words and sit in silence as conversations carry on around me. Chelsea talks to Farrah, Gage to Malachi, Julie and Duncan to Lucian. I couldn't feel any more disconnected from everyone around me. I side-eye Gage, wanting nothing more than to take back my words. My little finger twitches from side to side, inching closer toward his thigh before quickly retreating. I'm so conflicted where Gage Calloway is concerned. I want to hate him, and yet deep down I like when he's close, I like how he places his hand on the small of my back in a way that makes me think it belongs there. Yet this man, this individual has the power to destroy everything I've spent my whole life building, and for that reason alone I need to keep him at arm's length. To eliminate the temptation to touch him, I clasp my hands together and sandwich them between my thighs.

I jump when a hand lands on my lap, and notice Gage is once again touching me. I look at him under my lashes and am immediately hit by an explosion of heat at how he is looking at me.

"What do you say?" He gives my thigh a squeeze.

I shift in my seat, trying to subtly get him to remove his hand, but he doesn't. I clear my throat when I notice all eyes are on me. "Say to what?"

"About spending the day as tourists tomorrow. I'll rent out the London Eye and Kew Gardens so we have exclusivity for the day. Or what about Harrods for our own personalised shopping experience? We'll have dinner at Bacchanalia and finish off the day at the Royal Opera House."

Chelsea laughs. "You can't call yourself a tourist without riding an open-top bus and seeing the Changing of the Guards at Buckingham Palace."

Chelsea's suggestion surprises me and makes me think that unlike the Calloways, she wasn't born into money.

Gage shrugs. "I was thinking something a little more upmarket and extravagant, but we can do that too, if you want."

Chelsea breaks eye contact with Gage to look at her phone. By the goofy grin on her face I'd say she's checking times and availability for excursions.

Gage leans in to me. "What do you say, Mildred?"

As wonderful as that all sounds, my stomach instantly tightens at the thought. I can only imagine the number of people lining the streets, and my idea of a fun day out doesn't consist of being around loads of strangers. "I, er…"

"Say yes, say yes." Farrah claps her hands excitedly. "We'll make a day of it."

"We?" I question, and look to Gage.

"Yes, us, Farrah and her bodyguard."

"Don't forget us," Chelsea chimes in.

"We have plans tomorrow," Lucian interrupts, his gaze momentarily on a golden pocket watch.

Chelsea's eyes go wide. "Please, Lucian. I'm sure Annabelle would love to ride in an open-top bus. Imagine the look on her face when she sees the sights."

Sighing, Lucian opens the lapels of his jacket and slides the pocket watch into the inside pocket. "Chelsea, sweetheart, are you forgetting the meetings I've pencilled in for the new cruise liner?"

"I'm sure your business partner Angus can hold the fort."

The serious edge on Lucian's face melts away the second Chelsea juts out her lower lip and gives him puppy dog eyes. He pulls her in for a hug and nods. "Count us in."

Gage turns his attention to Malachi. "Well, seeing as it's turning into a family day out, how about it?"

Malachi's expression is stoic. "Thanks for the offer, little brother, but I'll pass. Fortunately, I have more important things to do with my time than spend it amongst commoners."

Chelsea scoffs. "If there were bread rolls on the table, I'd have thrown one at your head."

Malachi shoots a knowing glance at Lucian. "Point proven."

Lucian tenses. "I hope for your sake that you're not calling my wife a commoner?"

"Not directly. I was merely making an observation."

"How about we step outside, and I'll give you an observation?"

Malachi smiles devilishly, then winks at Chelsea. "That won't be necessary, little brother."

It's clear Malachi takes pleasure riling his brother up, and it is working. The tension is palpable. Whereas Malachi remains blasé, it feels as though any second Lucian will jump to his feet Hulk-style and rip Malachi a new one.

"Gentlemen, remember yourselves," Duncan says harshly, but his words do little to ease the anger simmering in Lucian's stare.

Uncomfortable seconds pass, and I'm sure Lucian is about to speak when the doors to the restaurant swing open. We all observe as a dark-haired woman enters the room holding the most beautiful little girl I think I've ever seen. The woman lowers the child down. The second her little feet touch the floor the child runs with speed toward the table. She holds her arms out while heading for Chelsea, but is scooped up by Duncan, who lifts her onto his lap.

"How is my best girl?" he asks.

"Gra-da," she bleats and buries her head into his suit jacket. The harsh lines that were present on his face moments ago have been washed away and he's smiling, an open-mouth smile displaying a mouthful of pearly white teeth. It took him long enough, but he finally gives off that kindly grandfather vibe.

It seems the conversation of moments ago has been forgotten as everyone's attention is on the sweet little girl and her infectious smile. Everyone including Malachi, though he isn't smiling—no, he is far too superior for such emotion, instead he simply observes.

I turn my attention to Gage. "What's up your brother's ass?" I don't feel the need to specify which brother.

Gage shrugs. "I don't know. Malachi isn't usually this hostile. What I do know is since Lucian married Chelsea, our father is putting a great amount of pressure on Malachi to marry an heiress, specifically an heiress he despises."

"That can't be nice," I say, imagining how I'd feel if I was being pressured to marry someone I hate.

"Tell me about it. My father wants me to marry one of Lucian's old flames, a girl called Samantha Matthews."

His words are painful and cause my stomach to tighten. "What's she like?" I can't help but ask.

Gage shrugs. "She's beautiful."

Of course she is. Not that I care. Why would I? It's not as though I have feelings for him, or any claim over this man.

"Fortunately for you, I'm not a man who will be told what to do by anyone."

"Fortunately for me?" I counter back.

Gage smiles, and I swear I see a glimmer of evil in his eyes before he speaks. "Come on, Mildred, you know you want me."

My brows shoot up indignantly. "Excuse me?"

He leans close. "It's okay. I want you too."

FIFTEEN

Gage

Mildred Edith Mills! What is it about this stubborn, pain-in-the-ass woman that has me craving her so badly? She is the polar opposite of the kind of woman I usually find attractive, and I'm not talking about her physical attributes—no, I mean her personality. She's headstrong, stubborn to a fault and says the first thing that pops into her mind with little to no filter.

These qualities alone should deter me, but they don't, they only make me want her more. I like that she's headstrong, I like to see how much I can rile her up before I get a reaction. Seeing her angry or pissed off makes me horny as hell. I want an angry Millie to yell at me while tearing open my shirt in a lust-filled rage. My mind bubbles with ideas of all the things I want to do to her.

I side-eye Millie, who appears to be in deep conversation with Malachi, of all people. I listen in on how she describes the island and hotel to him. Pride shines in her eyes as she speaks, though my brother doesn't share her enthusiasm. Malachi pulls off the mildly interested look while not-so-subtly glancing down at his watch.

My attention is diverted as a hand waves in front of my face. "Earth to Gage."

I look up and get a flash of Chelsea's face and warm smile before my niece Annabelle is plonked on my lap. The kid looks like a bright pink marshmallow in a very large, very ruffled fuchsia dress. Her curly brown hair has been scraped back in a ribboned headband. I smile at the toddler, who is trying desperately to turn around and face the table. My guess is that she has her heart set on the raspberries. Pity they're swimming in glasses filled with champagne.

"How's my best girl?" I manage to get her attention long enough to boop her nose.

"Stawbewwy!" she demands, and I can't help smile at her mispronunciation.

"Not so fast." I take hold of her outstretched hand, which was inches from the stem of my glass.

"Oh, my God, she's adorable," Millie purrs. "How old is she?"

"A little over one." Her birthday party wasn't too long ago. Lucian of course went all-out for his baby girl. He hired everything from ponies to entertainers, not forgetting the ridiculous number of bubble machines.

With Annabelle struggling to break free from my hold, I flag down a waitress and ask her for a bowl of berries. While waiting I bounce her on my knee. She smells so sweet, a mixture of soap and youth. I can't help wonder how it'd feel to have a daughter of my own. To have her look at me the way Annabelle looks at her father—like I'm her world. To earn the title Dad. It was something I thought would be a reality by now, but sadly that reality was snatched away from me.

"Uncle Malachi's turn," Chelsea announces as she again appears out of nowhere. She plucks the child from my lap and, pass-the-parcel style, carries her over to my older brother.

"Malki!" Annabelle exclaims, and the second she is placed on his lap she wraps her arms around him. Malachi places one arm around her back while continuing his conversation with Millie. Annabelle's attention doesn't waver from my brother's face, and the way she looks up at him is spellbinding. Occasionally Malachi glances at her, which causes her to explode into a fit of giggles, though Malachi still looks bored. My brother has never cared much for children, and has made it crystal clear that he has no intention of continuing the Calloway name. Although my father has a beautiful healthy granddaughter, he is constantly dropping hints about how he wishes for a grandson.

A waitress places a saucer full of berries on the table in front of Malachi. Even with the brightly coloured fruit, Annabelle's attention remains locked on him. He eyes the fruit and then our niece. "Are these for me?" he asks.

Annabelle grabs a raspberry and offers it to Malachi.

A ghost of a smile tugs at his lips. "You eat it, sweetheart." The tenderness in his gaze is there for a second before he turns his attention to me. "I've heard enough from your girlfriend."

By 'girlfriend' I assume he's talking about Millie. I open my mouth to correct him, but of course, she beats me to it.

"I am not his girlfriend."

Malachi doesn't acknowledge her words, nor does he break eye contact with me. "Give the girl her hotel, and focus your attention on endeavours worthy of your time and money."

Millie's body tenses, and I can already feel the words bubbling, about to explode. As entertaining as that would be, it's my sister's birthday, and I don't want anything to ruin her special day.

I wrap my arm around Millie's shoulder and pull her into me. Sitting poker straight, she attempts to pull herself free. I lean down, and when my lips locate the shell of her ear I whisper, "Remember where you are."

"I know," she says through gritted teeth. Her body relaxes slightly, and she shuffles out of my hold.

"So when's dinner?" I glance around the table. Everyone is deep in conversation, everyone except for my father, who looks from me to Millie with obvious annoyance on his face. Of course he wouldn't approve if anything were to happen between Millie and I. But unfortunately for him, I'm Gage Calloway, and I don't give a flying fuck what he thinks.

It doesn't take long for our calamari appetisers to arrive. Chelsea lifts Annabelle from Malachi's lap as the waiter brings over a high chair. With the little girl secured in her seat we begin eating. All except Chelsea, who is thoroughly cleaning her and Annabelle's hands with antibacterial wipes.

I turn, about to tuck in, when I notice Millie forking fried calamari rings around her plate. Of course, she hates seafood. As we're a family who love fish, Farrah requested a set menu, and it's unfortunate for Millie that the appetiser and entrée feature the one type of food she hates.

While everyone is eating I flag down a waitress. "Please take Mildred's plate away, and bring her the menu from one of our other restaurants."

Millie side-eyes me and smiles. She mouths 'thank you'.

I place my hand over hers and squeeze. "Don't mention it."

To my surprise she doesn't flinch, nor does she pull away. Her brown eyes sparkle in appreciation. Our eye contact is broken when Malachi clears his throat. I glance across the table to see him looking in our direction.

"Please correct me if I'm wrong, but you come from a fishing family."

Millie slides her hand from mine and places it in her lap. "That's correct."

Malachi pokes the prong of his fork into a calamari ring and moves it toward his lips, though stops inches away. "Please forgive me for my bluntness, but publicly refusing to eat seafood is bad for business. Look at us Calloways for example. Young Lucian owns the cruise liner business, Gage the hotel chain, and myself the housebuilders' company."

"Your point?" Millie is quick to ask.

"My point is that as a family we support each other's business ventures. I think the fact that you won't eat fish is unsupportive."

I lean forward in my chair. "You expect the girl to eat something she doesn't like?"

Malachi nods. "She should learn to like it. Business is about sacrifice, and people don't just look at the owner of said business, but the extended family. Take me, for example. I don't care much for the ocean as I get terrible seasickness. Regardless, I make a point of going on a cruise at least twice a year to show my support for my younger brother."

"You're so hard done by," Chelsea chimes in, but her words serve as mere background noise. Malachi's attention remains solely on Millie.

"I'm not trying to hurt your feelings, Millie. But unfortunately for you, you'll be scrutinised by association and, like it or not, will be seen as part of the brand. A brand you are clearly failing." With those final words, he pops the calamari ring into his mouth and chews.

Millie shows no outward sign that my brother's words have affected her—the expression on her face is completely stoic—but from the way her face is contorted, I'd guess that she is biting the insides of her cheeks to prevent herself from speaking. She wouldn't have taken those words had they come from me. Although I've only known the girl for a short time, I know that she'd have verbally fired back and given as good as she got. But unlike me, Malachi oozes a natural authority, one which for some is intimidating.

I finish my last calamari ring and switch my plate with Millie's. A plate I asked the waitress to remove.

"There, you've eaten yours," I say, and Millie's eyes briefly meet mine. Eyes that are swimming in unshed tears. Her gaze remains unblinking as she stubbornly refuses to allow her tears to fall. These aren't tears of sorrow. No, the girl is seething.

I smile and push a fallen lock of hair behind her ear. "Ignore Malachi. He lives and breathes work, but here in the real world the guy pretty much talks out of his arse."

She smiles tightly, which causes her chin to quiver. When she can't keep her eyes open any longer she blinks, causing those tiny pearl-drop tears to fall. They roll slowly down her cheeks before disappearing into her lap. Instead of meeting my gaze she looks down, seemingly defeated by allowing herself to cry.

"Millie," I whisper.

Her gaze snaps to mine. She takes in a deep inhale of breath. "What… what did you call me?"

I shrug. "I called you Millie."

A ghost of a smile tugs at her lips. "But you said that was a pet name, reserved only for friends and family."

"Call me soft, but I see you as a friend."

She looks at me sceptically. "Since when?"

"Since now. Right now."

Our eye contact is broken when a waitress places a menu between us. Millie smiles up at the redhead, who holds a small electrical device to place her order. The menu is a subtle shade of green, white and red, which of course coincides with the Italian flag. It would seem Millie is spoilt for choice as her gaze flashes up and down.

"Any suggestions?" she asks under her breath.

I don't even need to think. "The spinach and ricotta gnudi with tomato-butter sauce," I say and hand the menu back to the waitress. "In fact, make that two."

Millie's cheeks flush red. "Gage—"

"Make it three," Chelsea calls across the table. She glowers at Lucian, who nods. "Italian it is."

"And me," Farrah adds.

I look over to Julie, who signals the waitress that she would also like the same. The table goes quiet as all eyes land on Malachi and my father. Their expressions remain unchanged.

Father shakes his head. "I'll stick with the lobster."

Malachi remains silent. Of course he does—he's Malachi Calloway, and I know my brother, he won't explain himself to anyone. When it becomes abundantly clear he isn't going to change his order the waitress taps on the electronic screen before heading out of the room.

"You didn't have to do that," Millie whispers under her breath.

I shrug. "I wanted to."

It is now Millie's hand that seeks mine under the table. She squeezes once in a silent appreciation before placing her hand back into her lap.

Have I finally chipped away at the wall she's built between us? Does she finally see me as an ally and not an enemy? I'm not sure, but what I am sure of is that something has changed between us, and as small as it may be, I like it. I like seeing Millie happy, and I like seeing a smile on her face, especially if I am the one responsible for putting it there.

SIXTEEN

Millie

Despite the less-than-ideal start to dinner, the evening has been lovely. I've chatted with Chelsea, Farrah and even at times Lucian. Gage has been wonderful, and I've thoroughly enjoyed his company. I dab the corner of my mouth with my napkin and lower my silver dessert spoon into my now-empty bowl with a clink.

"Nice?" Farrah asks.

"Ten out of ten. In fact, I think that was the best crème brûlée I've ever tasted." I chuckle to myself, a sign the wine is starting to go to my head. "I had to fight the temptation to pick up the bowl and lick it clean."

I regret the words the moment they leave my lips. The table falls silent. Of course they wouldn't find my comment funny. I'm amongst one of the wealthiest families in England. What was I thinking? *Stupid, stupid Millie.* I really should slow down with the wine, though my unease only prompts me to drink more.

I lean back in my seat and flash a glance at Gage. I'm

expecting him to be embarrassed, but the way he looks at me has goosebumps blossoming over every inch of me. He looks at me as though I'm the only girl he has ever seen, and the fire simmering in his crystal blues is simply no match for the fire that's burning deep in the pit of my stomach. It's got to be the alcohol. That's the only explanation as to why I'm feeling so giddy and drunk on him. Although those feelings were there before a single drop of wine touched my lips.

Farrah places her hand to the side of her mouth as if to tell me a secret. "I sometimes do that in private." Although her confession isn't loud, it's loud enough for everyone to hear.

Duncan scoffs. "I should hope not. I brought up a lady."

Farrah's expression straightens instantly, and, pushing a lock of hair behind her ear, she turns her attention to Chelsea.

I don't know where to look, so keep my gaze trained in my lap. Jeez, aren't this family allowed to laugh and joke? I can't help but compare Gage's family to my own. Growing up with three brothers, our dinners were so much more relaxed. But amongst the Calloways there is an invisible forcefield of restraint cocooning us. It's Farrah's birthday, for God's sake, and even she isn't allowed to break from this expectation.

Dinner couldn't end soon enough, and as soon as I get a hint of someone getting ready to leave—by way of a chair's legs creaking against the wooden floorboards—I jump to my feet.

"Thank you for a wonderful evening," I say, and smile at Chelsea, Farrah, Julie, and of course the darling little girl. My gaze happens upon Duncan and then Malachi. I have to force my lips to stay poised in an upward position when what I really want to do is glower at them. In any other circumstance I'd have given Malachi a piece of my mind, but today is not about me, today is about Farrah and coming together to celebrate her birthday. For that reason alone I keep my opinions to myself.

Lucian stands. "Chelsea and I would like to second that sentiment," he says, and while Chelsea lifts Annabelle from the child's seat, Lucian makes his way over to Farrah's. He leans down and places a hand on either shoulder. "Happy birthday, little sis," he says and places a kiss on the top of her head.

I want nothing more than to leave—not walk, but run out of this room and never look back. But I'm held captive by that forcefield of expectation, and I stay rooted to the spot as everyone says their goodbyes.

Goodbyes only serve as another excuse to strike up conversation. The only difference is that we are standing as opposed to sitting. The Calloway men talk business, while the ladies try to drag me into conversations about our impending trip to London tomorrow. My heartbeat begins to thump in my ears and my palms begin to feel clammy. Whereas they talk of the attractions and the fun we'll have, all I see is doom and busy streets lined with lots of people. I see myself being swallowed up by a sea of faces with no way out. I smile and answer 'yes' and 'no' on cue, but in this moment feel the most homesick I have ever felt.

I've come to London. I've seen the Calloway hotel and done everything I set out to do. Now I just want to return to my island and home.

Long minutes pass, filled with even more monotonous conversation. I'm about to retake my seat, seeing as it seems pointless to remain standing—that is, until Annabelle throws the mother of all tantrums, giving Lucian and Chelsea no other choice than to leave.

My hope is that everyone will follow suit, and I'm not wrong. Julie isn't far behind. She is followed by Farrah, who is met at the door by her bodyguard, leaving me alone with Duncan, Gage and Malachi.

Gage meets my gaze several times and it's clear he's trying to get away but is dragged back into conversation with his father and brother. I want to leave, need to leave. I open my mouth to speak, but before the first syllable leaves my lips, Gage turns to face me. "Millie, why don't you go ahead and wait for me in our suite."

Finally.

I smile politely and head for the door to leave. I'm halfway down the hallway when I realise that Gage has the key card to get into said suite. There is no way I'm going back to the function room, so instead head for the lobby. Gage will have to pass when he makes his way to our suite, so it makes sense for me to wait here. I locate an empty table and take a seat in a faux-leather chair. When drumming my fingers becomes boring, I turn my attention to my phone screen and begin scrolling. Of course my curiosity takes me to Stanton and Mills on TripAdvisor and I search for the most recent customer reviews. Logic tells me that the hotel hasn't gone up in flames since I left, but it's still nice to check in.

There are no new reviews. The latest was from a gentleman named Steve, written over six months ago. The fact people aren't leaving reviews isn't good for business. I surmise that I need to give our holiday makers an incentive to leave feedback, be it entry into a prize draw or a complimentary drink upon departure.

To date, Stanton and Mills has three hundred and eight reviews. Seventy percent of those are five stars. The other thirty percent are scattered evenly throughout the other star ratings. I'm not a person who dwells on negativity, so have never read the reviews below four stars, but for some unknown reason, I feel compelled to look. The feedback seems pretty consistent for three stars and below. 'Great holiday', 'amazing scenery', 'shame about the dated hotel'. A one-star review goes into great detail about the—and I quote—'god-ugly décor, ripped carpet and uncomfortable beds'.

Each review feels personal, every word a punch in the stomach. When I'm done with self-torture, I type in the name of the Calloway hotel we are staying in and hit enter. My eyes widen. Twenty-two thousand reviews. Ninety percent of the reviews are five stars. I scroll down to the one and two stars and notice the general trend is people complaining about the wait on food and room service. One guest complains that it took eight minutes for them to receive their room service brunch. I can't help but eye-roll at that comment. A whole eight minutes? Is this guy for real? *Rich people!*

I keep scrolling. There isn't a single negative review about the décor in the hotel. Not one. Is Stanton and Mills really that bad? Sure, it's a little dated, but that's part of the charm, isn't it?

An incoming call from my brother Travis flashes on the screen. I'm about to answer when a shadow looms over me from behind. I swipe the call notification and send Travis to voice mail, then turn around. I was expecting to see Gage, but am instead met by a tall balding man.

"Miss Mills, it's a pleasure to meet you. I'm Nicolas Spaulding from *London Weekly*."

Great, just what I don't need—the press. I smile out of politeness.

"Is that seat taken?" Nicolas motions toward the seat opposite me.

"Actually, it is," I say, though Nicolas is either hard of hearing or blatantly ignoring me as he rounds my chair and sits down. He signals to a hotel employee.

"Two glasses of wine, whenever you're ready."

I raise my brows at the presumption of the man. I signal to the same employee. "Make it one glass, I was just leaving."

Nicolas leans forward and places his hand on my knee. "Don't be like that. I only want a few minutes of your time."

If Travis has taught me anything, it's how to look after myself. I smile sweetly and lean forward. "Unless you want a broken nose, I suggest you remove your hand."

Nicolas' eyes go wide and he holds both hands up apologetically. "Please forgive me. I just want to talk, is all."

I fold my arms and raise my brows expectantly. "You have two minutes."

Nicolas' face breaks into a smile, and, opening the lapel of his jacket, he pulls out a small notepad and pen. "I hear Mr

Calloway is investing in your hotel chain. Tell me, is your relationship strictly professional?"

He certainly doesn't mess about. "My relationship with Mr Calloway is none of your…"

Nicolas glances past me, and I instinctively turn. I'm met with Gage. I'm surprised when he leans down and places a kiss on my cheek. "I'm so sorry to keep you waiting, sweetheart."

Sweetheart?

Gage looks to Nicolas, a smug expression plastered on his face. "Would you look at that, you're sitting in my chair. I believe the term 'fuck off' would be appropriate in this moment."

Nicolas stands immediately. "Well, I never…"

"Indeed. And unless you want me to sue your ass, you will stay the hell out of my personal life and refrain from running another story on me. Do I make myself clear?"

I'm shocked by the seriousness of Gage's tone and the harshness of his expression.

"Beverly," Gage calls across the lobby. When a tall brunette glances over, Gage does a come-hither type motion. Gage waits until she's within hearing distance before he speaks. "Please see that the exterminator is called first thing. We seem to have a large rodent running loose in the hotel." Gage makes it crystal clear that the rodent is metaphorical as his attention remains unwavering on Nicolas.

Grunting, Nicolas replaces the notepad and pen in his jacket pocket and mutters under his breath.

"I'm sorry," Gage says to Nicolas, and makes a point of cupping his hand around his ear. "I didn't quite catch that."

"I said Miss Mills has struck gold. It's obvious that she is only with you to further her career."

I sit bolt upright, about to give Nicolas a piece of my mind, when Gage speaks. "That's where you are wrong. Millie doesn't need me to further her career, she can do that herself. She is the most honest and hardworking woman I have ever come across.

Not only is she amazing, but she's charismatic, intelligent and downright determined to make a success of her business. And I am the lucky one to be in her presence."

The bravado and strength I felt moments ago is instantly quashed. Gage's words have penetrated somewhere deep inside, a place that has remained dormant for a very long time. My emotions are conflicted. On one hand I'm seeing red, yet on the other I feel giddy, as though I'm floating on a cloud. *What the hell is wrong with me?*

As Nicolas leaves, a staff member arrives carrying two glasses of wine on a silver tray. It would seem she didn't hear when I declined the drink.

"Perfect timing, Trudy." Gage casually sits down. "Millie and I will have these before we retire for the evening."

I take the fluted glass by the stem. My gaze remains locked on the man sitting opposite. "Thank you, 'sweetheart.'" I make a point of rehashing his term of endearment, and even go so far as to add air quotes.

Gage runs his fingers over his beard. "Sorry about that, and for kissing you in public. I realise I overstepped. It won't happen again. I just wanted to give that smug-ass reporter a picture he couldn't print."

"I never said that. I kind of liked it when you kissed me." Did I actually say that aloud? No doubt my cheeks are beet red. Despite my obvious embarrassment, I do nothing to take my words back and instead take a large sip of my wine. It's the drink talking and not me. I would never be so forthcoming normally.

Gage's expression sobers and his eyes darken with lust. "You wouldn't be flirting with me, would you?"

His directness has tingles of excitement running through me from my head all the way to my toes. Though it's too soon to meet his directness with an answer, so instead I say the first thing that pops into my head. "I'm tired. Can we just go to bed? I mean, can we go to sleep in our own beds that are in separate rooms?"

Gage places his empty glass down, makes his way around the chair and stops when he is standing in front of me. He holds out a hand for me to take. I look at him questioningly before taking his hand and allowing him to help me to my feet.

He leans in closer, and instinctively I lean back. My retreat does nothing to stop him from closing the space between us. I freeze when his lips land on the shell of my ear and he whispers, "I very much like the idea of your first suggestion. But seeing as you're under the influence of alcohol, I will wait until you're sober."

I try to sneer indignantly, but manage a schoolgirl giggle. What the actual hell is wrong with me?

He's right, I'm inebriated. I will feel different in the morning. Less giddy, less agreeable, less into him.

We make our way to our room in silence. The whole time Gage's hand rests on the small of my back. Only this time I don't tell him to give me space. No, instead I walk in step with him to make sure we keep contact. I like having him next to me. I like breathing in his aftershave and that uniqueness that is Gage Calloway.

My heartbeat picks up with each step we take closer to our shared hotel suite, as though I am anticipating something is going to happen between us, but that's absurd. I hardly know the guy. No, we are going to say our good nights and go to bed.

We stop in front of the door, and although I can feel his eyes burning through me I keep my gaze trained on the gold-plated room number. The number one holds my attention, not because that number holds any significance—it doesn't—but because it's something to focus on, something that isn't Gage or my stupid feelings.

There's a beep, and I take an audible breath in as Gage swipes the room card. The door opens and we enter. The penthouse suite is big, huge in fact, but as we stand toe to toe the space feels very small all of a sudden. Very small and very hot.

"Millie," Gage whispers. The back of his fingers caress my cheek, but instead of flinching or backing away, I lean into his touch.

Like the ends of two magnets, we lean into one another until the space between us has been eradicated. This is the closest I've willingly been to Gage and we are dancing on dangerous territory. Whatever happens now changes us, changes everything. There's a voice in my head telling me I should say goodnight, telling me that I need to leave this situation before any lines get crossed. Unfortunately for that voice, I choose not to listen, and instead all I can hear, all I can focus on is the ebb and flow of our breaths as they collide.

Gage's lips are inches from mine. When I don't back off, he leans in for one final time. His lips hover before grazing mine for the briefest of moments. It's as though he is seeking approval. Approval I am silently granting.

"This is a bad idea," I whisper, and, pursing my lips, I allow Gage a chaste kiss.

"Tell me why," Gage says, and without warning sucks my lower lip into his mouth. I pull my lip free and we kiss, though this time more than a peck, this time our lips press firmly together. I can taste the sweet essence of wine on his breath, mixed with spearmint. Gum or mints, I can't be sure. I can't help but wonder if Mr Calloway was hoping for a goodnight kiss this evening.

I pull away for the briefest second, allowing my brain to catch up with the here and now. Logical me needs to speak up and tell him why this is a bad idea. And in this instance logic has the upper hand. "We have nothing in common."

Gage kisses me again, and with our lips locked, he walks forward, causing me to walk back. I don't stop until my back collides with the wall. I have nowhere to go.

"Stanton and Mills, that's what we have in common," Gage says, and I immediately pull away.

"No. Correction, you're trying to take my hotel from me."

Gage's expression is unreadable. "Is that what you think?"

When I say nothing Gage continues. "I want to make the hotel, *our* hotel, the best it can be. I promise that I won't do anything without your permission."

I can't help but scoff.

"Millie, you have my word as a friend and as a gentleman." He holds out his hand, which for some reason unbeknown to me I take. I can't help notice how his large hand engulfs mine as we shake.

"A billionaire's promise," I say, looking at him from under my lashes. "Let's see if you stay true to your word."

"I'm always true to my word." Gage leans into me to once again claim my mouth. But I place my pointer finger on his lips.

"Just to let you know, I don't make a habit of making out with random men."

"There you go, yet another thing we have in common."

I nudge him playfully, but can't hold back any longer. I practically throw myself into his arms. Our lips crash together, our teeth colliding as we share a lust-filled kiss.

SEVENTEEN

Gage

I break the kiss, not because I want to, but because I know where this is leading.

I stand back for a moment and take in the sight that is Millie. I take long seconds to appreciate her shapely legs, the delicate curve of her hips, and the narrowing of her waist. She watches as I drink her in, from her head all the way down to her toes.

"If you only knew all the things I want to do to you," I say. She looks up at me, her eyes so dark and sultry. Her lips are swollen, her cheeks are flushed red, and the lids of her eyes appear hooded.

I rock on my heels once, twice before speaking. "Goodnight, Mildred." I use her full name purposely, seeing as though it's becoming increasingly difficult to keep physical distance. We need to at least establish some kind of emotional distance. And by the way her shoulders slump it would seem that my words have done just that.

"Wow, how quickly you demote me back to Mildred."

Despite her trying to compose herself, I can't miss the crack in her voice. She's silent for a second as if coming to terms with my words. Words it would seem have served more as a blow. She drops her arm to her side and smooths the skirt of her dress, pulling the material further down.

"Goodnight, Gage." Her words are emotionless. The heat that was radiating between us moments ago turns to ice.

"Forgive me. I want our first time to be amazing, and not a drunken mistake."

Her eyebrows shoot up. "There won't be a first time," is her curt reply. It's clear that I've hurt her because she won't even look at me and instead turns to face the opposite direction.

With nothing else left to say I take backward steps and head for my room. I wait for her to look at me, but as stubborn as she is, she keeps her gaze trained on an imaginary spot on the adjacent wall. It isn't until I enter my room that she turns to face me. We hold one another's gaze for long, intimate seconds until I'm inside and the door clicks shut in its frame. I stand, my fingers clasped around the door handle. It takes all of my willpower not to go back to her. Not to finish what we'd started.

Damn it.

I need to focus on something, anything that isn't Millie, I pull out a cigar, but not just any cigar. One of Malachi's imported Gurkha Black Dragons. I don't smoke much these days, but when I do it's always a Dragon.

Sitting on my bed, I pull the lighter from my pocket and hold it on the cigar butt until it sizzles, then, closing my eyes, take a long and deep inhale. In my head I picture all the things I'd be doing to Millie now. How I'd take my time with her, kissing my way up her body one delectable inch at a time. But instead I'm here smoking this damn cigar with my fingers clasped around my dick. *When did that happen?*

It strains so tightly against the waistband of my trousers that I have no choice other than to release the fastening. Blowing out several rings of smoke, I begin to stroke myself, working my shaft up and down. In my mind I'm working Millie's underwear down her thighs. When she is free of them I kiss my way up her legs until my lips are in line with her sex. I blow warm air onto her exposed flesh before swirling my tongue around her clit. My hand picks up pace and I jerk myself in time with how I picture myself tongue-fucking her.

God, what I'd give to taste her, to slide my rock-hard cock inside her slick wet opening. To fill her with complete and utter abandon. My jerks become more vigorous as I push for my release. I let out a guttural grunt when I'm nearing my climax. In my mind I'm balls deep in Millie. It's a shame my imaginings and reality aren't two of the same thing.

I'm pumping harder and faster, but my eyes snap open when a door slams. I have no choice other than to stop what I'm doing, shove my cock back into my pants and zip my trousers up. I rearrange the way I am reclined on the bed to look a little less like I'm fisting my dick.

Millie enters my bedroom like a hurricane. She has changed out of her evening dress and in its place is a body-hugging red nightie. Jesus, is she trying to kill me? My gaze lingers on her cleavage. Her very nice, very inviting cleavage.

"Gage, I need to leave. I have to leave now."

I shake my head. "That wasn't part of the plan. We aren't due to return until Wednesday at noon."

"Screw the plan," she snaps. "I need to go home."

The second I get to my feet she begins pacing the room. "Is it because we kissed? Because if it is…"

"No, Gage!" Her words are sharp.

"What's going on?"

She runs her fingers through her hair, once, twice, three times. "It's my dad. He's had a stroke and is in hospital."

I clasp her shoulder and spin her around so she has no choice other than to face me. Although we're facing one another she isn't looking at me, more through me.

"Millie, breathe," I say in a calming voice. "I need you to tell me how long ago this happened and which hospital he's in." Stupid question now I think about it, seeing as there is only one hospital on the island.

"What if something bad happens and I don't make it to him in time?" Tears stream down her face as she continues talking, only her words are completely incomprehensible.

I clasp her upper arms and don't release her until she reluctantly meets my stare. "Pack your case. I will make a call and have us back on the island as soon as humanly possible."

Millie sniffs, and, wiping her nose with the back of her hand, says, "Okay, Gage."

We arrive on the island soil several hours later. We are out of the helicopter and running toward the hospital in no time. A few people pass us on our way in, but for a hospital this place is deathly quiet.

Millie's brother, Travis—clad in his dark yellow fisherman's overalls—meets us in reception and leads us to a private waiting area. He holds open the door, and as Millie enters, he steps to the side, blocking me from going any further.

"Family only." Travis smiles big and claps me on the shoulder. "I've got this, mate."

I return his smile and hold out my hand for him to take. He reluctantly takes my hand, but instead of shaking I give his arm a firm tug and pull him out of the way. I enter the room to find Millie's mum sitting in the far corner completely inconsolable and Millie's brothers Austin and Bruce with their arms around her. Millie makes her way over to them and is soon engulfed in the family hug.

"Tell me everything," she says.

"Dad started to feel funny earlier today, but you know Dad…" Austin talks in a low voice, so low that I can't make out exactly what is being said.

From the corner of my eye I notice staff going about their usual duties. It would seem no one is in a rush to speak to us. I can see this being an all-night affair. I turn to leave the room, but bump full on into Travis, who is standing behind me.

I nod toward the door. "I'm going to…"

"You're not going anywhere." Travis wraps his arm around my neck and marches me across the room. The essence of salt water and fish are pungent on his clothes as he pushes me down into an empty chair. A chair that is opposite to where Millie hugs her mother.

I pull out of his hold and dust my suit down. "What the hell is your problem?" I whisper-shout.

Travis takes a seat in the chair next to mine, leans back and leisurely crosses one leg over the other. "The problem, rich boy, is that this room clearly states 'family room', and that is something you are not. I told you politely to leave. Still, you thought it was your God-given right to enter. So now you're here, you're staying."

I narrow my eyes. "I had no intention of leaving. I was going to find a drinks machine so that I could bring everyone back a coffee."

"Fuck your coffee." Travis's voice rises an octave, and everyone goes quiet.

"Will you stop!" Edith's voice booms around the room. For a petite lady she sure has a strong pair of lungs. She looks at me momentarily before her gaze homes in on Travis. "Your father has had a stroke, and when he is ready to receive visitors he needs to know his family are all here to support him. Not bickering like children."

Travis grunts. "Gage is *not* family."

Edith, dressed in a fluffy sage robe, shakes her head. "Like it or not, he's here to support your sister."

Millie stands from her group hug. I'm expecting her to tell me to leave. And she'd have every right to after the way I dismissed her in London.

"Gage stays," she says and motions toward the door. "How about we go and get that coffee? I dare say we'll need a constant supply."

I smile sweetly at Travis. "Would you like one sugar or two?"

Travis's face twitches in annoyance, but he doesn't answer. I don't see the need to antagonise him further, so together we leave the family waiting area and take to the brightly lit corridors. Millie's steps are sprightly, and I quicken my pace in order to keep up.

Her back remains toward me as we make it to a Costa vending machine. "It's two pounds each," she says, her voice strained.

I place my hand on her shoulder. "He'll be okay. I know I haven't known your old man long, but what I do know from the short amount of time I spent with him is that he is made of tough stuff."

Her body begins to jerk as she silently weeps. "They say time is the most important thing when somebody is having a stroke."

"True," I say.

"They were out at sea when it happened. It took them three hours to get back to land and a further half an hour to get him to the hospital. Over three and a half hours, Gage. I don't even want to think about the damage that's been caused during that time."

I gently spin her around so that she's facing me and she throws her arms around my neck. I wrap her up in a tight hug as piece by piece she breaks.

"He's in good hands, Millie. But if you're not happy I could have him airlifted to a private hospital in London. There he will receive the best treatment money can buy."

Millie shakes her head vehemently.

"Very well," I say and, leaning down, kiss the top of her head.

She pulls back, her gaze on me. Her cheeks are blotchy and damp from the tears she's cried. It guts me to see that she's hurting and there's nothing I can do to make that hurt go away. I stroke her cheeks with the backs of my fingers, only for her to capture my hand in hers. She doesn't move my hand away, nor does she request space. It's as though my closeness brings her comfort.

We stand like this for several minutes, as though this moment serves as a pause in time and a break from reality. But unfortunately reality is something we cannot escape, no matter how much we want to.

EIGHTEEN

Millie

"What do you mean I can't see him?" I choke out. "We've been sitting in the waiting room for hours."

The blonde-haired nurse, whose name tag reads Lucy, smiles sympathetically. "I'm sorry. He only wants to see his wife."

Tapping my shoe against the floorboards, I fold my arms in front of my chest. "Fine, but you tell him from me that I'm not going anywhere until he sees me."

Lucy nods once, then she and the small team of doctors exit the family room. They told us that Father will have to stay in hospital for a minimum of three days. The first twenty-four hours will be an observation stay before he will be admitted to the strokes unit. Despite his speech and mobility being affected, they predict that he will make a full recovery. Even though the outcome seems to be positive, I still want to see him. I need to see him.

I glance at my mother, who's as white as a ghost. She didn't utter a single word when the doctors came to speak to us, in contrast to myself and my brothers, who bulldozed the team with question after question.

"Mum," I whisper, but she doesn't meet my gaze. I turn my attention to Travis and hold out my arms in question. "So, what now?"

Travis nods in a kind of acceptance. "We go home. We have businesses to run, and not only that, we need to build our strength up to be here for Mum when she needs a break."

Travis's reply surprises me. Out of my three brothers Travis is by far the most argumentative. In fact he makes an argument out of thin air, yet now when it actually matters he says nothing.

"Just like that?" I say, my tone sharp. "You're accepting what the nurse said? Don't you want to see Dad?"

Travis sighs before rubbing his temples. "I'm tired, Millie, and our business isn't going to run itself. On top of that, we've lost a full night of fishing. And after his stroke who knows when Dad will be able to return to work again, if ever."

I can't look that far ahead into the future. We need to focus on the here and now, which has me thinking. "With Mum being here, who's going to run the shop tomorrow?"

Travis shrugs and turns his attention to Austin and Bruce. "Guess we'll have to take it in turns between the fishing boat and shop, or work double shifts."

"Work night and day?" Bruce's eyes look as though they're about to pop right out of his head. "I can't function without at least eight hours of sleep."

"Sleep when you're dead," is Travis's harsh reply. He isn't being nasty per se, I can see how stressed he is.

Gage takes a step forward. "I'm sure I could pull some strings and fly someone in to help."

His offer is met with Travis's glare. "No, thank you, rich

boy. This is a family-run business. I don't want some outsider interfering."

Gage steps back and raises his hands. "Suit yourself, but the offer is there."

"Don't worry, boys, I can still run the shop," my mother announces. She can't be serious. She's planning on spending all night in the hospital with Dad, only to go home in the morning and then work?

"No way," Bruce says.

My mother and brothers talk amongst themselves, deciding who will be best manning the shop. But it just isn't going to work. 'Square peg, round hole' comes to mind.

I turn my attention to Gage, who nods. I don't have to utter a word; it seems he knows what I'm going to say before the words leave my lips. Now all that's left is to give said words volume.

I clear my throat. "I'll work in *Genie*'s Catch of the Day for as long as you need me."

The room goes quiet. I feel the need to repeat myself. "I said—"

Travis raises his hand. "I heard what you said, but you struggle setting foot in the fishmongers for five minutes. How are you going to work there for an entire day?"

I shrug, because honestly I don't have an answer. Fish has a very distinctive scent, a scent that turns my stomach. But if my family need me, then it is something I will have to get over.

"I'll manage," I say, trying to sound as sincere as possible.

"And what about the hotel?" Austin adds. "Who's going to run the hotel?"

"Well, it hasn't gone up in flames since I left the island." I smile up at Gage. "And besides, someone once told me that a successful business with good staff runs itself. I'll call a meeting first thing in the morning, but I know Stanton and Mills will be in good hands."

Gage and I linger at the hospital for another couple of hours. I refuse to leave on the off chance that my father will come to his senses and agree to see me. Of course I have no such luck, the stubborn stick. I have no choice other than to admit defeat and, deflated, I leave.

I do, however, take some comfort from the words 'we're confident he'll make a full recovery'. Those words loosen the knot in my stomach and ease the worry I felt when returning home from London.

It's a little after four a.m. when Gage and I make it to Stanton and Mills. My hotel appears silhouetted against its dusky backdrop, though as eerie as it appears, there is something disturbingly beautiful about it.

"Cheers," Gage says, and, leaning forward in the seat, pays the taxi driver. It's so surreal being back and I know beyond any doubt that I never want to leave the island again.

Gage gets out of the car and rounds the vehicle to open my door. It feels as though everything around me is playing out in slow motion as I take Gage's awaiting hand and shimmy off the cool leather.

I look at Gage while he looks at me. Morning birdsong plays around us in a choir of tweets and chirps. The waves crash in the ocean's serenade. The sound of heaven. The sound of home. Yet in this moment all that I want to do is stare unblinking into the eyes of this man.

It takes several seconds for me to release the breath I was apparently holding.

"I'll get our luggage." Gage's hushed words snap me out of my trance. I nod and hurry ahead to the hotel. The door to the entrance remains unlocked due to the occasional guests who are brazen enough to go for an early morning dip—or usually skinny-dip. Though the doors to the entrance are open, the reception is unmanned. Our reception opening hours are nine through to midnight. No one ever signs in past that time.

I flash a glance at my watch and sigh. It's too early to go to bed in my actual room, seeing as Hayley has to get up for work in only a few hours. Feeling Gage's presence behind me, I round the reception desk to see which rooms, if any, are vacant. Of course, the key cupboard is empty. At the peak of the season, we are always fully booked.

"Is there a problem?" Gage asks.

I run my fingers through my hair, once, twice before answering. "All the rooms are taken. And as much as I want to go to my own room, I can't wake Hayley up at this hour."

Gage shrugs like it isn't a big deal. "Okay, so share my room for the night."

I swallow. "But there is only one bed."

Gage smiles big. "I'm good with that."

I can't share a bed with Gage. I can't lie in such close proximity to him without wanting to touch him. I know we kissed earlier, but how I feel now is different. Returning home and finding out the terrible news about my father caused a rush of adrenaline to course through my body. Adrenaline that is still there and needs unleashing one way or another. Aside from that, I have a mix of emotions about this man. I don't want to want him, I shouldn't even like him, yet I can't control how my body reacts to him. This is dangerous. But with no other rooms available, what do I do? Sighing heavily, I nod.

The key to Room 201 jangles as Gage pulls it from his pocket. "Okay, let's go." The wheel of my suitcase squeaks as he heads toward the lift. But he stops only moments later, as though sensing that I am not following. "Millie…"

I love the sound of my name spoken by him. He looks at me with a question in his eyes. "So, are you coming? Or are you planning on sleeping at the reception desk?"

I force a frown, trying to put some emotional distance between us. "Of course not."

I round the reception desk and push past Gage. Inwardly I'm freaking out because I know that when we enter that room we aren't going to be able to keep our hands to ourselves.

Gage captures my wrist as I pass and stops me from taking another step. My stupid, confused heart pounds in my chest and my breath catches in my throat.

"What's wrong?" Gage asks.

I don't meet his stare, I can't. Instead I keep my gaze trained in front of me. "There's only one bed." My words shake.

I can feel Gage's breaths against my neck as he nears. But I don't back away, and instead find myself leaning into him, welcoming his closeness.

He takes a long and deep breath in before speaking. "Millie Edith Mills."

Gooseflesh explodes on my skin and the tiny hairs on my arms stand up on end as I anticipate what he is going to say next.

"I would love nothing more than to ravish you." He wraps his arm around my waist and pulls me into him. The hard bulge in his trousers presses deliciously into my back. Instead of pulling away, instead of chastising him I arch my back in desire.

His arm tenses. I must be affecting him in the same way as he is affecting me. He lowers his hand and keeps lowering. His fingers glide over my jeans, and without warning he slides his fingers between my thighs and rests his hand right below my sex. Jesus, I want him so much. The only thing that separates us is a few thin layers of clothing. He rubs his hand backwards and forwards, applying more pressure each time.

"Fuck. I can feel how wet you are for me," he practically growls into my ear. My clit aches at the pressure he's applying and the way he moves his hips. "I want nothing more than to eat your sweet little pussy and then take you in every room and in every position."

And just like that his claim on me is gone, and he slides his hand out from between my legs and from my aching sex. "But now isn't the right time. Tonight has been a whirlwind of emotions, and if I took you I know I'd be taking advantage."

I ponder how wrong of me it would be to tell him I want him to. I want him to take advantage of me, I want him to take me. I want his lips, his tongue between my legs, I want him to soothe this goddamn ache I have. "Gage…"

"I will sleep on the sofa tonight," he says, and without another word continues toward the lift.

"But what if I want you?" The words leave my lips before I have a chance to stop them. I slap my hand over my mouth, but it's too late. He heard.

He stops walking and turns to face me. "Oh, I plan to fuck you, Millie. This"—he motions between us—"this will be happening. And very soon, I can assure you. But right now you need to sleep off the alcohol you drank last night and get your head around everything that's happened with your father."

He's right. I'm not thinking clearly, because it isn't like me to jump into bed with a guy I hardly know. I've only known this man for a few short days, but as crazy as it sounds, I feel as though I've known him for years.

"Millie, come." Gage presses the up arrow button on the lift.

I follow closely behind, and when I'm standing by his side he places his palm on the small of my back. I wriggle free of his hold, and, frowning, he looks at me with a question in his eyes. But that question is answered when I link my fingers with his.

"Thank you," I whisper.

"For what?"

I give his fingers a squeeze before replying. "For respecting me."

The smile that spreads across his face is immediate. Without a word he lifts our joined hands and places a kiss on my knuckles. Inwardly I feel as though I'm on fire, yet on the outside I remain as calm and collected as possible. He can't see how much he is affecting me, although the glint in his stare tells me that maybe he already knows.

The lift doors ping open, and together we step inside.

NINETEEN

Gage

I wake the next morning to the sound of running water, a stiff neck and a rock-hard erection. This thing gives new meaning to the term 'morning wood'.

I was so tempted to join Millie in bed. So tempted to strip her of the covers and every last thread of clothing. The thought got me wondering if she sleeps naked. The problem is that the rooms at Stanton and Mills aren't as spacious as those in the Calloway hotel, and as a result of that, the bed and the sofa are in the same open-plan room. Being the gentleman I am, I afforded Millie the time to get ready for bed by going into the bathroom and having a shower. By the time I emerged she was all tucked up in the covers and fast asleep.

I lay down on the sofa, which gives new definition to the word 'uncomfortable'. I managed to overlook that my neck felt as though it was going to break, and with the light from the partially open blinds I watched Millie sleep for most of the morning before finally drifting off myself.

Now the bathroom door creaks open, and Millie emerges. Steam like small clouds surround her as she nears. She is dressed in a towelling robe, a small towel wrapped around her hair. She's so fucking sexy.

She meets my gaze and immediately looks away. She reaches the bed, and, turning her back on me, starts rummaging through the items in her suitcase, which lies open on the mattress.

"Morning, beautiful," I say, and get nothing but silence back.

I run my fingers over my beard. Is she ignoring me?

"Hello? Earth to Millie." I jump up from the sofa and spin her round. The tie of her robe comes loose, exposing her half-naked body.

The barely-there tangerine bra and matching undies does little to hide what's beneath. She grabs her robe to cover herself up, but I capture her wrists before she has the chance.

"Don't," I choke out.

Our gazes lock for a fleeting moment before my gaze once again lowers.

She snaps her hand free and places it on her hip. "Do you like what you see?"

"Very much." My lips part before my brain has time to think. "You do yourself a discredit with the frumpy old-lady clothes you wear."

Her jaw goes slack. "Excuse me?"

My dick is bulging against the waistband of my boxers, and she only needs to look down to see just how much she is affecting me. Everything about this woman is unintentionally attractive, from her smouldering dark brown eyes, to the dusting of freckles on her nose, to her smoking hot body. Sure, her personality could do with a slight rewire, but the more time I spend in her company, the more I'm enjoying having her around.

"Baggy jeans and knitted cardigans, really, Millie? All I'm saying is it's about time you embrace what you have, instead of hiding it away." I close my mouth, satisfied that I've paid her a compliment, in a kind of roundabout way.

"Noted," she says with an air of sarcasm, and, pulling her other wrist free from my hold, flings the Egyptian cotton material of the robe over her body.

"Have dinner with me," I say.

"Why?" She's biting back a smile. She enjoys this back-and-forth just as much as I do. It's a fucking turn-on.

"Because I want to discuss the hotel, and…"

"And what?" Her tone is sharp, though her expression is faltering.

"And because I'd really like to have dinner with you."

"Why?"

I take a deep breath in, and sigh. "Because against my better judgement, I like you. Sure, you're more outspoken than my usual type. You're hot-headed, argumentative, rude and—"

"Wow, let me stop you right there, Casanova, and say I'm honoured. I mean seriously, how can I refuse after how you listed my best qualities? What I'd really like to know is why *wouldn't* you want to have dinner with me?"

By now the tension between us is electric. I feel it, and I'm sure she does too. I reach forward and drag her lower lip down with my thumb. She lets me. With the same hand I yank at the tie of her robe so the material hangs loose. Again she lets me. I wrap my arm around her under the fabric. Her skin is warm as I pull her into me.

"We definitely shouldn't do this," she whispers when our lips are only inches apart. She smells so damn delicious, a mix of rose and citrus. I wonder where else she's applied that same body wash.

"We definitely shouldn't," I say, about to press my lips to hers when there's a knock at the door.

"Housekeeping," comes a voice from the other side.

Millie's gaze snaps to me. "Please tell me you put the deadlock on the door."

Said door opens, answering her question without me having to utter a single word. Millie springs out of my arms and wraps herself up in the robe quicker than I can take a breath.

Hayley stands in the doorway, a duster in one hand and a basket of products in the other.

"Guess the 'do not disturb sign' would have come in useful right about now," I joke and place my hands strategically over my groin, covering any visible outline as to what lies beneath.

"Oh, my God. I'm so sorry." Hayley's eyes go wide, as if she's as shocked to see us as we are to see her. "You weren't due back until tomorrow."

"Plans change." Millie motions toward the door. "Will you just leave?"

Hayley's shocked expression dissolves and is replaced with a smug-ass smile that spreads across her face. "Oh, it's like that? Am I interrupting something?" She motions the duster between us. She's clearly taking everything in she's seeing and jumping to the right conclusion.

Millie's cheeks flush red. "No, we were just… I mean, nothing happened… I mean…"

"Mm-hm. Well as the head of housekeeping, I really should report this to my superior. It is a clear breach of the 'no fraternising' rule."

Millie's expression turns to thunder, and I know she's about to explode when Hayley continues.

"But seeing as you're both my bosses, I think it best I say nothing more on the matter." She winks exaggeratedly before making her way out of the room. Before she is fully out of the door she stops. "Oh, and by the way, seeing as the rules seem to be more open for interpretation, I'm having Travis round later. You may want to stay away as we aren't exactly quiet…"

The door clicks closed.

Millie sighs before yanking the towel from her head, causing her wet hair to fall free. "Great, great, great."

I take a step in her direction, only for Millie to jump back with her hands in the air.

"Millie…"

"Don't. Just don't." She spins around. With her back toward me she whips off her robe. My attention lowers to the globes of her ass, which are on full display due to the thin lacy cotton thong. I'm afforded a small window of time to visually explore her body, and what a body she has—her shapely thighs and ass, the tiny dimples at the base of her back… In a split second her torso is covered by a black T-shirt and a frumpy sage cardigan. She pulls on a pair of dark jeans and flip-flops, then hurries to leave.

She opens the door that leads out to the hallway, only for me to push it shut in its frame.

Millie spins round again. "Gage, what do you think you're doing?"

"I think I should be the one asking you that question." I close the distance between us. As close as we are, she seems unable to hold eye contact. I use my pointer finger to lift her chin. "One minute you're hot, the next you're cold. Will you at least have the decency to tell me where I stand?"

Her shoulders drop, but it's now she meets my stare. "We're not in London anymore, Gage. Here, I can't be seen to…"

"To what?" My voice rises an octave. "Be happy? Shit, Millie, you're allowed to have a personal life. You're a hotel owner, not a nun!"

"I know." She reaches behind her for the handle. "I just need to speak to Hayley."

I release my hold on the door. "So then go. Go tell her that there is nothing going on between us." I take a step back, allowing Millie the space she needs to leave. She doesn't.

"I'm not going to do that, Gage. One thing I can't do is lie.

Physically nothing has happened—well, nothing more than a kiss. But I feel as though emotionally something has happened between us. I want to see where this can go, but I don't want to rush into anything. And it's for that reason I don't feel as though I can share a room with you. Not again, not tonight."

Talk about an ego stroke. I cock a brow. "And why would that be?"

Her cheeks glow red.

"You want me," I tease.

"I, er…"

She can't answer. Cute. That's okay though, as I'll answer for her. "I want you, Millie Edith Mills. In my bed, and in my life. So go tell Hayley that Travis is free to stay with her as long as he wants, because your presence is required elsewhere." I capture her hand and pull her toward me. "See you later, beautiful," I say and press a kiss on her forehead.

Her cheeks are crimson. I'd say from her reaction that she is not used to male attention. She shakes her head, as though shaking away her embarrassment.

"See you later, Gage." She stands on the tips of her toes to kiss me on the cheek. Such a sweet and innocent gesture. She lowers herself down to her normal height, and stands almost frozen to the spot. It's as though she's trying to leave the room, but is unable to muster the willpower to make it happen.

Seeing as she is unable to leave, I reach past her and do what I should have done hours before, which is to flick the deadlock on the door.

"What are you doing?" Her voice comes out as a whisper.

"I thought that was obvious."

"Gage… Please, don't do this. You don't know how hard it is to resist you when I want you so badly."

I quirk a brow. "So then stop resisting. Stop putting unnecessary time between us as a barrier, as if a day, a week or even a month will change how we feel about one another."

Her eyes are wide and filled with emotion, yet she remains silent. It's as though she's waiting for me to make the next move.

"If you want to leave, then leave. I won't stop you." I take a small sidestep away from the door, but instead of allowing Millie time to get caught up in her own internal war I crash my lips into hers.

I'm half-expecting her to pull away, but she doesn't. Instead she moans into my mouth and kisses me back. Millie fisting her fingers into my hair is the go-ahead I need to lift her off her feet and march her toward the bed. With me clutching the globes of her ass, she wraps her legs around my waist. Her groin presses deliciously against my cock. If she failed to notice my bulging erection before, there's no way in hell she is missing it now.

I continue toward the bed, undoing her cardigan buttons one at a time. "Fucking cardigan," I growl, and, losing my patience, tear it from her.

"Gage," Millie scolds as buttons pop off and fall to the floor. "Will you be careful? This belonged to my grandmother."

"Why am I not surprised?" I accidentally say aloud. But when her expression transforms to one of annoyance I add, "We'll tell your grandmother we're sorry."

She squeals as I throw her onto the bed. "Gage!" She attempts to sit up, only for me to push her back down.

"Lie back and enjoy while I pleasure you." One-handedly I unfasten the metal button from her jeans and lower the zip. Millie props herself up on her elbows and watches as I work the denim down one painfully slow inch at a time. She lifts her ass, making it easier for me to undress her. Her tangerine undies become more and more visible as I work the material down her thighs, to her calves and finally off.

Silence. Nothing but silence passes between us as she watches me as I hungrily watch her.

I use my pointer and middle finger to walk my hand up her leg and toward her sex. I stop when my fingers rest on the lacy frill of her undies. "We seem to have run into a problem," I tease. Without another word I grab her legs and drag her further down the bed so that her ass rests on the edge of the mattress.

"Problem averted," I say and in record time have her legs resting on my shoulders.

"I thought you were a gentleman," she says when she's in the most compromising position she could be in.

I laugh mockingly. "Sweetheart, I left the gentleman at the door." I pull her panties to the side and bury my face in her pussy. I'm not soft, nor am I gentle as I nibble mercilessly on her clit.

"Gage," she cries out, her body tensing and trembling.

"Fuck, you taste so good," I growl, sucking and nipping. She attempts to pull away from me as she writhes in pleasure, but she isn't going anywhere. I grab her thighs and hold her in place.

"Gage, God, this is too much." Her quivering thighs clamp around my face, her fingers fisting my hair, pulling me closer. She's so fucking wet, and I happily drink in every drop of her orgasm.

I'm so fucking turned on that I fist my cock in my hand and begin working myself up and down until pre-come dampens the tip. I need to slow down before I explode.

I use my free hand to open her folds and push two fingers inside her. I pull out and suck my fingers into my mouth.

"Fuck, Millie," I growl. "I need to be inside you." I peer up, meeting her stare, and wait for permission.

"Yes, Gage, yes."

"Don't move," I tell her.

I leave her momentarily to grab a condom from the nightstand drawer and tear the packet open with my teeth. Millie has scooted up the bed so her head rests on the pillow. She leans up on her elbows and watches as I remove my boxers. She sucks in her lower lip when my cock springs free.

"Like what you see?" I say and work my shaft up and down for her before sliding the condom on.

She nods shyly.

"All yours, baby." I get onto the bed and make my way toward her. I part her legs with my knee and line the head of my cock up with her entrance.

TWENTY

Millie

I knew sharing a room with Gage would be dangerous, I knew it the second he suggested it. And yet here I am doing just that.

I had one job this morning, which was to get out of bed, have a shower and get the hell out of his room. Epic fail on my part, but it's impossible to want someone this much and not act upon it. I want this man more than I've wanted anyone before.

He inches his cock forward. The sheer size of him causes me to tense. I wasn't expecting him to be this big or this thick.

He looks at me for long seconds, in a kind of 'this is your last chance to stop this' kind of way. But why the hell would I do that?

I take a deep breath and nod while inwardly bracing myself for what's to come. I will my body to relax, clutching the bedsheet between my fingers, and take shaky breaths as he fills me inch by inch. My wetness makes it easy for him to slide in, yet the burn has me white-knuckling the sheets.

"Is this okay?" he asks, when he's fully inside me. I peer up into his eyes, at crystal blues that I would happily get lost in.

He looks genuinely concerned, which has me only wanting him more.

He awaits my answer, though neither of us say a word as he holds himself perfectly still inside me.

"Yes," I say finally, loop my arms around his neck and pull him down for a kiss.

He purposely avoids my lips and kisses my forehead, then works his way down my face. He stops at my temple to kiss each of my eyelids.

I laugh. "What are you doing?"

He looks at me as if to say, *Isn't it obvious?* "Kissing every inch of you is what." It's now he begins gliding his cock in and out of me in hot delicious strokes.

He kisses down the bridge of my nose. Thrust. He kisses each cheek. Thrust.

His lips hover over mine, but he doesn't bridge that final distance. He's such a damn tease. I lift my head to kiss him, but he retreats just enough that he's out of reach.

"Not yet," he whispers. "I want to watch you."

He thrusts in and out. The whole time his gaze is locked on mine. His thrusts begin to pick up pace and he starts to fuck me harder and faster.

"Gage," I moan. "This feels…" I pause and, closing my eyes, suck in my lips.

It's now Gage's lips crash against mine. When I attempt to kiss him back he captures my lower lip between his teeth and gives my lip a playful nip before kissing me. His tongue, like his cock, plunges deep inside me.

This is too much. I moan into his mouth while attempting to kiss him back with the same amount of passion he's kissing me. But I can't, instead I am falling apart in his arms, trembling with pleasure.

He breaks our kiss momentarily and growls into my ear. "I'm going to come."

"Okay," is the only word I can muster. He sandwiches his hand between my ass and the mattress and lifts me up. With my back arched he's able to deepen the thrusts, and by doing so hit my most sensitive spot. It feels incredible as he thrusts harder and faster over and over. I'm a bundle of nerves that falls apart at the same time as Gage. We orgasm together and spend the next ten minutes wrapped up in each other's arms.

I use his chest as my makeshift pillow and he slowly brushes his fingers through my hair. My head moves up and down with each breath he takes.

"That was amazing," he finally says, breaking through the silence.

I nod in agreement.

He stops caressing my hair. "As much as I want to stay here"—he jerks his head in the direction of the bathroom—"I really should…"

I bite back a smile. "Yes, you should." I lift up, giving him just enough space to slip from the bed. I watch his bare arse as he walks across the room and disappears into the bathroom.

The second the door clicks shut I pull the bedsheets all the way up and over my face, blocking out the room and reality. I have to pinch myself to believe that what happened actually happened. I slept with Gage Calloway, a man I've only known for a few short days. And yet here I am, in his bed. I've spent my whole life as someone who is renowned for not taking risks, yet here I am jumping headfirst into the unknown.

I spend the next five minutes, maybe longer, swaddled in the sheets and lost in my thoughts.

The sound of the bathroom door opening and closing does nothing to inspire me to move, not so much as an inch. I hold my breath as the echo of feet against the tiled floor gets louder. The sheet scrunched between my fingers tightens and is pulled all the way down. Gage smiles down at me, and then, leaning into my personal space, plants a kiss on my forehead.

"Why don't we go for a morning run?" he suggests, opening and closing drawers. He pulls on items of clothing, first skintight black boxers, followed by grey tracksuit bottoms and finally a light grey T-shirt.

I sit up and stretch. "What time is it?"

He flicks his wrist and peers down at his watch. "A little after nine."

"A little after nine? We needed to be in the fishmongers for nine o'clock start."

Gage shakes his head. "Bruce texted me this morning. He said they're going to hold the fort until this afternoon. That gives us time to go for a run to discuss the hotel and to hold a staff meeting."

I frown. "My brother texted you?"

Gage flashes me a wicked smile. "Of course."

He says that like my brother texting him is no big deal, but it is. Bruce has never given his number to any of my boyfriends in the past, not even Joseph, whom I was with for a year. Yet here Gage is, fitting in like he's part of the family.

Then I remember what his sister and Chelsea said about Gage being married, and it wasn't all that long ago. Was that a whirlwind romance? Did he sweep her off her feet and walk her down the aisle only for it to end in divorce? I need to know.

"Gage?" I ask. His back is toward me as he opens the minibar to grab a drink. "Your ex-wife. Tell me about her."

His body stiffens, and he releases the bottle of orange juice and instead grabs a bottle of Jack Daniels.

"It's a little early to be drinking," I note.

Gage unscrews the lid and takes a large gulp. "So, what about our run?"

He avoids my question, so I ask again. "Why can't you answer me?"

"There's nothing to say on the matter." He tips his head back and takes another gulp of whiskey. He must see from my expression that his answer is not enough. He opens his arms in question. "Have I asked you about your past boyfriends?"

I open my mouth, but he answers for me.

"No, I haven't. And do you know why?" His tone is so cold it chills me to the bone. I capture the bedding in my hands and scrunch it to just below my neck. "Because all the past can do is hurt you. It's best to leave memories where they belong and focus on the here and now."

I remember when my mother asked him about his parents, to which he replied his mother died when he was nineteen and his father was an arrogant arsehole. There was no softness to his tone, only terseness. I can't help but agree with him about his father, but his mother? I can't help wonder what she was like.

"What did she do?" I choke out.

"Excuse me?"

"Daphne, your ex-wife. What did she do that hurt you so badly?"

His beautiful crystal-blue eyes narrow into slits. They darken in colour, as though a storm is brewing in them.

The glass bottle clinks against the marble worktop as he places it down. "Don't confuse my indifference with pain. One has to care in order to feel hurt. I'm going for a run. I need to clear my head. You're welcome to join me. I'll go slow so you can catch up."

He makes his way toward me and leans down to kiss my forehead. The storm that was brewing in his eyes moments ago has cleared and he's back to his happy-go-lucky self, like he hasn't a care in the world. How can he turn his emotions off so easily?

He turns his back on me and heads for the door, picking up his trainers on his way. He leaves me to lie alone in bed with only my thoughts as company.

I don't join Gage for a run and instead have a long soak in the bath and spend my morning working at reception with Tanya.

We're both quiet, seemingly both lost in our own thoughts. It's me who finally fills the silence. "How's James?" I enquire.

Tanya shrugs. "I honestly don't know. He's been working later and later at the office, and when he's home he's glued to his phone."

I haven't got the heart to tell her what is blatantly obvious, that her husband is cheating. With no proof, I can't just throw accusations around willy-nilly. "Maybe suggest a time at home where he needs to turn off his phone?"

Tanya lets out a laugh. "There's no way. He says it's his lifeline to work, but honestly there are times I question if it's me he's married to or that damn device."

I give her a sympathetic smile, but can't help wonder if sometimes ignorance really is bliss. It makes sense that she's choosing not to see what's right under her nose. Tanya's father died some years back, and her mother and maternal family reside in Ireland, so James is all the family she has here on the island.

I take a few bookings for next summer, one of which is a wedding party of twenty. I manage to arrange the guests' rooms so they're all within a short walking distance of each other. I hang up the phone and notice Tanya is in much better spirits. With a smile on her face, she tucks her mobile phone into the pocket of her trousers. I figure she and James have sorted things out, for now at least. No doubt he has apologised, bought her flowers, and booked a table this evening at Christopher's.

"So, are you going to tell me what happened in London?" Tanya asks.

I let out a long sigh because I knew this was coming. "I stayed at the Calloway hotel. I was shown around and met Gage's family and came home."

Tanya folds her arms in front of her chest. "And is that all?"

"Nothing happened in London," I protest, and, well, technically I'm not lying, nothing did happen. Apart from when we kissed, and what a kiss that was. But that's a snippet of information Tanya doesn't need to know.

"Judging by the goofy grin on your face, I'd say there is something you're not telling me."

I can feel my cheeks begin to pink, but am saved by the ringing of the phone. I turn my back on Tanya and, planting a smile on my face, lift the phone from the receiver. "Good morning, this is Millie from Stanton and Mills Hotel. How can I help you?"

"I'd like a room." A familiar deep voice from behind has me almost dropping the phone. I spin around only to come face to face with Gage's brother. Malachi looks as dark and intimidating as he did last night.

"Certainly, sir," Tanya begins, but his gaze is fixed on me.

"I'll deal with this," I cut in, handing Tanya the phone. There's no denying that the Calloway brothers are attractive, but there is something about this Calloway that chills me to my core.

"It's nice to see you again, Millie," Malachi says, but I know it's more out of politeness than him being sincere. "How's your father?" Again, more lip service, and Malachi pretending like he gives a damn.

I decide to cut to the chase. "What are you doing here?"

"My, my." Malachi tsks. "My brother certainly underestimates your charm."

"Yours too, I'm sure."

Malachi's expression remains unchanged. "I would like a room."

"Why? Why here? Shouldn't you be in a Calloway hotel showing your support to your brother?"

Malachi runs his fingers over his trim beard once, twice before answering. "I believe this is soon to be a Calloway hotel. And as to the nature of my trip, that is frankly none of your concern."

What a charmer! I open my mouth to speak when Tanya interrupts.

"Room 205 will be available at three o'clock."

My mouth goes dry. That's only a few doors down from Gage's room. "But that room—"

"Is perfect," Malachi interrupts. "I will go for a tour of the island while I wait."

I force a smile. "Knock yourself out." *Literally.*

Malachi places his elbows on the reception desk and leans forward. "Gage doesn't know I'm here, and I would like it to remain that way, so would appreciate your discretion."

"No balloons or bunting then." Sarcasm drips from my words.

Malachi doesn't respond, and if anything, he looks positively bored. He turns and leaves the lobby.

"Oh, my God, what is in the water these Calloway men drink? He is so freakin' hot. No doubt I'll have the housekeepers asking me to find out everything about him," Tanya bleats, but her words act merely as background noise.

Why is Malachi Calloway, of all people, here on the island and staying in my hotel? I won't mention to Gage that his brother is here. Not because Malachi has asked me to do so, but rather because I want to figure out what his agenda is.

TWENTY-ONE

Gage

The staff meeting goes as well as expected, and Millie and I leave confident the hotel is in safe hands.

It's one o'clock by the time we arrive at *Genie's* Catch of the Day. Millie's brothers are out front piling polystyrene boxes into the boot of a car. Travis sees us, smiles at Millie, but glowers at me.

I smile big. "Howdy. Fine weather we're having."

Millie side-eyes me. "Howdy?"

I shrug. "Just being polite." And sarcastic as hell, but I leave that part out.

"Is there any news on Dad?" Millie asks.

Travis shakes his head. "There's no change. As much as I want to stay and chat, we have orders to deliver."

Millie looks from Travis to the dozen boxes stacked in the car boot. "Are you being serious? Why didn't you do deliveries this morning?"

"We didn't have time." He nods toward the shop window and

the large display of produce. "We've been preparing fish all morning. All you need to do is weigh it on the scales before selling."

Millie nods. "Thank you, but that must have taken hours. You didn't need to do that."

"I figured rich boy wouldn't get his hands dirty." Travis flashes me a glance. "I don't know why you brought him, he won't be much use other than looking pretty."

I squeeze my hand into a tight fist, trying to think of why I shouldn't use said fist on Travis's smug-ass face. But he's trying to goad me, and for that reason I will not take the bait. "You think I'm pretty?" I pucker my lips and bat my eyelashes, my way of flipping him the middle finger. I won't throw the first punch, but I will sure as hell throw the last.

"I think you're pretty." Millie nudges me playfully, and I nudge her right back.

"My God, tell me you two aren't fucking." Travis's words are sharp.

"Will you keep your voice down?" Millie warns.

Travis ignores Millie. His attention is solely on me. "I gave you strict instructions *not* to touch my sister."

"I'm sorry, but you must have me confused with someone who actually gives a fuck."

Travis closes the distance between us. I figure he's ill-equipped to have a verbal conversation and would rather talk with his fists. That is a language I can talk fluently, if provoked.

"Oh, my God, will you two stop it?" Millie barges past us and into the shop.

Travis snarls, "Hurt my sister and I'll bury you."

I tap my chin thoughtfully while remembering his previous threat. "Is that before or after you drop my body into the ocean? Because those seem mutually exclusive, don't you think?"

The honk of a horn has us both turning. Austin and Bruce are sitting in the car. I'm assuming they're waiting for Travis to join them.

"I'm coming," Travis hollers, then returns his attention to me. "Enjoy looking pretty today while the real men work and get their hands dirty."

I shouldn't laugh, but I can't help it. "Yes, you run along and get on with your little deliveries."

Travis's nostrils flare. "Are you mocking me?"

I say nothing. I'm a firm believer that silence speaks louder than words.

"You actually think you're better than me, don't you?"

I allow more silence to pass while picking at invisible lint on my suit jacket.

"Okay, rich boy. Why don't you join us tonight on the fishing boat and see how your manicured hands fare?"

How hard can catching some fish be? Travis wouldn't know the definition of a real day's work, but I intend on showing him. "Challenge accepted. But in return you will spend an afternoon with me in London."

Travis's eye twitches. He doesn't answer, so I hold out my hand. "One afternoon in London, in exchange for a night on your little boat."

There I go again, using the word 'little'. But if he wants to patronise me about my looks and my hands, then I'll patronise him right back.

He wipes his palm over the back pocket of his trousers before slapping it into mine. His grip is firm as we shake, and I can't help noticing how rough his skin feels. "Be on the harbour at midnight."

I flash him my teeth. "It's a date."

The car horn honks for a second time, and Bruce is hanging out of the driver's side window. "Come on, Travis. Let's get the show on the road."

I wait long enough to wave Travis goodbye. I'm going to have so much fun pissing him off tonight that I can't wait.

I enter the shop with a spring in my step to find Millie

standing behind the glass serving display cabinet. She does look the part dressed in white, a blue and red apron secured around her waist and her hair scraped back into a bun.

"You know, you make dead fish look good," I say, and, smiling, look her up and down.

I can't help the gag she tries but fails to conceal. I have nothing but admiration for the girl. I know how hard today is going to be for her.

"Not funny, Gage," she chokes out, her eyes watering.

"Sorry, I shouldn't talk ill of the dead." I do a hail Mary sign to the fish corpses that have been cut up and displayed ready for purchase.

"I'm not talking about the fish."

I frown. "Okay, then what?"

She gags again before wiping her eyes. "This beef you have with Travis stops now."

I laugh. "Righto."

"I'm serious, Gage. Me and you, this isn't going to work. I'm very close to my family, and I can't be with someone they don't get on with."

I am not losing this girl because of her arsehole brother. I think fast. "And what do you think I'm trying to do?" I counter back.

Millie frowns. "From where I was standing, it looked as though you were doing everything in your power to get under Travis's skin."

"That's where you're wrong. I'm going on the fishing boat with your brothers later to get to know them better."

Millie goes from looking pissed to concerned. "I'm sorry, what? You're going on the fishing boat? What for?"

"To help out, of course. I figured we could play a round of cards and have a drink while the fish swam into the nets."

"Is that what you think my brothers do when they're working? Gage, fishing is one of the most dangerous jobs to do."

I let out a laugh. "Dangerous? Really?"

Millie rounds the counter so she's standing directly in front of me. "How do you think Travis got that scar on his face? He nearly lost his eye when one of the ropes snapped. There are so many hazards, too many to list, from weather conditions to equipment failure and…"

I lift my hand and cut her off. "I'm a big boy, Millie, I'm sure I'll be fine."

The bell above the door chimes, and an elderly woman enters the shop.

"Mrs Sumners," Millie says, and makes her way back around the display counter. "What would you like today?"

The elderly lady smiles. "Oh, I'm not sure yet, dear. I'm going to have a mooch around to see what you have."

Millie meets my gaze. "There is a uniform in the back. You need to change before you can serve."

When I reenter the shop—fully kitted out in the white attire, apron and hairnet, looking like a class-A bellend—Millie is deep in conversation with a tall, balding middle-aged man. The man smiles and nods animatedly. I stand in the doorway and watch their exchange.

"I couldn't," Millie protests as the man appears to be handing her some kind of plastic storage box.

"Please, I insist. Your brothers were only too happy to accept my generosity earlier. And besides, if the shoe was on the other foot your father would do the same for me."

"What's going on?" I ask and join Millie.

Millie wipes at her eyes. "Collin Grimsby heard what happened to my father and has kindly brought us some extra produce to sell."

Grimsby? It takes me a second to place his name. "Aren't you the other fisherman on the island?"

He nods. "Guilty."

I narrow my eyes. It's not normal for competition to be

helping each other out. Something is definitely amiss. "No pun intended, but what's the catch?"

Millie nudges me, while dear Collin looks offended. "No catch, boy. I heard *Genie* lost a full night of fishing. I just want to offer my support."

Like hell he does. If I've learnt anything, it's that there are no friends in business. I stare at him blankly. "How much do I owe you?"

Collin lifts his hands, signalling he won't accept a penny. "Nothing at all. Just that if we find ourselves in an unfortunate situation, you remember this." The classic 'I scratch your back, you scratch mine'.

Millie smiles and accepts the box. "Of course."

"There's plenty more where that came from, and if you need more you only need ask." The bell above the door dings as Collin leaves.

Well, shit, there are genuine people in the world. Who knew?

Five o'clock soon comes, and Millie and I have a nice little routine in place. I stand behind the serving unit and serve customers while Millie stands in the doorway between the shop and the back room. I place the fish on the scales, which with her back toward the customer she weighs and types the price into the till. It's a clever way of her being present, yet not on display. She is able to hide her gags by sneaking off into the back room before returning with a miscellaneous item of cutlery to look as though her going into the back room was for a purpose.

I follow the last customer as she leaves and flip the sign on the door from 'open' to 'closed'.

"Thank God that's over with." Millie yanks off her hairnet and leans against the wall. She brings her palms to her face and inhales loudly. "I don't think I'll ever get the smell of fish off my skin."

"Probably not," I agree.

Millie flips me the bird, to which I can't help but laugh. "Why don't we go upstairs to my old room?"

I raise a brow. "Are you trying to seduce me?"

"Smelling of fish? No. My old room has a small en suite. I was going to suggest us getting showered before we leave."

I recall how small the rooms are upstairs and picture myself squeezing into a dinky shower. "I have a better idea. Why don't we go back to the hotel, have a shower together, and then go out?"

"No," Millie snaps. "I don't want to go back there, not yet."

She still wants to keep us a secret. "People are going to find out eventually."

Millie sucks in her lower lip. "It's not that."

"Then what?" I prompt.

Her shoulders drop. "I can't tell you, and in any case, you'll find out soon enough."

She doesn't elaborate and begins packing away. Like Millie, I have no plans to go public with a relationship, not yet anyway, but it's different here on the island. There's no Nicolas Spaulding or his little minions watching my every move. No *London Weekly* with my face spread across the cover. It feels so nice to finally disappear under their radar and just be a man, slowly falling for a woman.

I'm starting to think that Millie was right about this place being a small slice of heaven.

A heaven I never want to leave.

TWENTY-TWO

Millie

There is a taxi waiting outside my parents' shop after we have showered and changed. Gage has changed back into his shirt and grey trousers from earlier, me into a yellow summer dress that was hanging up in my old wardrobe. I haven't worn this dress since I was a teenager, but Gage appreciates how the thin material caresses my thighs.

"You look cute," he says, a stupid grin on his face as I lock the door leading to the flat behind me.

I flash a glance at the taxi. "Where are we going?"

"It wouldn't be a surprise if I told you, now would it?" Gage's tone is playful as he opens the back driver's side door for me. "After you, my lady." His eyes twinkle as he takes me in. I can't help wonder if his words are true. Am I his lady? Are we a thing? Or are we nothing more than a bit of fun? Honestly, I would be crushed if he sees me as the latter, but I can't bring myself to ask him.

"Thank you, kind sir," I say, and slide onto the car's leather seat.

He closes the door behind me and gets in the other side. The car pulls away from the kerb the second Gage's door closes.

Although it is fast approaching eight o'clock, it is still light out. A few of the locals mill around, either for an evening stroll or to go to Christopher's restaurant. Maybe that's where Gage is taking me? He mentioned earlier that he wanted to take me out for dinner, and seeing as Christopher's is the only restaurant in town, it'd make sense that he'd take me there.

As predicted, the taxi pulls up outside Christopher's. It's a quaint sage-coloured building and like all businesses here on the island is family-run.

I spin around in my seat and can make out the sign for *Genie's Catch of the Day*. I can't help but laugh. "Was a taxi really necessary? We could have just walked."

"It's too far to walk," Gage says, and unfastens his seat belt.

Sighing, I do the same. "We've polluted the Earth, for what?"

"Excuse me?" Gage looks genuinely confused.

I shrug. "I know it's a different way of life in London. But here on the island we're all about looking after the planet. For one, hardly anyone drives here as everything is within walking distance. And anything that isn't, we have a bus for. For another, we limit the use of plastic."

Gage shakes his head. "Do you think I'm that conceited that I can't walk down the street?"

When I don't answer Gage opens the car door and slides out. "This is a quick pit-stop. Wait here," are the words he leaves me with.

I make eye contact with David, the driver, through the rear-view mirror. I went to school with David; he was in the year above. He had dreams of being a pilot, but instead has taken over his father's taxi company.

"Millie Mills," he says enthusiastically, holding the last syllable of my name for longer than necessary.

"David Andrews," I say with less enthusiasm, more in acknowledgement.

"How's life treating you? Don't see you much these days with you working at your uncle's hotel."

My hotel, I want to correct him. But as long as Stanton remains in the hotel's name, people will always assume it belongs to my uncle. And I, like my name Mills, am a tagged-on afterthought.

I change the subject. "Can you tell me where we're going?"

David's green eyes crinkle in the corners. "I could." David doesn't say another word, which is his way of saying he could but isn't going to. He was always a smartass at school. I lift up my leg and give his seat a nudge. "Hey, you mark it, you buy it."

"Is that right?" I nudge his seat again. "How about the time you spray-painted a life-sized penis on the side of the hotel?"

The smug smile David wore seconds ago has gone.

"Now, I'll ask you again, where are we going?"

David takes a deep inhale. I'm sure he's about to answer when the car door opens and Gage slides in next to me. The scent of food wafts up from the brown paper bags he's holding. He sets both bags in the space between us and refastens his belt. David slides the gear stick into first and pulls off.

"So, is anyone going to tell me where we're going?"

The silence that follows is all the answer I need. I do all I can in that moment, and that is to sit back in my seat and wait.

It takes half an hour to make it to our destination. Excitement bubbles up inside me when I look at the large body of the lighthouse. Bright light like liquid pours into the taxi one moment and is gone the next.

I side-eye Gage and can't help wonder if he has the ability to read minds. I've wanted to come here for as long back as I can remember. How did he know? I had envisioned coming with Daniel, but seeing as my best friend is MIA and is far too busy to so much as send me a text message, coming with Gage is the next best thing.

"I hope here is okay." He rakes his fingers through his hair. "It's just you run toward the lighthouse every morning, but never actually make it all the way, so I figured—"

I don't let him finish. The paper bags crackle as I practically throw my arms around him and pull him into a hug. "It's perfect."

We get out of the taxi. Gage holds the bags containing the food.

"Ah, I had envisioned eating our dinner inside the lighthouse." I can hear the disappointment in Gage's tone.

It's easy to imagine the lighthouse is derelict. But that isn't the case. The large structure is attached to a small bungalow which is occupied by the Walkers, Patricia and Rodney, the island's eldest residents.

We glance around, but at the top of a cliff there's no houses close by. There is nothing to see apart from miles of turquoise blue. From all the way up here Stanton and Mills looks like no more than a tiny speck in the distance.

My hair begins to dance around my face as the wind picks up. I look to Gage, who looks back. "So, what now?" I ask.

"Simple. We find somewhere to sit."

We walk a little way down the cliff and stop when we find a wooden bench. The name 'Bertha Walker' is engraved into a small silver plaque, along with her date of birth and the date of her death. A single red rose has been secured to one of the wooden slats.

"Do you think Bertha would mind if we sat here?" Gage asks.

I shake my head, remembering good old Bertha. "As long as you don't talk with your mouth full. That was a real pet peeve of hers."

"Noted," Gage says, and is careful not to crush the flower as he sits. I sit also and leave a gap, so I don't knock the stem.

Gage lowers the bags to the ground and pulls out tray after tray of food. There must be a dozen trays laid out between us. Black Sharpie writing on the lids tells us what's inside, from beer-battered mushrooms and loaded jacket potato skins to fish and chips, gammon and egg, and not forgetting the desserts.

My stomach rumbles, but I can't help laugh. "Are you planning on feeding a small army?"

Gage pops the lid off the beer-battered mushrooms and hands me a knife and fork. "No. It occurred to me that I don't know anything about you, what your interests are, your favourite colour. Not even the foods you like."

I stab the prongs of my fork into one of the mushrooms and stop when it's a few inches from my lips. "You only need to ask. My interests are…"

I jump when Gage gives my thigh a soft squeeze. "Now where would the fun be in getting to know you if you told me all your secrets and your little idiosyncrasies?"

He has a point. He plucks the fork from between my fingers and guides the mushroom toward my lips and into my mouth.

"She likes mushrooms but doesn't like fish. How strange," he mutters under his breath.

I begin chewing. "A mushroom is nothing like fish."

Gage tsks. "No talking with your mouth full, remember. Dear Bertha, God rest her soul, won't be pleased."

No, she won't. Jeez, does Gage remember everything I've said to him?

I finish chewing as Gage bites into one of the loaded jacket potato skins. "What are you doing?" I ask.

Gage doesn't answer right away. He makes a point of chewing as slowly as humanly possible and dabbing the corners of his mouth with a cotton napkin. "I'm eating."

I give him an 'are you for real?' look before stabbing my fork into another mushroom. "I'm talking about this." I motion the fork between us.

"I told you already, I want to get to know you."

"Why?" The doubt is so evident in my voice that I hear it too.

"Because I want to be a fucking amazing boyfriend."

I almost choke. Did I hear correctly? "Since when did we become an item?"

"Since right now." Gage doesn't say another word, and instead reaches for my hand and laces his fingers with mine.

I haven't had a boyfriend in so long that I almost forgot what it felt like to have another person call me theirs. I've always put the hotel and my career before my love life, but peering down at our hands, I can't help wonder if I'm finally able to have both.

I feel hot all of a sudden, hot and floaty, like if he released my hand I would float right up to the clouds. I squeeze his fingers in acknowledgement.

I don't know what to say, so say the first thing that pops into my mind. "My favourite colour is white. And before you ask why, it's because it's a blank canvas."

A ghost of a smile tugs at Gage's lips. "You're so impatient to give away the goods, aren't you?"

"And what's that supposed to mean?" I can't help but feel defensive. "I hope you're not referring to how quickly we slept together, because sleeping with practically a stranger is not something I make a habit of doing."

I loosen my grip on his hand, whereas he only tightens his, his way of silently telling me there is no way he's going to let me go. "I wasn't talking about that. And *that*, for the record, was fucking amazing. I fully intend to feast on your pussy for dessert."

The blush that explodes on my face is immediate. Gage Calloway isn't shy and certainly doesn't mince his words.

"Have you ever played the game 'pass the parcel' as a child?" he asks, making small circles on my palm with his thumb.

I'm too embarrassed to answer, so with my gaze trained on the floor say nothing.

Filling the silence, Gage continues. "The music plays, and you take it in turns to pass a wrapped-up gift around a circle. When the music stops playing someone tears off a layer of paper."

I nod, my throat feeling way too dry for me to conjure up words.

"Well, I want to get to know you. I want to slowly tear layer upon layer off until I make my way to your centre." His gaze lowers to between my legs and I feel very hot all of a sudden.

I fan my face with my hand before nodding toward the bags. "Have you got anything to drink in there?"

"I have red wine and white. I also have a bottle of sparkling water and—"

"Water, please."

He passes me the bottle, and I unscrew the lid. After taking a gulp, I relax and admire the scenery. "You know, you couldn't have brought me anywhere more perfect."

"Oh, yeah?" Gage reclines back.

"You said London is the beating heart of England. Well, the lighthouse is the beating heart of the island. It can be seen from virtually anywhere and to me represents home."

Gage blows out. "Home. What a fickle word."

His statement has me frowning. "And where would the great Gage Calloway call home?"

Gage shrugs. "It's wherever I rest my head for the night. I move from estate to estate, hotel to hotel. There isn't a property or location I feel strongly enough toward to afford it that title."

"That's kind of sad," I say and pick up my knife and fork.

"Not at all. It's just the life of a hotelier."

He may say that, but I feel as though it is his biggest pretence. The problem runs much deeper than his profession, of that I am sure.

We spend the next half an hour eating. We talk about everything, yet talk about nothing. We tell each other random bits of information from our past. Nothing too deep, or personal, so the topic of Gage's ex-wife doesn't get brought up. Instead, he tells me of the time his brother Lucian had a horse-riding accident and ended up in a coma. He tells me about the time he got drunk and vomited all over his mother's prized begonias after he set her trellises on fire, all while naked as the day he was born.

Gage is so endearing with his stories that he somehow has me ready to start crying in sadness, then crying tears of laughter.

"Tell me something about you," Gage says, after finishing off the tray of fish and chips.

I poke at the gammon and egg I was eating and try to think of something exciting about my life. But try as I might, I come up with nothing.

"There's not much to tell, really. I was a good girl." My shoulders slump. How am I going to keep someone so interesting and full of life interested in boring old me?

"Being good isn't bad," Gage says, and lifts my chin. "I like that you were a good girl in the past. It simply means that it's my sole responsibility to corrupt you." He offers a wink.

Corrupt me or change me? The words are on the tip of my tongue when he speaks.

"Tell me how your parents met."

I smile and relax. My parents' love story is romance novel-worthy. "Like me, my mum used to work at Stanton and

Mills Hotel. Her name was Stanton back then, so the hotel was just called Stanton Hotel."

Gage nods. "And Mills was added when she got married, I'm assuming."

I wring my hands together in my lap. "That's right. My uncle didn't bother having a new sign made up, instead he paid for a makeshift sign to be added with the words, 'and Mills.'

"Cheapskate," Gage mutters, and I don't disagree.

"Anyway. My father had loved my mother for years, but was too damn stubborn to tell her how he felt or ask her out on a date. So, instead, he wrote his feelings on a sheet of paper and put that piece of paper in a bottle. That night when he was working on the fishing boat, he threw the bottle out to sea and left the rest in fate's hands."

"And your mum found it, and they lived happily ever after?" Gage finishes for me.

I nod. "Mum used to run on the beach every morning like I do now, and one morning she stumbled across the message in the bottle. After reading the letter she and my father began dating, and I guess the rest is history."

I leave out the part where my father planted the bottle on the shoreline where he knew my mother would find it. That's my and my dad's little secret, one I promised I would take to the grave.

Gage wraps an arm around me. "Now that's a love story you tell the grandkids."

I smile, thinking that Mum and Dad haven't yet had the chance to do that. My brothers haven't been in a rush to have children, and neither am I. Sure, I want them one day, but not for a while. "It's where the name Genie came from. It was Father's nickname for our mother."

"That explains the name on the boat, and the fishmongers," Gage notes.

"That's right."

Gage places the empty trays of food back into the paper bags and guides me into his lap. He wraps his arms around me and rests his chin on my shoulder. We sit in silence and listen to the crashing sound of the waves from below. Everything is so perfect in this moment that I never want it to end. He lifts his hand and brushes a lock of hair behind my ear. "Right here, right now, Millie, is where our story begins."

I can't help but smile, but my smile falters. The problem with my and Gage's story is that we are worlds apart. He doesn't have a home, and if he did it certainly wouldn't be here on the island. As for me, I don't see a future in London. Someone is going to have to bend. And as always, that someone isn't going to be me.

I wonder if there is a way in the chaotic reality of our lives that we are able to meet somewhere in the middle. Though that is a conversation for another day. Because today is perfect, and I will not ruin it with the bitter taste of reality.

TWENTY-THREE

Gage

I make a point of arriving at the harbour at ten minutes past midnight. I intend to let dear Travis wait. Though it would seem the joke is on me, as he still hasn't arrived fifteen minutes later.

I stand alone at the harbour. It is pitch black, lit only by sporadic streetlights that lead off into the town. With nothing else to do but stand and wait, I watch *Genie* as she bobs up and down on the water. In this sliver of time, I scroll through my emails. I respond to several of my hotel managers before opening an email marked 'urgent' from my father. He has sent the details of a charity gala that he expects me to attend in the coming weeks. Although I can't stand these mind-numbing functions, I make an exception for the annual Pink Ribbon Breast Cancer Charity Gala, a charity my family and I hold dear, as breast cancer was the illness that caused my mother's untimely death. I reply without even thinking.

> Gage: I'll be there.

I will be expected to take a plus-one. I will ask Millie, of course, but I know she will not be up for going to London in the foreseeable future, or any time in the future for that matter. She is an island girl through and through, and I can't say I blame her.

Without a plus-one my father will no doubt try to pair me with Samantha Matthews—a suitable match in his eyes, a woman whose uncle has substantial wealth and a great deal of connections. Father would have us married in a heartbeat. But porking my brother's ex-girlfriend isn't at the top of my to-do list.

"Rich boy." Travis's voice pulls my attention from my phone screen, and I look up as he approaches. He is clad in shiny yellow overalls with dungaree-style fastenings. Draped over his arm is a replica of the garish outfit, which I assume is for me.

Jesus, what have I gotten myself into?

I'm far too proud to tell him I've changed my mind, so tap the face of my Rolex. "You said midnight."

"I did, didn't I? But when you didn't arrive on time I popped into Mum and Dad's for a coffee. I figured if you wanted to keep me waiting, then it's only fair I return the favour."

I narrow my eyes, but have nothing to say in response. Travis is as petty as I am.

"Due to your tardiness, I don't have time to give you a guided tour of the boat. Austin and Bruce will be here any minute. You need to change before we set sail."

Travis flings me the fluorescent yellow overalls, which I catch one-handed. The material is cool and rubbery to the touch. I lift the outfit, making a mental note at how small it appears and with very little room to give. "Are you sure this will fit me?"

Travis shrugs. "Sure it will. It belonged to me long before I went to the gym and bulked up. I have no doubt your scrawny body will fit."

I am a gentleman, I remind myself. *I never deliver the first punch.* But my gentlemanly manners and reservations are starting to crumble. I want nothing more than to punch this guy square in the face.

The overalls squeak as I squeeze my hand into a tight fist. I'm a millisecond away from giving Travis a black eye when Bruce and Austin approach.

Travis plasters on a tight-lipped smile. "I really am going to have fun tonight."

"That makes two of us," I retort.

The tension is gone the second Bruce pulls me into a tight hug. "It's good to see you, bud. Travis tells me you're keen to help out and learn the ropes."

Overstatement of the century, but I don't correct him. Nor do I try to put distance between us, even as his thick beard digs into my neck. I surprise myself when I lift my arm and wrap it around his back.

"Good to see you too, man," I say, and clap my hand on his shoulder blade several times before releasing him.

I have no idea why I let Bruce hug me, or why I reciprocated said hug. Maybe it's because his father has had a stroke, and I know too well how it feels to lose a parent. Or is it because I'm slowly falling in love with his spitfire of a sister?

Fuck me. It suddenly dawns on me that what I feel for Millie is intensifying at an alarming rate. That not only do her feelings concern me, but so do those of her brothers. I want them to like me—no, more than that, I want them to accept me. Austin and Bruce, that is. As for Travis, he can swan-dive from the lighthouse cliff into shark-infested waters for all I care.

But then I remember Millie's words that she and I won't work if Travis and I can't see eye to eye. So, swallowing my pride, and any self-respect I had several moments ago, I nod my head toward the boat. "I guess I'll get changed."

"Right this way." Austin climbs aboard, hurries toward the helm and powers her up. Fluorescent lights positioned around the boat flicker several times before powering on. The boat is bigger than I had anticipated, with a large deck area and narrow steps leading into another area below. Storage boxes line either side of the deck. While some are iced, others are empty.

"I gather that is where we'll store the fish," I say.

Travis scoffs. "I didn't know we brought Einstein with us."

I squeeze the yellow overalls so tightly now that my fingers feel as though they'll snap right off. "I'll go below deck to change," I say, trying hard to remain civil.

Travis winks. "You do that, princess. Try not to break a nail."

"Will do." I give a one-fingered salute, which I use to creatively flip him the bird.

"Here." Bruce hurries in front of me. "I need to nip down anyway, let me show you where the head is."

"The head?" I question.

"Sorry, fisherman talk. I mean the toilet."

Although I follow, I can't help think it's a fishing boat—surely it can't be that hard to locate the toilet myself. But I quickly eat my words. Whereas the top deck area has some kind of order, down below is a mess. Nets are stacked up in a pile, with several workstations and storage boxes, too many to count, stacked haphazardly.

"Bruce, this is—"

"A hot mess, I know. The head is right there." He points to a door at the back of the boat, a door partially blocked by more stacked-up boxes.

I move the boxes aside and manage to slip inside. I leave my T-shirt on, though slip out of the trousers. I push my feet into the yellow overalls, but have to yank the material up inch by inch and then some in order to get it on. As expected, the overalls do not fit. They're incredibly tight, making any movement, be it walking or even breathing, next to impossible. Every time my knee bends the rubbery suit squeaks in protest.

Without warning the boat begins to move, causing me to jerk forward, my elbows crashing against the thin walls of the toilet.

"Are you okay in there?" Bruce hollers.

"Fine." I open the door and join Bruce.

"As I was saying, it's usually tidy below deck, but with Dad's unexpected stroke, you could say we all went into panic mode."

I nod. That makes sense. I motion toward the stairs. "After you."

Bruce shakes his head. "You go ahead. I'm going to stay below deck and tidy up."

I leave Bruce on his hands and knees scrubbing the floor. I don't know how I do it with this ridiculously tight-fitting outfit on, but I manage to climb the stairs from the lower level up to the main deck. Austin is at the helm, steering the boat, whereas Travis is sitting on a small wooden box untangling a net and feeding it into a machine.

"Can I help?" I ask.

Travis kicks a wooden box my way. "Knock yourself out."

I can't help but think he means those words in the most literal sense, but say nothing as I take hold of the rope and with Travis begin untangling.

I'm sure the overalls tear as I sit, but I say nothing about that. "So, are you going to tell me a little about what we're going to be doing? Or am I meant to just guess and hope for the best?"

Travis rolls his eyes. "I knew bringing you would be a mistake."

"Well, it was you who asked me to join you here. The very least you could do is tell me a little bit about what we're going to be doing."

Releasing the rope, Travis stands. He points to a steel roller mechanism beside him. "The net will be released into the ocean when we are a little further out. When the machine is turned on the net will be brought up the roller system, and tangled up will be the fish, crabs and scallops. It's our job to untangle them and deposit them in the correct storage boxes. When the boxes start to fill up Bruce will take them below deck, where he will start to work on them."

My eyes widen. "You don't waste any time." The saying rings true—time is money. "I take it that Bruce semi-prepares the fish on the boat before heading back to shore, then you take them to the shop for the final touches ready to be sold?"

Travis nods. "Precisely. Now can you stop talking?"

We untangle the net in silence, and it isn't until the sun comes up that the machine is switched on and the net starts to be fed through the roller. As Travis said, fish and crabs are tangled up in the net. It's our job to untangle them and put them into the correct boxes. I have no idea what I am doing, so watch.

Travis claps his hand on the helm, causing Austin to turn. "I feel like the fishing gods are smiling down on us this morning."

"That's what I like to hear." Austin fist-pumps the air several times before turning his attention back to the open water.

One by one Travis and I get to work untangling crab and fish from the net. I follow Travis's lead as to where to deposit the fish once they are free. The crabs are placed in large buckets, lobsters in another, the rays in storage boxes. Travis makes a special journey for the monkfish, which he takes to the very back of the boat. It isn't long before Bruce brings an empty storage box up and takes down one we have filled.

I haven't sat down from the second the machine was turned on. That and the fact I haven't slept for twenty-four hours is making this extremely tedious and tiring work.

"How's your old man doing?" I ask and use the back of my hand to hide a yawn.

Travis untangles a crawfish from the rope before answering. "He's doing really well. Mum said he could come home as early as tomorrow."

"That's great, Travis."

Travis eyes me sceptically. "What is it you're after, rich boy? Because coming here sure as shit wasn't a male bonding session."

I take the net and begin to untangle a ray. "I just want to make your sister happy. And us getting on would definitely help in achieving that."

Travis is quiet for a second. He deposits the crawfish into a bucket before speaking. "I don't like you, Gage. And I dare say the feeling is mutual."

My silence answers his question.

"But I love my sister. And if being with you makes her happy, then I will try to get along with you for her sake. If you hurt her, I will murder you and chop you up into tiny pieces."

Travis and his many threats. Though he may have forgotten his previous promises to end me, I have not. "Is that before or after you bury me or toss my body into the ocean?"

"I've not decided." A ghost of a smile touches his lips.

"Can I be blunt?" I lean my elbows on my lap.

Travis raises a brow. "If you must."

"You're a dick, and so am I. That said, can we put all of this bitterness behind us and start again?" I hold out my hand, and to my surprise, Travis accepts.

Hours later we return to the harbour with storage boxes full to the brim. I nip downstairs to the head to change out of the yellow overalls and back into my trousers. Upon squeezing out of the overalls I notice a tear to the rear. That explains the chill I felt when sitting. It felt as though my bollocks were going to drop off through lack of circulation.

I leave the overalls draped over the sink and make my way off the boat. The brothers are carrying the storage containers from the deck and onto the harbour, then from the harbour into *Genie*'s Catch of the Day. I, meanwhile, feel like shit. I'm beyond tired and in need of a stiff drink. But, as a Calloway, I refuse to show a sliver of weakness. I crouch down and pick up one of the storage boxes.

"I've got this," Travis says, and claps me on the shoulder. "You look like shit."

I place my hand over my heart in mock offence. "And just when I thought we were getting along so well."

Travis laughs. "Go get some sleep. Seriously, we've got this."

I don't argue, and with my shoulders slumped make my way toward the hotel. I walk through the town for a little bit of the way before continuing on the beach.

I pass Mr Porter and George. Mr Porter waves, and George barks. I nod my head in acknowledgement but have no intention of stopping to chat.

I am no stranger to working out, but am surprised how much my legs and arms ache from working on the boat with Travis. It's given me a new appreciation of just how hard and physically demanding their job is. They fish through the early hours of the morning, then when they're back hand-deliver orders to the townspeople and our hotel. They get a few hours' sleep in the afternoon before starting the whole ordeal over again.

My feet are starting to feel heavy in the dry sand. My eyes are so heavy from lack of sleep that I'm sure if I don't get to my bed soon I'll collapse right here on the sand. Which wouldn't be the worst idea, but I don't want to wake up with sunstroke either.

"Gage…" The sound of her voice has me spinning around. Millie approaches, dressed in her tracksuit for her morning run.

I open my arms and, smiling, she runs right into my embrace, a little too enthusiastically as the force of her body crashing into mine has me recoiling.

"Tough first day?"

"Tough first and *last* day," I correct. Although my words are light-hearted, there is no way I am setting foot on *Genie* any time in the future.

I wrap my arm around her shoulders, and together we make

our way inside the hotel and head straight for my room. The only thing I can think of now is my bed. I must be tired, as not only am I falling in and out of sleep while walking, but I'm sure I see my brother emerge from one of the rooms.

I blink several times, but when the figment of my imagination doesn't disappear it becomes clear to me that he is actually here. "Malachi?"

He eyes me sceptically. "Gage, what the hell happened to you? You smell almost as bad as you look."

I hadn't considered the pungent smell of fish emitting from my clothes. A scent Millie actively detests, and yet here she is with her arm wrapped around me.

"What brings you here?" I say and pull my room key from my pocket.

Malachi straightens his silk tie, maybe to highlight how put together his appearance is right now compared to mine. "Oh, you know, a little bit of this, a little bit of that." He spins on his heel. "It was nice catching up with you, little brother. Now I really must get on; I have a jam-packed day of exploring the island planned."

Malachi strolls toward the lift and I side-eye Millie, who sighs. "He arrived yesterday."

"And I guess he didn't want you to tell me?"

"You guessed right."

"He's up to something," I say. "Is there any land for sale on the island?"

Millie shrugs. "I don't think so, I tried to look yesterday but couldn't find anything."

"It's because you're not looking in the right places." I push the key into the door and let myself in. "I'm too tired to think. Don't worry, I will find out. But first I'm going to catch up on some overdue sleep."

I stumble toward the bed and, fully dressed, fall onto the mattress. Millie lies next to me, and with her wrapped up in my arms I close my eyes.

TWENTY-FOUR

Millie

While Gage sleeps, I spend the morning working at the hotel's reception. Tanya appears much happier today; she has a smile on her face and sporadically hums to herself. Though her change of mood brings out her talkative side and she doesn't stop bleating on about Malachi the whole time we are working.

"Is he single?" she asks for what seems like the millionth time. I don't get Tanya's interest in Malachi. He's been nothing but standoffish with everyone since his arrival.

"I'd imagine so," is the same reply I give every single time.

Tanya nods, but I can see that she is not content with my answer. She taps her pen on the reception desk several times. "But how do you know for sure?"

I place my palm over my face. "Because he is a crotchety piece of work and I don't know any sane woman who would put up with him. That's how I know."

"Could you ask Gage for me?"

I throw my arms in the air. "Ask him yourself if you want him so badly."

She points to her wedding band. "I couldn't care less whether he's single or otherwise. It's just I have a ton of staff and guests who are pestering me to find out."

"This is a respectable hotel, not *Love Island*." I round the reception desk and head toward the door leading out of the hotel.

"Where are you going?" Tanya calls after me.

"Anywhere that isn't here," I call back.

I told Tanya I'd work at the desk with her until one, that is the time my brothers are minding the shop till. But I decide they've worked hard enough today that I'll relieve them from their duties early. It will also give me a chance to get away from the broken record currently standing at reception.

I push the lobby door open and head for the concrete steps that lead down to the beach. Holidaymakers are everywhere. Clad in beachwear, some are swimming in the pool, others are paddling in the sea and those who don't want to get wet are reclining on sunloungers. The hotel staff take turns patrolling different areas serving food and drink. Everything is running like clockwork, and everyone appears happy.

Continuing on, I take a slow walk to the shop, something I rarely do. I am always in a hurry, a hurry to get up for my morning run, a hurry to get back to the hotel to start my shift. I am in such a hurry to do everything that I never stop and enjoy the simpler things in life, mainly what I have right here at my feet.

With that sentiment in mind, I think back and can't remember the last time I dipped my toes in the sea. I stop walking and pull off my shoes. I roll my trousers up to my knee and walk to where the water caresses the shoreline, then, one step at a time, make my way into the ocean. I walk until the waves lap against my thighs, wetting my trousers, but I don't care. For once I don't care about rushing anywhere. I take a deep breath in, inhaling the strong scent of the sea. Has the air always smelt this fresh and the sea this salty?

I blow out, slow and controlled. I've rushed around for far too long, taking all of this for granted. No more. I'm going to cut myself some slack. I intend to not be so rigid with schedules and times. Gage said the hotel can run itself, and he was right. I'm not here to babysit the staff. Although I don't intend on giving work up any time soon, I plan on taking some time out for me. But it's not just me I want to make time for. I want to make time for Gage. I want to join him for evening walks along the beach. I want us to enjoy more picnics at the lighthouse. I want it all.

When I finally make it to the shop I notice Mum working behind the counter. The bell dings as I rush in.

"Mum," I screech, and with my arms outstretched run toward her. I'm sure she's about to topple over from the sheer force of the hug. "I'm so happy to see you. How's Dad?"

Mum pulls away. "He's upstairs, sweetheart, why don't you ask him yourself?"

Tears stream down my face. "He's going to be all right?"

Mum sandwiches my cheeks between her palms. "Yes, sweetheart. He is."

I return to the hotel at seven p.m. and am surprised to see Gage sitting in the lobby with Malachi. They really stand out here, where the unspoken dress code is smart casual, though it would seem they left the 'casual' at the door. Both men are impeccably dressed in dark tailored suits. Malachi sits poker-straight, while Gage is hunched forward with his elbows resting on the table. Red-faced, he gesticulates with his hands as he speaks.

It would seem they're having a heated discussion. So as not to disturb them, I make my way behind the reception desk.

"How long has he been here?" I ask Tanya.

No answer. Of course not—her attention is fixed on Malachi and Gage. She is deathly quiet and it's as though she is trying to overhear what they are saying. She chews on her bottom lip, fidgeting with her long ebony braid.

I snap my fingers in front of her face and ask again. "How long has he been here?"

"About fifteen minutes," Tanya answers, though her gaze remains fixed. "Did you find out if he's single?"

"I don't know. But to stop you from repeatedly asking, I'm going to get the answer straight from the horse's mouth."

"Wait, what?" With panic in her voice Tanya grabs my wrist. "Millie, don't."

Ignoring her words, I free myself from her hold. Without a backward glance I head toward the table where Gage and Malachi are sitting. Malachi looks up briefly and catches my eyes. He doesn't smile, doesn't so much as acknowledge me. He just continues his conversation with Gage. Gage, on the other hand, must sense my approach as he turns in his seat. In contrast to his brother, his face breaks into the sexiest smile I think I've ever seen.

"Hi, babe." He stands and opens his arms. I walk quicker, needing his touch, needing his warmth as much as I need my next breath. I'm a ball of emotions right now, and I don't know whether to laugh, cry, or both. I walk into his arms and pull him close to me.

The control I had moments ago fractures and I find myself tearing up. I can't stop the involuntary gasps that leave my lips as I try but fail to keep my composure.

"Why are you crying?" Gage asks, and I can sense him trying to lean down to see my face.

I sniff and wipe my eyes. "It's my dad."

Gage's body stiffens. "Is everything okay?"

"He's home, Gage, he's home." My mind flashes to when I

saw him earlier. "Apart from his speech being slightly slurred, you wouldn't know there'd been anything wrong with him."

"That's fantastic news." Gage leans down and kisses me hard. I don't pull away; I don't care who sees. Instead, I kiss him right back. It's a closed-lipped kiss filled with a thousand unspoken words and a thousand emotions.

In my mind the kiss goes on forever, but in reality, it's only several seconds. He pulls away, and I swear I see his eyes tearing up, though can't be sure as he quickly turns his attention to the reception. "Tanya, have a waitress bring us a bottle of your finest champagne. A celebration is in order."

Tanya nods. "I'm on it."

I glance around and see eyes on me from every direction, be it guests going about their evening or staff passing by. Still, I do nothing to put distance between me and Gage. I want everyone to know we're together—hell, I want the world to know.

I'm snapped from my thoughts when Malachi clears his throat. "Please, take a seat." He stands, looking a million shades of arrogant as he pulls out a chair for me to sit.

I smile sweetly. "Don't mind if I do."

I ignore the chair and instead make my way around the circular table and pull out the chair beside Gage. Malachi and I hold eye contact until I am seated. His dark gaze holds a chill so cold I swear I feel it in my bones.

"Obstinate, like an unbroken horse," Malachi notes. "Fortunate for you, dear brother, all horses can be tamed."

I fold my arms in front of my chest. "I'm no horse."

"And she has tenacity. Not at all like your ex-wife. Remind me of her name, Gage. Florence? Mabel?"

"Daphne," Gage corrects and takes a seat beside me.

I narrow my eyes at Malachi. "If you're trying to embarrass Gage, it's not going to work."

Gage places his hand over mine, his way of silently telling

me to stop talking. But I'm too riled up. I hate sibling rivalry and arguments; I want this nipped in the bud right now.

"On the contrary, Millie. My intention is not to belittle my brother. The truth is I didn't care for Daphne one bit. She was a conniving little intriguer."

I frown. I have no idea what that word means.

"Whereas you," Malachi continues, "I have the utmost respect for you."

Malachi looks at me expectantly. I gather he's waiting for me to say something. My head is blank, so I say the first thing that comes to mind. "Are you single?"

Malachi's serious expression falters and he actually smiles, an open-mouthed smile showcasing a set of pearly white teeth. "Steady on, Millie, I said I respect you. It wasn't a declaration of love."

I can feel the tips of my ears begin to pink. "I wasn't asking for me, I was asking for—"

"Where's that champagne?" Gage interrupts, and as if on cue a waitress arrives holding a bottle of our most expensive bubbly.

One glass turns into two, then three. The more we drink the looser our tongues become.

Malachi and Gage talk of their childhood, of memories growing up in Knightsbridge, London. Of the mischief they'd get into, especially Gage. The more they tell me, the more I fall in love with the man sitting at my side.

Despite all the crap he's been through in his life, he's managed to turn out an amazing person. An amazing person I get to call my boyfriend. I reach under the table and place my hand on his thigh. He responds immediately by placing his hand over mine.

He side-eyes me. The look in his eyes tells me he doesn't plan on us staying in the lobby for longer than absolutely necessary.

"So"—Gage turns his attention to his brother—"are you going to clear the veil of suspense and tell us what you're really doing here?"

"I told you already, I'm here for a short vacay." Malachi flashes a glance at his watch. "Would you look at the time. On that note, I'm going to head to bed." Malachi stands, pulls his wallet from his back pocket and tosses several notes on the table. Without another word he makes his way toward the lift.

My shoulders drop, and I turn to Gage. "Guess we're no closer to finding out why Malachi is here."

The second he is out of earshot, Gage leans in close. "I've done some digging of my own and have discovered that a substantial plot of land has been purchased here on the island. I can't see the date when the land was acquired, or by whom, but I have my suspicions."

I shudder inwardly. Malachi's company builds houses, it doesn't take a genius to figure out what he's planning.

"The island doesn't have the amenities in place for more people to live here." My words are strained. I think back to my time in London, at the busy streets, and all the traffic on the roads. Is that what Malachi is trying to do? Turn our island into a mini-London?

"I know my brother, and he wouldn't start any of the works before calling a town meeting."

I raise a brow. "A town meeting? Why?"

"To get in people's good graces first, of course. He'd have slideshows and a 3D model put together to show his plans, and then he'd listen to the townsfolk's thoughts on the matter."

Finally, a glimmer of hope. "And if everyone was against his plans then he wouldn't put them into action?"

Gage breaks eye contact for a beat before saying, "People are fickle, Millie. When they hear of his plans firsthand and see how he intends to improve the island, most will be on side."

"But I know the locals. No one will want the island to be changed. If we all signed a petition, would that stop him building?"

"It wouldn't stop his plans. But please don't worry, we have time on our side."

I force a smile. Worry doesn't quite cut how I'm feeling right now. I'm freaking out.

"Knowledge is power, Millie. When we know more we will act accordingly."

I hold out my arms. "So, what do we do in the meantime?"

A wicked grin spreads across Gage's face. "Oh, I can think of plenty of things we could do to pass the time…"

TWENTY-FIVE

Millie

Three weeks pass in a flash, and life is good. Better than good, it's perfect.

It doesn't take long for Gage and I to fall into a routine. We start our days at six a.m. sharp, when we go for our morning run. Without fail we bump into good old Mr Porter. He always stops me for a chat, and while we're deep in conversation, Gage takes over fetch duties with George.

After our run I spend the morning with Tanya working at the hotel reception, during which time Gage is up in his room busy with conference calls. By afternoon we go to my parents' shop to help out and spend our evenings having dinner in Christopher's restaurant or at the lighthouse.

Everything has been perfect until right now.

With his arm wrapped around my shoulder, Gage pulls me into him. "It'll only be for a few days."

That's a few days too long.

My heart feels as though it's being squeezed a little tighter with each rotation of the helicopter's blade. A helicopter that is here to take Gage away from me. We haven't spoken about the longevity of our relationship, nor have we spoken about how we're going to make this work logistically. Will Gage stay on the island with me, but make regular trips back and forth to London? The thought of him leaving is killing me. How will I cope if this becomes a regular occurrence?

Wind from the helicopter blades pick up, causing the skirt of my dress to fan out. A skirt Gage is very quick to hold in place.

"What are you doing?" I ask and give him a playful nudge.

"I don't want anyone to see what's mine."

By 'anyone', he is referring to his brother Malachi, who decided to join us so that he could see Gage off.

Gage releases my dress momentarily to remove his jacket. "Here." He drapes the heavy material over my shoulders, and I'm instantly swaddled in the scent and warmth of my boyfriend. Gage would have had nothing to worry about if single Millie flashed her underwear because she wore big frumpy buttcheek-covering pants, but 'in a relationship' Millie, she's a different kettle of fish. She wears see-through lace thongs and frilly knickers. I wouldn't have worn said frilly knickers and dress tonight if I'd known Gage would be jumping in a helicopter.

We were en route to my parents' for dinner when Gage had a call from one of his assistant managers. He was told there was an emergency at one of his hotels and the police had been called. That was enough to have him call for a helicopter to arrive on the island ASAP.

My shoulders drop as the landing skids touch the ground. Gage gathers me up in his arms. "I'll be back as soon as I can." With that he releases me and makes his way toward the helicopter. My instinct has me wanting to run after him, to go with him, but memories of the busy London streets have my feet well and truly rooted to the ground.

A hand rests on my shoulder. "He'll be back before you know it."

I smile at Malachi. "I know."

Malachi has grown on me over the past few weeks of him coming to and fro. I wouldn't call him a friend, but I wouldn't call him an enemy either. We share a mutual respect for one another, and that's enough for me.

The door to the helicopter opens and Farrah and her bodyguard climb out. I can't help but wonder whether Gage invited her here to keep me company in his absence, but the look on his face tells me he is surprised to see her. Gage and Farrah exchange words, but from where I'm standing I can't hear what they're saying. Still talking, she motions toward Malachi, who waves in acknowledgement.

I side-eye my boyfriend's brother. "It was you, wasn't it?"

"Excuse me?"

"You invited Farrah to keep me company while Gage is away."

He's silent for a beat. "Yes, I invited her."

I nudge him playfully. "I knew there was a decent person in there somewhere."

Malachi opens his mouth but doesn't speak. It appears that he is lost for words.

Gage gets into the helicopter. I run toward Farrah. She has the same idea and runs toward me.

"Oh, my God, what an unexpected surprise." I'm blinded by her long black hair as we hug.

"It's so lovely to see you again, sis," she says, only this time I don't correct her.

"You too." I pull free from the hug, and we watch as the helicopter lifts off the ground. Farrah and I wave as the helicopter takes flight. Our feet remain rooted to the spot until the helicopter is no more than a speck in the distance.

Then it dawns on me that Gage is gone, and just how much

I'm going to miss him. I stop my bottom lip from wobbling and keep my composure. *It's just a few days,* I keep reminding myself. The time will surely fly and Farrah will be the perfect distraction while Gage is away. It's just a shame Dante is here as her permanent shadow.

Farrah places her hand on her stomach. "I'm famished, what's for dinner?"

"We were going to eat at my parents', but I don't think it's your kind of thing."

Farrah's eyes go wide. "Are you serious? I'd love to join you for dinner and meet your parents, that is if you think they'd have me."

I contemplate calling my mother, but the point of getting together this evening is so my parents can meet Hayley. They of course know of her in passing, but they don't know her as Travis's girlfriend. She is the first girl my brother is bringing home, and it's a pretty big deal. I can't overshadow their evening.

"Actually, I have a better idea." I side-eye Malachi. "What do you say to dinner at Christopher's? My treat."

Malachi looks at me as though I've sprouted a second head. "Dinner at Christopher's, yes, but do not offend me by opening your purse. Dinner is on me."

I fold my arms over my chest. "Seriously, Malachi, we're in the twenty-first century, not the eighteen hundreds."

Malachi's expression hardens. "Still, it is not a lady's place to pay."

I flash a glance at Farrah, who shrugs. "I'm hungry. Let's get food and argue about the bill after."

We make it to the restaurant ten minutes later. Farrah's jaw looks as though it's about to hit the floor as we enter. She claps her hands excitedly. "Oh, my God, I just love this."

Her and me both. Christopher's appears like a regular restaurant from the outside, but on the inside has a retro 1960s theme. Black and white chessboard-style tiles line the floor, with electric pink and blue chaired booths scattered around the open space. A mahogany jukebox stands proud in the corner of the room, blasting rock and roll music from the day.

The owner, Christopher Junior, kept the interior exactly the same when the premises were passed down to him by Christopher Senior. And everyone loves the restaurant's quirkiness. The young love it for its loud and vibrant colours, and the elderly appreciate the history of the place. I guess for them it's like stepping back in time to their youth.

Farrah's shoulders drop when she looks around. "It looks a little busy in here."

It's busy all right. There isn't a table spare.

Malachi reaches for his wallet. "Don't worry, sis, I could always ask someone to go home early."

By 'ask', I gather he means 'bribe'. I glower at Malachi. "No, you won't. We'll sit at the bar and wait patiently, like everyone else who isn't loaded does."

"Fine, but I need a stiff drink first to be able to eat in this monstrosity of a place." Malachi heads toward the bar and grabs a menu en route.

During his on-off stay on the island Malachi has eaten exclusively at the hotel. Apart from breakfast, which he has in the hotel restaurant at eight thirty, he has room service deliver his lunch and dinner at the same time every day: twelve fifteen lunch and five thirty dinner. The guy is like clockwork.

Malachi sits on one of the electric blue bar stools. Farrah and I join him. Cindy the barmaid smiles in acknowledgement. Like the restaurant, Cindy's attire is 1960s-themed. She is clad in a pale blue tunic-style dress with a sewn-on apron.

"What can I get you?" She mops up a spillage with a white paper towel.

"A table for four, please," I say.

"She means a table for three," Malachi corrects.

"But what about…?" I let my words trail off.

Malachi follows my gaze to where the bodyguard is standing. His arms are crossed over his chest and he stands poker-straight against a nearby wall.

"We don't dine with the hired help," Malachi says under his breath. "Dante won't be joining us."

Cindy clears her throat and nods toward a corner booth. "Table five are just finishing up with their desserts. They won't be long. Would you like a drink while you wait?"

Malachi points toward the back wall, where all the bottles are lined up. "A glass of your finest merlot."

I glance at Farrah, whose eyes are wide as she takes in the chrome milkshake machine. "A banana and strawberry milkshake with sprinkles, please."

Malachi covers his eyes with his palm. "You're twenty, not two. Don't you want a more adult type of drink?"

Farrah shakes her head. "No. I want a milkshake with sprinkles."

Cindy's gaze meets mine. "And for you, Millie? Do you want your usual?"

By 'usual' she's referring to a glass of water with a slice of lime. I've never cared for sugary drinks, but am a believer in solidarity. I smile at Farrah before pointing toward the milkshake machine. "Make that two."

One by one our drinks are placed in front of us, first Malachi's glass of merlot, followed by the milkshakes. Sprinkles and whipped cream slosh over the rim of my glass, and I roll up the sleeves of Gage's jacket before taking a sip.

The family sitting at table five pay their bill and leave. A waitress clears the dirty plates and cutlery away and wipes the table down before calling us over to sit.

Malachi sighs before muttering, "Guess we're slumming it."

I side-eye Farrah, who shakes her head. "Honestly, unless

it's a Michelin star-rated restaurant, you can't take my brother anywhere."

Farrah and I slide into the booth, and Malachi slides in beside me. Bonnie, our waitress, hands out our menus, telling us she'll give us a little time to decide what we'd like to order.

The menu is split into two parts, classic dishes from the 1960s on the left-hand side and modern-day dishes on the right. Although I scroll through the options, I know what it is I want—the beer-battered mushrooms to start, followed by garlic chicken breast and triple-cooked chips for my main. If I have enough room I will order the cheeseboard for dessert. I've always been a creature of habit. But a nagging voice in the back of my mind tells me I should try something new, and I plan to do just that. When the waitress comes to take our order I point to the 1960s section of the menu.

"I would like the stuffed celery and cherry tomatoes to start, followed by the meatballs with grape jelly for my main," I say and pass my menu back to Bonnie.

"That sounds positively revolting." Farrah hands Bonnie her menu. "I'll have what she's having."

It doesn't surprise me that Malachi doesn't follow suit. He orders a prawn cocktail to start and the avocado and chutney salad for his main.

Bonnie asks, "Any desserts?"

"Maybe," I say, and, taking a gulp of my milkshake, try not to grimace. "We'll see how we feel after our mains."

Bonnie nods. "That's wise." She jots our orders down in a notepad before leaving.

We sit in silence for a moment, except for Farrah, who sings along to the song 'Help' by the Beetles. Farrah sighs when the song finishes and another isn't played. She rests her chin in her hands and bats her long lashes at her brother. "Be a star and play a song on the jukebox."

Malachi crosses his arms over his chest. "What did your last servant die of?"

"Disobedience," Farrah deadpans, before stifling a laugh. "Go on, Malachi. Go play something from the Rolling Stones."

I'm surprised someone so young has an appreciation for the older generations' songs.

"Can't beat a bit of the Rolling Stones." He shuffles out of the booth and heads for the jukebox.

I reach across the table for Farrah's hand. "So now that you're here, what do you want to do tomorrow? I could take you on an island tour. We could go to Sprinkles for ice cream, after which I could show you the lighthouse. Name it, and I'll make it happen."

"I thought you'd like to come with me to see my new house. Well, soon-to-be house," she corrects.

"New house?"

Farrah's brows knit together. "On the plot of land Malachi purchased. He promised me a sea view. How cool is that? I can visit you any time I like then."

Farrah searches my gaze for a light bulb moment. When the light bulb moment doesn't happen, and I sit deathly silent, she asks, "Didn't Malachi tell you? It's the reason I'm here."

"No, he seems to have forgotten to mention that to me." Guess that explains why he was at a loss for words earlier.

"I was meant to arrive in the morning, but when Malachi called and said Gage needed the helicopter tonight, well, it made sense for me to come. It's just a pity that Gage won't be here tomorrow for the big meeting."

"Meeting?" I say, sounding more and more like a parrot.

Farrah flicks her hair back and laughs. "My God, Millie, have you been living under a rock for the past few weeks?"

The song 'Confessin' the Blues' from the Rolling Stones begins to play in the background, and when I don't answer

Farrah continues. "Malachi is calling a town meeting to discuss the development on the land."

I don't need to say a word. I'm sure the expression on my face speaks for itself.

"Oh, my God, he hasn't told you."

My throat goes instantly dry and I watch Malachi as he makes his way back toward our booth.

"No," I say to Farrah. "He hasn't told me anything."

TWENTY-SIX

Gage

I've spent the last few hours sat in the security room of my hotel surrounded by screen upon screen of footage. The purpose is to spot someone who looks out of place, but that's next to impossible with the sheer number of people coming in and out of this hotel on a daily basis. With the two hundred cameras we have installed around the corridors and lobby area, it's like finding a needle in a haystack.

I'm not a stranger to death threats—they are part and parcel of being a billionaire. But this is the first bomb threat we have received. This evening a mysterious package addressed to me was found on the floor of our sushi restaurant. The package was handed in at reception and immediately handed to my security team. When they opened said package there was a note with the word 'BANG' in capital letters.

The police were notified right away, and they arrived within minutes. As well as asking for a full list of the hotel staff, past and present, they seized all of our security footage, but lucky for me, we always have a backup.

As a result I have increased the alert level of my security guards. They are currently stationed in and around the hotel. No one is able to enter or leave without being interrogated. This is extremely bad for business. If word got out we received a bomb threat we could lose thousands, hundreds of thousands overnight. The knock-on effect throughout my hotels would be catastrophic, not only financially, but reputationally.

"Here, sir." Clifford, my head of security, places a steaming mug of coffee in front of me.

I tap the empty seat to my right. "Come, join me."

And he does. We watch the footage of the last twenty-four hours in slow motion. We pause numerous frames and zoom in and out of faces, but still get nothing.

I take a gulp of coffee, hoping it will stop me from falling asleep. One mug turns into two and soon three. It has certainly done the job of waking me up, but I don't know if that's the caffeine or the number of toilet breaks I am taking.

My phone vibrates on the table in front of me, I'm about to cut the call when Millie's name flashes on the screen. The device slips from between my fingers in my haste to grab it. I leave the videos running and accept the call.

"Gage?"

It's only been a matter of hours since I was with her, and yet all I want is to have her back in my arms. "Hey, babe." I run my finger over the cursor of the mouse, zooming in and out of several frames.

"You were right," she says, her voice strained.

I release the mouse and recline back in my chair. "Right about what?"

"Your brother. He's bought land on the island and is arranging a town meeting tomorrow evening. Please tell me you'll be back. I need you here."

I rub my temples, silently cursing Malachi for the opportunist he is. "I'll do my best, but it's important I stay here until everything is cleared up."

"Important? What could be so important that you can't come home?"

Home. The word has me smiling. I haven't called a place home since I was a teenager. I've never cared enough about a place I stayed. I've hopped from hotel to hotel, estate to estate, and that suited me. That is, until now.

"Gage." Millie's voice pulls me from my thoughts. As much as I want to get back to the island and back to her, I know I can't, not yet.

"I'm sorry, but my hands are tied. The hotel in Birmingham has received a bomb threat."

"Oh, my God, Gage. Tell me you're not in that hotel."

I could lie and tell her that I'm not, purely to give her peace of mind. But I'm not a believer in deception, so decide on telling her the truth. "Where else would I be?"

"I want you to come back right this second. Do you hear me?" Her voice is laced with pure panic.

"Yes, Mum," I tease. I'll never admit it out loud, but it's kinda nice having someone worry about me.

"Gage, I'm serious."

"Relax, the place is swarming with my security. All my hotels are, as of tonight. Not even a fly will be able to enter the premises without me knowing about it."

She's quiet for a beat. "Funny you're in Birmingham."

"Oh, yeah?" I say, half paying attention to the call and continuing my perusal on the monitors. "And why is that?"

"Because it's where Daniel is studying."

I sit poker-straight, my interest immediately sparked. "Daniel, as in your best friend Daniel?"

"That's the one."

Surely it has to be a coincidence. But out of all the hotels

I own, it's funny that the one in Birmingham has received the threat. "You know I'd never question your past, or want to know about your previous partners, but have you and Daniel ever…?"

"Ew, no, he's like a brother," she cuts in. "We have only ever been friends."

So 'scorned lover' is out of the frame.

"And besides, I doubt Daniel has a chance to deliver bomb threats, with his apprenticeship and my uncle crashing at his."

"Your uncle, as in the poker-playing, ex-hotel owner uncle?"

"The one and only."

I run my fingers over my jaw. "And why is he staying with Daniel?"

"Why not?"

Millie's answer irritates me. When I say nothing Millie continues. "Daniel heard what happened with the hotel, and offered him a place to stay while he got back on his feet."

"Quite the good little Samaritan," I say. "You wouldn't happen to know what your uncle gets up to during his free time?"

"I don't. He hasn't spoken to any of the family since he lost his share of the hotel. But one thing I know for sure is that he certainly is not sending bomb threats."

"I agree," I say. "The police are focusing their attention on staff. Mainly disgruntled employees. They could be a while, since the staff come and go over the months for one reason or another. But still, I don't think it would hurt to rule Malcolm out as a potential suspect."

Millie blows out. "If it will put your mind at rest."

"Have you got the address for where your uncle is staying?"

"Yes, I have. It'll be a wasted journey, but I'll forward it now."

I cut the call and jump up from my seat the second her message pings through. "I'm heading out," I say to Clifford.

"Are you sure that's a good idea?" he asks, matching my steps toward the door.

"Probably not, but when have I been known not to take

risks?" I stop at the threshold. "Thank you, Clifford, but I will take it from here."

I make my way out of the hotel toward my car. My driver Charles sees me and turns on the engine.

I slide into the front passenger's side seat and tell him the address. I spend the duration of the journey trying to find any snippet of information I can about Millie's uncle, but so far my internet searches for Malcolm Stanton have turned up squeaky clean. I hop on to social media, and it's there I discover that he had an on-off relationship with Daniel's mother for well over a decade. I figure that could be the reason Daniel has been so kind as to put him up.

The sound of the indicator has me looking up from my phone screen. The car slows before pulling up outside a block of flats.

"We're here." Charles looks around for a few seconds before pointing toward a row of shops. "I'll park up over there."

"If I haven't returned in half an hour, call the police." I hop out of the car and make my way toward his building.

On reflection, maybe it would have been wise to have brought a member of my security staff with me, or to have informed the police of my suspicions. Oddly enough, I feel a strange kind of loyalty toward Malcolm, and I put that down to the fact that I'm dating his niece. I can't have the police raid his place unless I'm absolutely sure. There is such a thing as coincidence, after all, and just because I received a bomb threat in the same city that Millie's uncle is residing doesn't automatically point the finger of blame in his direction.

I make it to the building's intercom, where I press the button for Room 489. It calls out several times before someone answers.

"Forget your key again?" a deep male voice asks.

"Sadly, no. I'm Gage Calloway. I've come to speak to—"

The intercom makes a loud buzz before I can continue, and without hesitation I open the door. The floor plan of the flats is printed on the wall, which tells me Room 489 is on the fourth floor. I take an inventory of the lobby and spot the lift. A sign on the double doors tells me the lift is out of order.

I make quick work of the stairs and am soon standing outside their room. The door opens before I have a chance to knock, and a slender red-haired man greets me. A red-haired man who isn't Millie's uncle. He looks to be in his late twenties, clean-shaven and semi-muscular. He is dressed in an Aston Villa football T-shirt and a pair of baggy tracksuit bottoms.

I hold out my hand. "I'm Gage Calloway. You must be Daniel."

He regards my hand as though it were dirt. "Come in."

The flat, although on the smaller side, is nicely decorated, with laminate flooring and magnolia-coloured walls throughout. I follow Daniel through a narrow hallway and into an open-plan lounge and kitchen area.

"Take a seat," he says, and motions toward a cream two-seater sofa. Balancing on the arm of the sofa is a can of beer and the TV remote. I notice that the television has been paused, and playing was the football.

I shake my head. "No, thank you, I prefer to stand."

I wait a beat for Daniel to do the cordial thing and offer me a drink. He doesn't, so I get right to the point. "I'd like to see Malcolm."

"He's out."

I wait for Daniel to fill in the gaps. He doesn't. It doesn't seem as though Daniel wants to make this easy for me. "When did you see him last, and when is he likely to be back?"

Daniel shrugs. "He's back when he's back."

I fold my arms in front of my chest. "You don't like me, do you?"

"No, I do not. Because of you Malcolm lost his business, his home and his pride all in one night."

I hold up my hands. "No one made him bet his share of Stanton and Mills on a hand of cards."

Daniel clenches his jaw. "No, but you didn't have to cash in your chips at the end of the night. What's half of a run-down hotel to you anyway?"

"I don't see a run-down hotel. I see potential. The opportunity to build a business from scratch."

Daniel sneers. "By being a damn cuckoo? Why don't you buy a plot of land and build a new hotel instead of stealing someone else's?"

"I think you need to look up the word 'steal.'"

"Let's cut the crap, shall we?" Daniel spits out, his face reddening. "How about you tell me the reason you're here."

So much for pleasantries. I take in a deep inhale. "My Birmingham hotel received a bomb threat earlier today."

"And you think Malcolm is responsible."

"I didn't say that."

Daniel narrows his eyes. "You didn't have to."

I raise my hands because it's clear we've got off on the wrong foot. "I'm not here pointing fingers; I just want to know where Malcolm was earlier today. The police are involved, and I would hate for them to turn up on your doorstep."

Daniel's expression changes, like he finally sees the seriousness in the situation. "Malcolm has been at work all day. He's a maintenance man for the city council. He works anything from twelve- to fifteen-hour shifts just to make ends meet."

I nod. "Thank you for your time."

Daniel is on my heels as I head for the door. "I suppose you're going to contact his employer to confirm this?"

"Nothing is stopping me, but no. You told me Malcolm was working and I believe you."

"Just like that, you're going to take my word?" Daniel studies me. "Why?"

The answer is simple. "Because Millie trusts you. Therefore, I do too."

There's a beat of silence between us. Daniel extends his arm toward the lounge. "Would you like to come in and have a drink?"

I smile. "I thought you'd never ask."

Daniel unpauses the football, and while he grabs me a beer from the fridge, I shoot Charles a text message informing him that my life isn't in imminent danger and he doesn't need to contact the police.

"Here." Daniel hands me a bottle of Bud, which I accept.

After getting off to an icy start, Daniel and I relax in one another's company. As we watch the match, Daniel begins opening up about life on the island and his apprenticeship. The guy he is working for has been messing him around, and Daniel is close to quitting.

"So then return home," I say, before taking a chug of my beer.

Daniel slumps in the seat. "That's the problem though. I return home and I become my parents and my grandparents. All they've ever known is the island. They were born there, got married and divorced there, and will no doubt die there. I want more for myself."

He's piqued my curiosity now. The sofa groans as I lean forward and lean my elbows on my knees. "And what is it you want?"

He smiles and looks skyward, almost like he's visiting a dream. "Enough experience that I can open my own restaurant one day."

Our conversation is interrupted when my phone vibrates. I pull it from my pocket and notice Ryan Winter's name flash on the screen. Ryan is the investigator assigned to my case.

I lift my finger. "I'm really sorry, I'm going to have to take this."

"Go right ahead." Daniel gets up from the sofa and heads toward the kitchenette, as if giving me some privacy.

I swipe the screen and accept the call. "Ryan," I say by way of introduction.

"Mr Calloway, I'm just calling to inform you that we have

found a clear set of prints on the letter. We have traced them back to an ex-employee, a man named Robert Whitehall."

"The name rings a bell." I scratch my head in thought. Then it hits me. The money launderer. I should have known.

"We take this kind of thing very seriously," Ryan continues. "I need to discuss whether or not you want to take things further."

Taking things further would involve the police and no doubt the media. "No. I will not be pressing charges," I say and cut the call.

Daniel is leaning on the kitchen worktop, clearly eavesdropping. "You're seriously not going to press charges?"

I smile. "There's more than one way to skin a cat, and trust me when I say I am not a man you want to cross."

One beer turns into two, and the football match goes into overtime. I must be making headway with Daniel as he pauses the game once again, only this time to put a pizza in the oven for us.

"And you call yourself a chef," I say, the look of disgust evident on my face when he throws the cardboard box it came in away.

Daniel feigns offence. "I'll have you know this is the best shop-bought pizza from around these parts. And besides, when I cook all day at work, it's the very last thing I want to do when I come home."

Twenty minutes later Daniel is slicing the pizza before handing me a plate. I'm about to take a bite when the door to the flat opens and Malcolm, dressed in grey overalls, steps inside. He is a small gentleman with sparse grey hair, a large nose and beady eyes. Despite his rodent-like features, he is a pretty happy-go-lucky kind of guy, or at least he seemed to be prior to me beating him at poker. Though his jovial expression turns to thunder when he claps eyes on me.

"What the hell is he doing here?" Malcolm's tone is clipped.

I open my mouth to speak when Daniel answers for me. "Hi,

Dad. So, Gage here thought you were responsible for a bomb threat sent to one of his hotels."

I shoot Daniel a 'fuck you' stare, and he smiles into the rim of his bottle.

Malcolm's eyes narrow. "You did?"

I shrug. There's no point denying that it crossed my mind, so I don't. "I'd like to make a peace offering."

Malcolm crosses his arms in front of his chest. "By peace offering I hope you mean give me my hotel back."

"No, but I've heard enough from Daniel about the kind of guy you are that I think you'll be interested to hear what I have to say…"

TWENTY-SEVEN

Millie

"That was exhausting," Hayley says, her hand on her hip.

"Really?" I can't help but laugh.

Dressed in a fluorescent pink tracksuit, Hayley joined me this morning for my run. Though I use the term 'run' extremely loosely. What we did in fact was walk along the beach while she harped on about dinner with my family. Not only was she gushing over Travis, but my parents and brothers too. She said they made her feel right at home and when the evening was over, she didn't want to leave.

I'm yet to fill her in about my evening at Christopher's or Malachi's plans, mainly because other than building Farrah a house, I don't know what his plans are. When I confronted him about it, he said I would find out at the town meeting along with everyone else.

The lift pings, and we make our way along the corridor and toward our room. "I need water," Hayley chokes out and grasps her throat to exaggerate the fact.

"Jeez, anyone would think you ran a marathon," I tease.

I unlock the door to my and Hayley's shared room and she dramatically falls inside. Sitting on the floor, she holds her arms up expectantly. "Aren't you going to help me?"

I lean against the doorframe and wait for her to pick herself up. I make a point of pulling my phone from my trouser pocket and checking if Gage has messaged me. But I have no new notifications, and the last text I received from him was late last night. His message read that the police had cautioned the perpetrator, an ex-manager, and it was business as normal.

"Fine," Hayley huffs when it's clear I'm not going to help her up. She gets to her feet and hobbles toward the sofa.

"Does my brother know what a prima donna you are?"

She turns and winks. "Naturally."

I laugh. "Travis has no idea what he's getting himself into."

Hayley's expression sobers. "Millie, I need to tell you something."

"That sounds ominous," I joke. "I'm going to jump in the shower, then I'm all ears." I shut the door. Except the door doesn't close all the way.

Blocking the door is a rather expensive-looking loafer. "Did I hear shower? Would you like some company?" Gage asks.

"Gage, you're back!" I squeak. God, he looks sexy as hell in his signature white shirt, unbuttoned at the neck, and dark blue jeans. His eyes appear heavier than normal and his hair dishevelled, which makes me wonder if he got a good night's sleep or whether he opted to come straight home.

He quirks a brow. "Do you intend on cutting the circulation off to my foot, or are you going to invite me in?"

"Oops, sorry." I release the pressure on the door and he steps inside. Without a word he lifts me off my feet and with me in his arms marches us toward the bathroom.

En route we pass Hayley, who holds out her arms. "And where am I meant to shower?"

"You have access to the empty suites. Take your pick." With those parting words Gage walks us into the bathroom and locks the door. "Now where were we? Oh, yes…" Fully dressed, he walks us under the walk-in shower and turns the tap. I squeal as freezing cold water cascades around us. Within moments we're drenched, causing the material of his shirt to become see-through. The wet fabric sticks to him like a second skin and clings to each one of the rippling muscles below.

Water drips from my lashes as I take him in. He wears the wet look perfectly and is so damn sexy, whereas I am dressed in a baggy tracksuit that, now wet, hangs off me like a sack. My matted hair and no doubt blotchy complexion will do nothing to enhance my appearance. Unlike Gage, who looks hot as hell, I'm sure I look more like a drowned rat.

"Oh, my God, Gage." I laugh when he tips me back in his arms, allowing the water to soak my hair. "You're crazy."

"Crazy in love with you." His words are so sincere and so confident that I know it wasn't a slip of the tongue.

My laughter subsides, and an air of seriousness settles around us. My breath catches in my throat. "Say it again."

Water that was freezing moments ago begins to heat up, causing a foggy cloud to form around us. And for a second it's as though we're transported into a dream.

"I said I love you. I love you, Millie Mills."

I begin to tear up, but not tears of sadness, no, these are tears of euphoria. They are joined by the water spray and together roll down my cheeks. "I love you too, Gage Calloway."

With my revelation I expect Gage to crash his lips against mine. I expect him to tear my clothes from my body and take me against the tiled wall. But to my surprise, that isn't what plays out. With me in his arms, he stands perfectly still, his eyes locked on mine. His stare is so intense that I can't look away. He loosens his grip on me momentarily and with his free hand caresses my cheek with the back of his fingers.

"Why are you crying?" he asks.

"I'm not. It's just the water from the shower is getting in my eyes." A blatant lie, but honestly I have never felt these kinds of emotions before and don't know how to process them.

"I call bullshit," Gage teases, and I snort out a laugh. He is so in tune with me that he knows exactly when to inject a bit of lightheartedness in a situation.

"It's just I've never used the L-word before. It's kind of a big deal," I admit, feeling happy but a little scared. This is completely new territory for me. I haven't fallen for Joe Average. I've fallen for an extremely handsome billionaire who could have any woman he wants. Yet he wants me.

"I haven't used the L-word before either."

I give him a 'yeah, right' look. I haven't forgotten he was once married. I'm about to challenge his statement, but don't get a chance as he crashes his lips against mine.

Our lips remain locked as he lowers my feet to the floor. Heavy, wet material slaps against the tiles as we begin to strip. There is nothing sexy about the way we undress, but there is something extremely raw in the moment.

Naked, we stand in front of one another, his hard cock pressing against my stomach. He towers over me, his body so tall and broad in comparison to me. Every muscle on his body is sculpted like a work of art.

"Is everything okay?" I ask when he doesn't make another move toward me. Maybe he's finally seeing how ordinary I am and is having second thoughts.

But the glint in his eyes tell a different story. He looks me up and down like he's starved and I'm his next meal. "I want to be inside you, but I haven't got a condom."

I suck in my lower lip. "That's okay." I reach between us and take his cock in my hand. "I'm on birth control."

"Fuck, Millie," he groans out when I rub my hand up and down the length of his shaft.

I look at him with hooded eyes. "Do you like that?"

The pre-come that settles at his crown answers my question. It is there for a second before the water washes it away. Without another word he hoists me up so my back presses against the cool tiles. He lowers me onto his cock and doesn't stop until I've taken every delicious inch of him. With his fingers grasping the globes of my arse he thrusts into me. The pressure, my God, the pressure is amazing.

I grip his back, digging my nails in his skin as he fucks me hard and deep. "Gage," I cry out when pleasure and love mix into an intoxicating feeling that has me all giddy.

Closing my eyes, I turn my head to the side. He sees that as an invitation to swirl his tongue along my neck. He sucks, nibbles and kisses my bare skin. Every single nerve ending is tingling, and it feels as though he has my whole body dancing to a secret melody, one only he and I can hear.

He thrusts harder before he stills. His cock pulsates inside me. Neither of us move. We stay as one, wrapped up in one another's arms until it's impossible to do so any longer. Then and only then does he loosen his hold on me and slowly lower me to my feet.

He leans in and kisses me one final time. When he breaks the kiss he reaches for the soap. "Now, I think we need to get you clean, Millie, seeing as how I got you all dirty."

He glides the bar of soap over my breasts, my stomach, and finally over my thighs. When he's finished cleaning me, I take the soap. I lather the bar in my hand before placing it back on the wall-mounted soap dish. With lathery hands I work my palms around his body, making sure to be very thorough and not miss a single inch of him. I'm amazed how hard and sculpted his abs are. My fingers glide in and out of all the pronounced bumps and ridges.

We make our way to the bed after the shower, and once under the covers we snuggle up together. He lies behind me in the classic spooning position.

"I met Daniel and your uncle last night," Gage says conversationally.

The duvet rustles as I turn to face him. "And you've lived to tell the tale."

"Indeed."

I reach forward and brush a long strand of hair from his eyes. "How were they?"

"Apart from wanting my head mounted on a spike, they were good."

Gage laughs. I don't. "I'm serious. How were they?"

Gage leans up on his elbows and rests his chin in his hands. "Your uncle was pretty pissed at me."

"That's to be expected, I guess."

"That all changed when I offered him the manager's job at the Birmingham hotel, complete with accommodation and a very generous company pension."

I blink, and blink again. "I'm sorry, can you repeat that?"

"Seeing as my manager is now my *ex*-manager, I needed someone to fill his shoes. Malcolm assured me he has a lot of experience in managerial roles and would be able to do the job."

"Oh, my God, Gage, I could kiss you."

"Yes, you could."

I lean in and place a hard kiss on his lips.

"Oh, and I forgot to mention that I offered Daniel the position of sous chef in my Italian restaurant." Gage winks exaggeratedly. "Here's the part where you kiss me again."

"I think your good deeds earn you a little more than a kiss."

"I think you're right." Gage rolls me onto my back and positions himself on top of me. "Are you ready for round two?"

TWENTY-EIGHT

Gage

Millie really tired me out after our sexathon. That and the fact I didn't sleep last night resulted in me having a late morning siesta.

Millie's side of the bed is cold when I wake up. Of course it is, she's working in reception. She really needs to take a step back where the hotel is concerned. But I know Millie, and she won't. Her dedication to her staff and guests is just one of the many things that I love about her.

I reach for my phone, which is on the nightstand. A text message from my brother is displayed on the screen.

    Malachi: Lunch?

I flash a glance at the time. It's four fifteen p.m. We only have two hours until the meeting at the town hall. But that gives my brother and I enough time to grab a bite to eat. I click reply.

    Gage: Hotel restaurant, fifteen minutes.

I roll out of bed and straighten the covers. I will need to go to my room to get changed. But then it dawns on me that I'm not wearing a stitch of clothing. Thanks to my and Millie's shower escapade earlier, I am completely naked.

With my hands placed over my cock I make my way toward the bathroom. My intention is to grab one of the towelling robes. But that's when I notice one of my suits hanging up on the wardrobe door.

Millie must have taken my room key from my trouser pocket when I was sleeping and grabbed some clothes for me. I could kiss her for being so fucking awesome. In fact, I'll do just that when I see her next.

I pull on my salmon shirt, grey suit jacket and matching trousers and head for the bathroom. After taking a leak, I wash my hands and, opening the vanity, help myself to a floss stick. I can't help but smile when I look at the shower. Shower sex is definitely on the menu for later.

I use a small dollop of Millie's Lotus Flower face wash and toss the floss stick into the bin. I stop, however, when something poking out of the lid catches my attention.

Is that…? No, it can't be. I crouch down and retrieve a small pink and white box that confirms my fears.

A pregnancy test.

The cellophane is torn and the cardboard edges frayed from where it's been ripped open. My heart rate begins to pick up as I peer inside the open box.

I pluck out the stick and locate the small window with the words 'pregnant 3+' displayed on the digital screen. My heart slams in my chest at the reality of what I'm seeing. Up until now we've been careful and used protection, but even if we hadn't, the test dates back to before Millie and I first slept together.

Reality hits me square in the face. The woman I love is pregnant with another man's child. Was her suggestion of unprotected sex earlier a way to pin the baby on me? I'm filled by a tsunami of emotions and memories of the past. I can't deal with either right now, so push the pregnancy test stick into the breast pocket of my jacket and head out of the room to meet my brother.

The hotel is particularly busy today, with guests constantly stepping in my way. With my patience wearing thin, I weave in and out of people on my way to the restaurant. Malachi is already seated when I enter. I nod a quick acknowledgement before heading toward the buffet stands. I grab a plate and dish myself up a prawn salad and then head over toward our table.

"Afternoon," Malachi says before popping a calamari ring into his mouth.

"Afternoon." I yank out a chair and sit down.

"Trouble in paradise?" Malachi drawls.

"Everything's fine," I snap, and stab the prong of my fork into my salad bowl.

Malachi eyes me sceptically. "Judging from how you're attacking your lettuce I would say you're the antithesis of fine."

I drop my fork, causing it to clang against the side of my plate. "Just say 'opposite.'" My words are razor sharp, but I don't care. "I don't know why you and Father use all these fancy words when you speak. Is it to confuse people, or to make you look superior? Because if it is, it's not working."

Malachi quirks a brow. "Well, if you wanted the award for pettiness, you have it. Now are you going to cut the pretence and tell me what is up with you?"

I glower at my brother. He knows me so well. Too well, in fact, since I can't hide a single thing from him. But instead of meeting him head on, I decide that a change of subject is in order. "Tell me, because I'm curious as hell. What are you planning to do with the land you've bought on the island?"

"Oh, that." Malachi dabs the corners of his lips with his cotton napkin before reclining in his seat. "First, tell me, when are you having this place fixed up?" He motions his hand around the restaurant's god-ugly décor. Which, funnily enough, has been the topic of conversation between Millie and myself over the past few weeks.

"We are closing the hotel for the month of November when it's quiet. The plan is to have Cole and his team of builders fix up and modernise the place in time for Christmas. Now quit changing the subject. What are your plans for the land?"

As hurt as I am by Millie, I can't stop the loyalty I feel toward her. The island is her home, after all, and the place she loves. I can't let Malachi do anything to destroy that.

Malachi lifts his tumbler from the table and swirls his drink several times before speaking. "I thought my intentions would be obvious. I plan to build, of course."

I give him a 'no shit, Sherlock' look before gesturing for him to continue.

"There is a rather large, rather desolate plot of land surrounding the cliffs."

"By the lighthouse?" I ask.

"Yes, there. I plan on demolishing the lighthouse and building a thousand new homes on the land surrounding the cliffs."

I suck in a breath, a piece of cucumber momentarily getting wedged in my throat before I'm able to cough it up. "You what?" is all I am able to muster.

I'm not sure which is worse, the fact he plans on building a shit ton of houses here on the island or that he plans on having the lighthouse demolished. "You can't demolish the lighthouse," I protest. "It's iconic here on the island."

"Iconic or not, it'll have to go. I can't have a bright light shining in all the homes' windows."

"But Patricia and Rodney Walker live there, they're the island's eldest residents. You can't expect them to leave their home."

Malachi laughs. "Oh, I'm willing to bet that for the right price they could be persuaded. And besides, I've already spoken with Rodney. He mentioned that they are struggling with mobility and finding it increasingly challenging getting to and from town."

"How convenient," I deadpan.

"Indeed. I think a generous cheque and a brand-new bungalow would help to seal the deal."

Of course my brother has made sure all his ducks are lined up. He'd never leave anything to chance. But there may be something he hasn't considered.

"Are you forgetting, dear brother, that the beating heart of the island is the greenery and the quaintness? You take away those two fundamental ingredients, then the island loses its charm. And besides, the islanders will never agree."

Malachi shrugs. "Oh, I'm sure I can get them on side. And if not, so what? The plans will go ahead regardless."

"If their opinions don't matter then why bother holding a meeting at all?"

"Simply to show them the new changes that are coming. I'm keen to hear suggestions of how we can expand the island further. I'm thinking another school to compensate for the influx of people, maybe even a small college. More restaurants, a brand-new shopping centre, more fishing boats on the harbour…"

"More fishing boats? You'll put Millie's family out of work."

"I will do no such thing. More restaurants will bring more demand, thus opening up more jobs. It's a win-win."

When I say nothing, Malachi leans in. "I've offered Farrah and Lucian a plot of land for a house. I'm going to do the same for you, but instead of a house, what do you say to a plot of land to build a real hotel? Not like this dilapidated old thing. I'm talking about showing people what real luxury is like. And I have the perfect location for your new venture."

I sink back in my seat. "Humour me."

"Where the lighthouse currently stands. The views will be out of this world. You wanted the opportunity to build a business from scratch, well, I'm giving you that opportunity. What do you say?"

Malachi holds out his hand for me to shake.

A knock at the door has me looking up. "It's open," I call from the edge of the bed where I'm sitting.

The hinges squeak and light from the hallway seeps into my room as Millie lets herself in. "Oh, my God, Gage, what are you doing sitting in the dark?" There's humour in her voice as she flicks the switch and turns on the light.

She stands with her arms held out, as if to say 'what the hell?' I regard her for a moment. She looks so cute dressed in a lime-green summer dress. My gaze homes in on her stomach, which at the moment is flat. I can't help picture how she'll look with a baby bump.

I lower my gaze to the floor, my concentration fixed on the bottom of the half-empty bottle of Jack. Mr Daniels is always good at keeping me company when I hit rock bottom.

The floorboards creak as Millie makes her way toward me. "Gage, what's going on? The town meeting is in ten minutes. We're going to be late."

I wave her off. "You don't need to waste your time. My brother is planning on building a thousand new homes and demolishing the lighthouse."

"What?" she chokes out. "He can't do that. We've got to stop him."

I laugh, but it isn't with humour. "I don't think you understand, Millie. It's already done."

I reach to the floor, grab the bottle of Jack by the neck and unscrew the lid. I can sense Millie approach, but don't look up. Instead I stare at two lime-green shoes that stop inches in front of me.

"Gage…" Her voice breaks, and finally I peer up into her eyes. Those beautiful, smouldering brown eyes that I fell in love with.

Concern is etched on her face. She looks past me. Her gaze

homes in on the bed and the rather large suitcase that is lying on top. "What's going on?" she asks for the second time.

I get to my feet. "What's going on, sweetheart, is that I'm leaving." I open the breast pocket of my jacket, pull out the pregnancy test and place it in her hand. "Congratulations. I hope you and the father are very happy."

TWENTY-NINE

Millie

With shaky hands I peer down at a pregnancy test. "What the hell is this?" I ask.

"I thought that was pretty self-explanatory."

I'm looking at Gage, but the irony is he doesn't look anything like himself. His jaw is tight, so tight that it looks as though it could snap right off. The vibrant blue of his eyes is dull, verging on grey. I peer up at him with so much love in my eyes, but all I get is an icy coldness staring back.

He zips his suitcase and lugs it off the bed. "Now, if you'll excuse me, I have a helicopter to catch."

Gage makes his way toward the door with me on his heels. He grabs for the handle, but I push in front of him, slamming the door in its frame.

"Gage…" I hold up the test. "This isn't—"

"What I think?" he interrupts. "Sure it is. Now that's been clarified, Mildred, I'd like you to step out of my way."

Mildred. The use of my full name is like a knife to the heart.

Tears cloud my vision, and when I blink they roll one by one down my cheek.

A smidgen of emotion touches his face. But that smidgen is gone as quickly as it appeared. "You'll find the deeds to the hotel at reception. You got what you wanted. Stanton and Mills is all yours. Do with it as you please."

"I don't want it," I snap. "Not like this."

Owning the hotel is all I've ever wanted. I should be elated, but I'm not. I've grown accustomed to the idea of being an 'us', and not an 'I', in business and my personal life. I look past Gage toward the bottles lined up beside the bed. Then it becomes clear why he's acting this way. "You're drunk. This is the alcohol talking, not you."

Gage laughs. "Really?" He marches over to where a bottle of Jack Daniels lies and lifts it between us. "Last time I checked, my good friend Mr Daniels couldn't speak." He lifts the bottle to his ear for a beat to prove his point. "See? Nothing but silence." He directs the bottle toward my ear. "Here, listen for yourself."

The hurt I felt moments ago transforms into anger. Molten hot anger. I squeeze the pregnancy test in my fist and use the same hand to swipe the bottle away from me. The bottle takes flight and smashes against the wall behind us. There are tiny shards of glass everywhere, swimming in a puddle of gold liquid.

Gage looks at me, dumbfounded. "That was a perfectly good bottle of whiskey."

I could slap him across the face I'm so angry, but instead raise my clenched fist and slam the pregnancy test against his chest. "I don't know what game you're playing, but it ends now. And for the record, this pregnancy stick isn't mine." I open my fingers and let the test fall into the empty space between us.

Gage laughs. "Sure, and I suppose it magically found its way into your en suite bin?"

I frown. My en suite bin? He must be mistaken. Why would a pregnancy test be there?

"Oh, my God," I say and slap my hand to my mouth as realisation hits me.

Gage must sense my shift in emotion as some kind of affirmation. He smiles a sad smile. "I'm sorry, Mildred. I just can't be with someone who lies. You understand that, right?"

"I'm not lying." My voice is strong. "The test you found is Hayley's. She wanted to speak to me earlier, I guess to tell me I'm going to be an auntie."

Gage's rigid demeanour relaxes slightly. "How do I know you're not lying? Will you do a test to prove it to me?"

"Oh, my God, Gage, will you listen to yourself? And the answer to your question is no, I will not do a pregnancy test. If you don't believe me then go." I motion toward the door. "Go to your helicopter and go back to your old life."

We stand in silence. I watch him as he watches me. His expression is one of conflict. It's as though he wants to believe me, yet the seed of doubt has been planted, the seed that has sprouted the roots of possibility.

"Believe what you want." I crouch down beside the broken bottle and begin piling up shards of glass.

Gage crouches beside me. In my periphery, I can feel his gaze locked on me. I'm sure he's waiting for me to crack under the heat of his gaze. Long seconds pass before he snaps out of whatever trance he was in. "Please, allow me to tidy this up."

"I'm not pregnant," I say for what feels like the millionth time, my voice cracking. He attempts to wrap his arm around me, but I shake him off. "Just leave me alone, Gage."

"The test isn't yours, is it?" Finally the penny has dropped. His expression sobers and the bravado he wore moments ago has been washed away.

"No, Gage. The test is not mine." My tone is sharp.

"Millie, I'm so sorry." Again, he attempts to wrap his arm around me, and again I shake away his touch. "What can I say, what can I do to make this right?" he asks.

I stand. "You can unpack your case for starters, and then stop drinking. Because if life has taught me anything it's that you can't run from your problems, and you certainly can't drink them away."

"What the hell would you know about my problems? You've lived your safe little life on your safe little island all your life. You wouldn't know the first thing about pain. About watching the light that shone so brightly in your mother start to fade until finally it's snuffed out."

I open my mouth to speak but have nothing to say, because as much as I hate to admit it, he's right. I haven't felt the pain of losing a parent, nor have I had anything life-altering happen to me.

"Just as I thought," he almost gloats.

"So then talk to me. Make me understand."

He makes his way toward the window and peers out onto the sea. He stands tall, as though trying hard to maintain his composure, but that composure falters when his shoulders drop. "I was a teenager when my mum was diagnosed with cancer."

That sentence in itself is a hard fact to swallow. My teen years were when I needed my mother the most. I can't imagine her not being around.

"We lived in fucking purgatory while she went through years of gruelling treatments. Treatments that were tough on her not only physically, but mentally too. But it all amounted to nothing because she died. Our lives as we knew it turned to shit, and nothing was ever the same again."

It has taken hitting rock bottom for Gage to finally open up to me. I make my way toward him and place my palm on his back. I expect him to turn around. He doesn't.

"Will you tell me about your mum?" I ask. "What she was like. What her interests were."

"I can't." His breath catches. "It hurts too much to think about her. And the only thing I can do to numb the pain is drink. Lots of alcohol. I drink and keep drinking until I can no longer feel."

Here I am, with my palm resting against the back of a man who outwardly is strong, confident and put together, but who on the inside is falling apart. I feel the need to tell him that drink isn't the answer to his problems, but don't repeat myself. Not yet anyway. He's finally opening up to me, I can't let the moment pass. "And Daphne?"

His body tenses at the mention of her name. "I don't want to talk about her."

I lower my hand, and with it break the connection between us. "You can't keep me in the dark, Gage, not anymore. If you are unwilling to face your past and tell me everything, then we don't have a future."

He turns around and finally I see his face. It's the first time I've seen him look totally broken.

There's nothing to say in the moment, so I do the only thing I can. I wrap my arms around him and pull him close. He doesn't return the hug and instead stands ramrod straight.

"What did she do to hurt you so badly?" I lift his arms in an attempt to entice him to hug me back, but he doesn't. Physically he's right here, but mentally he's so detached. "Please talk to me. Please let me in."

"And I will." He shuffles free from my hold. "Right after I get myself a drink."

"No, you don't get to do that." I make my way across the room and toward the minibar. I yank the door open and scoop up the remaining bottles. Glass clinks together as I march toward the bathroom. And then one at a time I empty the contents of each bottle down the sink.

Gage leans against the door with his arms folded across his chest and watches me. "Feel better?" he asks.

"Not even a little." I shake my head. "This stops now. No more hiding behind the bottle. Talk to me."

"What the hell do you want me to say?" His voice rises an octave and echoes around the bathroom. "That she was a one-night stand who tricked me into marrying her because she convinced me she was carrying my child?"

Gage makes his way toward the bed and sits. He hangs his head. I sit beside him. "I never wanted to be a father. That is until I peered down at the scan picture and saw what I thought was my baby. Then it was like a switch flipped and from that moment I was totally invested. I gave up on a stake in Calloway Housebuilders so I could be there for her. I went to all of the hospital appointments with Daphne and even fitted out a nursery in my Shropshire estate. Finally I had a reason to live, a reason to be a better person."

I swallow the lump in my throat. "What happened?"

"Malachi happened." There is an undercurrent of resentment in his voice.

"What did he do?"

"The saying 'ignorance is bliss' is so true. You see, my brother didn't trust Daphne from the word go. He ran a background check on her and even went so far as to have her phone bugged. In doing so he discovered she was leading a double life—one with the baby's actual father and the other with me. They planned for me to bring up the baby. Then when they rinsed me of millions, they would stop me seeing the child altogether. And as I wasn't the biological father, there'd be nothing I could do about it."

It baffles me how someone could be so damn cruel.

"It's for that reason I can't, I won't bring up another man's child. I couldn't lose both the woman and child I love." He holds out his arms to exaggerate his point. "There's only so much hurt one person can take."

His words wrap around my heart and squeeze so tightly that it hurts. A silence hangs over us, a silence that neither one of us wants to break.

Seconds turn to minutes, and then without a word Gage stands, makes his way across the room and, retrieving his suitcase, lugs it onto the bed.

I'm not sure if after his revelation he wants company or space, but I watch as he begins unpacking his case. He stops what he's doing for a second and, with his back toward me, reaches down and retrieves one of the half empty bottles of beer. My breath catches in my throat as I watch him bring the bottle toward his face. He pauses for a beat, as if thinking better of it, then turns around and makes his way toward the bathroom.

I hurry after him. "What are you doing?"

He passes me the bottle. "Do you want to do the honours?"

He doesn't need to ask me twice. I take the bottle and tip the remaining contents down the sink. I look at his reflection through the mirror. "Does this mean you're teetotal?"

Gage laughs. "I'm not an alcoholic, Millie. I don't need drink to function every day. The alcohol serves merely as a distraction. But I think it's about time I find something else to distract myself with."

He quirks a brow. That one small action has my stomach lurching. I spin around and, leaning my ass against the sink, ask, "And what kind of distraction do you have in mind?"

Gage closes the bathroom door, and, with a look of hunger in his gaze, makes his way toward me.

THIRTY

Gage

The town hall meeting finished hours ago. Millie and I did not attend and instead chose to indulge in some much-needed one-on-one time.

We lie in my bed together, her head resting on my bare chest while I run my fingers through her hair. There are so many things I want to say, need to say to her, except there are no words fitting enough to articulate just how sorry I am for the way I acted.

She rolls over so her chin rests on my biceps. "I've never been an auntie before. I wonder what sex the baby is," she muses. "I can so picture Hayley with a little girl. But I don't know how my brother will be with a daughter. She'll no doubt have him wrapped around her little finger."

I laugh and think of my own niece, Annabelle, and what softies she's turned all the men in the family into. Especially her father, my brother Lucian.

"I must remember to act surprised when she tells me."

I cringe, knowing I am responsible for taking that special moment away from Millie. "I'm so sorry," I begin, only to have Millie place her finger over my lips.

"Will you stop apologising? As far as Hayley knows, I'll have heard the good news from her." Millie pulls her best 'oh, my God, you're kidding' face. She even goes so far as to slap her hand over her mouth. "See? I'm a natural. I can definitely pull off surprised."

I roll my eyes. "Sweetheart, your acting skills leave a lot to be desired."

She nudges me playfully, and I nudge her right back.

"I'm sure I'll be more convincing in the moment. I mean, if I can fake a believable orgasm, I'm sure I can fake surprise."

It takes a second for her words to register, but when they do I give her bare ass a playful squeeze. "You and I both know there was nothing fake about the way you screamed my name when you came for me."

"I didn't scream your name." Her words are hushed and her cheeks glow crimson. I love that little bit of innocence she has intact. Even after our bedroom antics she still gets embarrassed.

Millie chews on her bottom lip. I can see there is something she wants to say to me, yet she is deciding how best to say it.

"You do want children, one day," she finally says.

"I do." I don't even have to think about my answer. "I want the loud, messy and disobedient kind."

She lets out a laugh. "Like their father then."

I don't know where this side of Millie has come from, but it's as cute as hell. "Me? Loud, yes. Messy, debatable. But disobedient? Never. Just say the word and I'll roll over."

By roll over I would take Millie with me, thus positioning me on top of her. The fact we are both naked would more than likely lead to another round of sex. To my disappointment Millie doesn't utter the words 'roll over', and instead lets out a low sigh. "I'd like kids too one day. But not any time soon. I see kids being at least five years off."

I nod. "I can work with that. Let's call it our five-year plan."

"And what about the years between?"

I kiss the top of her head and silently envision what our future will hold, the places I want to take her and the cultures I'd like her to experience. "Those will be our years," I finally say. "It'll be time that is ours to do with it whatever we please. I want to take you places—the Royal Opera House for a start, Paris, Rome. I want to show you the world."

She gives me a lopsided kind of smile. "And I suppose you're going to need your magic carpet to do that?"

Magic and fairytales died a long time ago for me. But I don't tell Millie that. "I'm afraid the magic carpet is out of order, so you'll have to settle for my private jet."

She breaks eye contact for a second and with her index finger draws invisible circles on my chest. "Will those places be busy? Because if they are…" Her words trail off, her whole body tensing.

I didn't realise how big of a deal being around a lot of people is to Millie. It's way out of her comfort zone to the point she feels uncomfortable. I won't do anything that'll compromise her happiness. "They are, but they don't need to be. I will book the entire Opera House just for us. And when it comes to travelling, I will book the most secluded places I can find."

"What about Stanton and Mills…?" Her words trail off.

"Your hotel will still be here when we get back," I assure her.

She shakes her head. "You mean *our* hotel."

"No. I signed the deeds over to you a week ago. I was planning to tell you at the surprise party next week."

"What surprise party?"

I tap the end of her nose. "The one that was meant to be a surprise. I wanted all eyes on the hotel for the big reveal."

"Big reveal?" she questions, only this time I don't explain.

"You will have to wait and see."

The next morning Millie and I go for our six a.m. run. Millie has an earbud pressed into her left ear and I have the other pressed into my right. I can't say that I'm in love with her classical playlist, but I'm learning to tolerate it.

It's a stunning morning. The sun is shining high and the sky is a vibrant blue. Oddly enough everything seems too perfect, kind of like the calm before the storm. And after last night's town meeting, I'm expecting a full-on tsunami.

"Keep up, slowcoach," Millie taunts.

"I'm going as quick as I can," I lie. We run in step with one another, though I often fall behind. Not because I'm struggling to keep up—no, I like to check out my girlfriend's arse in her tight little tracksuit bottoms.

We're about to turn around and head back to the hotel when we catch sight of some of the islanders. Mary Adams, Reverend Mortimer, and Rex Mitchell are gathered together in a small group. I know they saw us but are opting not to acknowledge us.

"Good morning," we call. I even go so far as to wave.

"Morning, Millie," Mary Adams calls back and completely blanks me.

I side-eye Millie, who shrugs. "What's up with them?"

"Guess they're not happy about the changes to the island my brother has proposed," I say, and, turning around, head back in the direction of the hotel.

"But that's him, not you," Millie says and runs at my side.

"The sayings 'tarred with the same brush' and 'guilty by association' come to mind."

Millie rolls her eyes. "That's stupid."

"It is, but that's people for you." To say I'm pissed is an

understatement. I'm not pissed at the islanders, but at my brother for his ludicrous ideas to ruin this beautiful island, and for what? Just so he can line his pockets? It isn't right.

"Here," I say, and hand Millie back her earbud.

She frowns. "But I thought we were listening to my playlist together."

"It's all yours; I'm going to run ahead." I don't tell Millie why, and instead pick up my pace and run back to the hotel.

Like Millie, I run where the sea moments ago left the shore, where the sand is firm and where it's easier to run. My breaths are heavy as I near the hotel, and when I look back Millie is nowhere in sight.

I jog up the concrete steps and make my way into Stanton and Mills. Right away I can pick up on the frosty atmosphere. Tanya, who always greets me with a smile, avoids eye contact with me altogether. Is this what life is going to be like from here on out because of my brother?

The large ornamental clock that hangs up behind reception says it's eight-forty. I head straight for the restaurant. I scour the sea of faces, but I don't need to. Malachi is sitting in the same place he sits every morning when he comes down for breakfast: the table beside the window that is the furthest away from the buffet stands. I jog my way toward him and, pulling out the seat opposite, sit down.

Malachi acknowledges me with a nod.

"The islanders aren't happy," I blurt out.

"They'll get over it," Malachi says, buttering a piece of toast.

I shake my head. "No, brother, I don't think they will."

"Change is hard for people to accept. But trust me, little brother, once they see that the changes are for the best, they'll thank me." Malachi takes a bite of the toast and takes his time chewing.

"But what if they don't?"

Malachi lets out a laugh. "I'm afraid that is for them to live with. And besides, we'll be long gone by then."

"No. It will be *you* who will be long gone," I correct.

Malachi's eyes snap to mine. "You're not seriously telling me you plan on staying here? Your life, your work is in London. You're willing to leave all that behind for some girl?"

"She's not just some girl, Malachi. She's *the* girl."

Malachi lowers his toast. It would seem that I finally have his full attention. "I'm sorry, but if she really is the one, then she'd know how important your career is and would move to London for you."

I shake my head. "But that's the thing, I wouldn't ask her to. I don't want her to leave the life she's built or her family behind for me."

"Yet you will do it for her?"

"In a heartbeat." I allow my words to sink in. I want Malachi to know just how serious I am. "Come on, Malachi, you and I both know I don't have a home back in London. I drift from estate to estate, hotel to hotel. I finally feel like I'm in a place I can call home, and it's right here with Millie."

Malachi steeples his hands on the table. "Let me get this straight. First you sign over Stanton and Mills to her, then you leave your life, your family behind. You're doing all this sacrifice for her. Tell me, brother, what is it she's sacrificing for you?"

Trust him to look at everything analytically. "It's not a contest."

Malachi narrows his eyes. "Good job it isn't, because you would win the prize for being the biggest pushover. Love is a two-way street of give and take, you know that."

"But she's given me the only thing I want from her."

I have sparked my brother's interest, and he rests his elbows on the table and leans forward. "And what would that be?"

"Her heart."

I expect my brother to start laughing, but he doesn't. He

studies me with a strange kind of fascination. "And I gather demolishing the lighthouse along with building the new houses would make your life here less enjoyable?"

I nod, and decide to put it in layman's terms. "You don't shit where you sleep."

"Indeed." Malachi removes his elbows from the table and sits tall. "It's quite the predicament we find ourselves in. It would seem we have a conflict of interests."

"So it would seem," I retort. "The question is, what are you going to do about it?"

Malachi's expression is stoic. "What do you propose?"

"Let me buy the land from you. Just name your price."

Malachi doesn't answer right away, and we sit surrounded by a strange wall of silence. He finishes his breakfast of two poached eggs, a slice of toast and a rasher of bacon. My mouth starts to water and my stomach rumbles at the scent of the food. Yet nothing provokes me to move, not so much as a muscle. Not until I have heard Malachi's answer.

"There you are," Millie says. I look up as she makes her way toward our table. Millie doesn't pull out a chair, and instead stands to my right. She places her hand on my shoulder, and I place my hand over hers. I turn my head so I'm able to see her. She frowns, looking between me and Malachi. The atmosphere must be so tense that she feels it too. "I'm sorry. Am I interrupting something?" Millie attempts to pull her hand free from mine, but I tighten my grip on her so she can't go.

"Not a thing, I was just leaving." Malachi dabs the corner of his mouth with a napkin before placing it on his empty plate. Malachi stands, as do I.

"No," I say my tone sharp. "You don't get to leave before you tell me what you plan to do with the land."

Malachi yawns. "Oh, that. I have had a change of heart and have decided that there is no money to be made here. The plot of land, like the island, is of no use to me. And for that reason, I will be signing the land over to you, brother. Do with it as you please."

My jaw is about to hit the table.

"Oh, my God, are you serious?" Millie screeches. Heads turn, and the attention of the restaurant lands on us.

I could hug the shit out of my brother right now. In fact, I'm going to do just that. I release Millie's hand and round the table toward Malachi, who lifts his hand, creating a barrier between us. That's right, I forgot my brother doesn't do physical contact.

"Malachi, I don't know what to say."

Malachi shrugs my comment off. "There is nothing to say. There is a substantial plot of land in Staffordshire with my name written all over it. I believe it's where the paper mill factory once stood. I will have my team of builders direct their efforts there."

It hasn't gone unnoticed that over the years Malachi has had my and my siblings' backs—granted, not every time we found ourselves in difficulty, but when it mattered. I extend my hand in way of thanks. Thanks for now and every time before. But as always, Malachi is too damn stubborn to accept. He politely declines by way of clasping his hands behind his back. "There is actually an estate home that has been put up for sale nearby. I'm growing quite bored of living in Scotland and feel like it's time for a change of scenery."

"In other words, you've managed to piss off all the locals and have no choice other than to relocate."

Malachi flashes me a devilish smile. "Naturally." With that, my brother leaves the restaurant.

Millie wraps her arms around me. "We'll have to tell everyone the good news."

I hug her back. "No need. We only need to tell one person."

She looks at me with a question in her eyes. "Who?"

That's easy. "Mary Adams, of course. If you tell her, I'm sure everyone will be fully in the loop by this afternoon."

Millie laughs. "Spoken like a true islander."

I smile. "About that…" I think it's time I spoke to her about my plans to live on the island. We need to discuss how our relationship will work with me having to commute from time to time to check in with my hotels. "What do you say we have a little chat over breakfast?"

THIRTY-ONE

Millie

A week has flown by, and so much has changed in that short space of time. Most important is everyone's change of attitude toward Gage and his brother. Once treated like the island outcasts, they are now held in very high regard. So much so that everyone goes out of their way to greet them.

Gage has had every islander want to speak with him privately. He is getting inundated with suggestions of how he could improve the island for its residents. Suggestions like an outdoor swimming pool and a leisure complex have been mentioned, as well as a nature reserve and even something as outlandish as a zoo.

With too many ideas to keep track of, Gage has arranged for a town meeting to be held in the coming weeks where residents can come together and brainstorm what we'd like to happen with the land, though Gage has made it clear he will only build on a small area, his words being that he 'doesn't want the island to lose its charm'. With the exception of a house he is building for us, he wants the land to remain mostly untouched.

I have been given very clear instructions not to snoop on the construction work going on. That our house, once complete, is to be a surprise. Which reminds me.

"How much longer are we meant to stay away from the hotel?" I ask.

Gage peers down at his watch. "At least another hour."

An hour to make ourselves scarce while the staff set up my surprise party, the one I'm not meant to know about. I've had practice with my 'fake surprise' face—in fact, I got to use it three days ago when Hayley and Travis finally told us their good news. It's official, I'm going to be an auntie. But one thing I didn't fake was the tears of joy that rolled down my cheeks.

"How much further is it?" Gage complains as I pick up my pace and walk ahead.

"Almost there."

Up until now the cliffs have stood in a long-unified line, like a chain-link fence. Though one of the links is broken, and in its place is a large fissure in the shape of a horseshoe. Inside is a mass of rock pools that are perfect for crabbing. I step off the soft sand onto jagged rocks and shingle. I dodge the rock pools as I step and am careful not to fall over.

"Please tell me this isn't it? That we haven't walked three hours for a bunch of rocks?" Gage's voice echoes around us, ricocheting off the cliffs.

"No, it's so much more. If you look closely at the cliffs, you'll see an opening." I take his hand and guide him inside. "This is a cave that only islanders know about. It's kind of our little secret. A secret that I want to share with you, now that you're officially an islander."

Gage follows me through a network of dank passageways. Our shoes splash in the puddles as we make our way deeper inside.

"What happens if the tide comes in?" Gage asks, his hand tensing.

I shrug off his comment. "Oh, you know, we'll get trapped inside and likely drown."

I don't tell him that very scenario almost happened to me and my brothers. As teenagers we lost track of time, and it was only when water started to make its way inside that we hurried to get out.

"Is it a good time to mention that I get claustrophobic?" Gage is barely able to squeeze through the narrow opening.

"You'll be fine," I assure him, and give his hand a tug. "We're almost there."

After walking through an even narrower passageway, we finally make it to a large cave. Gage stops walking, his mouth agape. "Wow, Millie, this is something else."

I feel so full of pride. "It really is."

Where I imagine the heart of the cliff to be is our secret cave. Light pours in from tiny fissures, light that when reflecting off the walls into the chasm below gives off a kaleidoscope of colour.

We walk a little further in, stepping between the stalagmites that reach up from the ground like crooked fingers. We stop walking when we reach the edge of inky water.

"My brothers and I would come here all the time when I was a child," I muse. "Fully dressed, Travis and Bruce would jump in, while Austin and I watched from a safe distance. You know, it's pretty deep in the centre."

I smile and think back to my childhood, to how close my siblings and I were and still are. "Travis was such a trickster. He convinced me the cave was haunted by ghost mermaids who only ate little girls. When we came down here, he'd make spooky noises that echoed off the cave walls."

Gage gestures toward the water. "Fancy a dip?"

I laugh. "Not on your life. The water is ice cold."

Gage kicks off his shoes and tugs off his socks. "Okay. How about a paddle instead? We'll stay in the shallow part so the mermaids can't get you."

"Very funny," I say with zero humour in my voice.

I kick off my shoes and Gage and I dip our feet into the water. The cold pierces my skin like a thousand tiny blades. While I recoil at the sensation, Gage seems completely unaffected. He rolls his trousers up and walks a little deeper.

I open my arms out. "What the hell? Were you a polar bear in your past life?"

"Maybe." He laughs. "But in this life I am accustomed to extreme cold, courtesy of the ice experience and plunge pools at my hotel spas."

The igloo room comes to mind. I don't know who in their right mind chooses a room filled with snow to relax in.

"What do you say to us building a spa at Stanton and Mills? We don't need anything as big as at the Calloway Hotel in Knightsbridge, but we could definitely add some luxury to the place."

I contemplate his words. "A spa would be expensive."

"I'll pay for it."

"No, you will not." My tone is sharp.

Gage wouldn't accept a penny from me for his share of the hotel, which has left me with a substantial amount of money I saved over the years. Money I am using to do the place up. I've budgeted enough to give each room new carpets, a fresh lick of paint, brand-new furniture and not forgetting top-of-the-range fixtures and fittings. I've also included new hoovers for my cleaning staff. I have been thorough with my attention to detail so that the next time I take a look at TripAdvisor all customers have to complain about is the time it takes them to get room service. But Gage is right, a spa would add a real sense of luxury to the place.

"Let's see how much money I have left over when everything is done," I say.

"How about you shut the fuck up and let me buy my woman a damn spa."

I choke out a laugh. "I said n—" Though the final syllable is stolen as Gage presses a kiss to my lips.

I wrap my arm around his neck and pull him closer. I love how familiar we are with one another. Even with my eyes closed I'd know his touch, his caress, the feel of his full lips against mine, and his scent. It's as though the uniqueness of Gage has been forever branded into my subconscious.

I love how he rudely barged his way into my life and somehow made me complete. I lower my hand between us and rub at the outline of his cock. I'm not surprised that he is hard.

Gage breaks the kiss. "As much as he wants to come out and play, sadly we don't have time."

I tug at his belt. The metal buckle clangs as I unfasten it. "Are you sure about that?"

Gage's eyes are hooded. "Millie Mills, you are a bad influence."

Water whooshes and rains down from my calves as he scoops me up. Instinctively I wrap my legs around him. Luckily, I had a suspicion that sex might be on the menu this evening, so as well as a dress I wore panties that would be easy to tug to the side. Gage walks us out of the water and around the cave. My guess is he's trying to find somewhere to lay me down.

"Fuck it," Gage growls, and leans me against the cave wall. There is no time for foreplay, no time for caresses and long lingering kisses. This is going to be fast, this is going to be raw, and this is going to be as hot as hell. One-handed, he pulls down his trousers and boxer briefs and sweeps my undies to the side. He uses the head of his cock to rub against my clit before pushing himself deep inside me.

My cries echo all around us as he takes me against the cave

wall. The rocks are damp and rough. The jagged edges dig into my back, but I don't care.

"Yes," I cry out, and fist my fingers in his hair. I lean my head to the side and Gage assaults my bare skin with molten hot kisses. He sucks and nips me, and I love it. I pull his ass closer with my feet, causing him to go deeper. There is something almost primal in the way he is taking me, almost like we have been transported back to cavemen time. Skin slaps against skin and teeth clang together in a frenzy as we strive to find our climax, our release. He thrusts harder until finally he stills. His cock pulsates inside me. I love that we no longer use condoms, that him going in bareback is just one less barrier between us.

"I love you, Millie," Gage breathes into my hair.

"And I love you right back. With all my heart." I can sense him pull away, but I'm not ready for him to go just yet. I cling on to him and keep him inside me for as long as possible. Finally when he is out, he tucks his cock back into his boxers, and re-fastens his trousers.

"You are a bad influence," he tsks.

I laugh. "I am."

Warm come drips down my thighs, and when Gage lowers me to the ground, I make my way into the water. I lift the skirt of my dress and wade out, not stopping until the icy cold laps against my knees. I scoop up the water to rid my thighs of any trace of our lovemaking.

"We will freshen up at the hotel before we join the guests. Now come on, Millie. You can't be late for your surprise party."

I join Gage and together we make our way out of the cave, through the network of passageways and back on to the beach. I can just about make out Stanton and Mills in the distance.

"It's a good job we hired a taxi to take us back or we'd never make it in time," Gage says, and we take a quick walk along the beach. It takes fifteen minutes to reach the wooden groynes that divide the beach and a further ten minutes to reach the steps that lead up onto the land. Our taxi is parked up on a side road waiting for us.

Gage links his fingers with mine, and, bringing our joined hands to his lips, places a kiss on the back of my hand. "Are you ready for an evening you'll never forget?"

THIRTY-TWO

Millie

"You look ravishing this evening," Gage says as we make our way through the hotel lobby. "Like a chocolate liqueur that has been nicely wrapped. One I will take great pleasure unwrapping later."

I blush at his comment. Upon returning to my hotel room, not only was it filled with dozens of champagne-coloured roses, but a champagne-coloured gown was laid out on my bed in readiness. An A-line gown that fits my body like a glove.

It's obvious that Gage has put a lot of thought into this evening. He hasn't left out a single detail. Not only are the dress and flowers colour-coordinated, but so are Gage's tailored suit and matching bow tie. We couldn't look more together if we tried, like two halves of a whole, and whole is exactly how he makes me feel.

Gage takes hold of the glass door that leads outside to the beach, though the door as well as the floor-to-ceiling windows have been covered with gold tissue paper to prevent me from seeing out. Gage doesn't make a move to push the door open, and instead stares straight at me.

Feeling on show all of a sudden, I try to push my hair forward so it covers my face, only for Gage to brush it behind my ear.

I side-eye him. "What are you looking at?"

His smile is so damn sexy. "I'm taking a mental snapshot of you in this moment. Because the next time you walk through this door, you will do so with your head held higher."

I frown at his comment. "What do you mean?"

Gage doesn't answer. He pushes open the door, and before I can take in my surroundings we are hit by an explosion of colour.

"Surprise!" voices bellow.

I can't see anything through the multicoloured confetti that rains down around us from every direction.

"Oh, my God, you guys." I release Gage's hand to wipe my eyes, but when I reach for his hand again it's gone.

Just as the confetti starts to settle, another confetti bomb is released. This time champagne-coloured confetti rains down around me. I smile, because I just know that one was from Gage.

Tiny paper squares settle on my shoulders, my chest and my eyelashes. I blink them away and am finally able to see.

There are hundreds of people lining the lounging area and gathered on the beach below. If I didn't know better, I'd say that as well as the hotel occupants every island resident and his dog is in attendance. I laugh at the irony of that as Mr Porter and George come into view.

Gage materialises at my side and gives my arm a soft squeeze. Oh, right, this is the part where I'm supposed to act surprised.

I slap my hand to my mouth. "My God, what a surprise."

I side-eye Gage, who does nothing to hide his amusement. Maybe my surprised act was a little OTT, but I'm rolling with it.

Gage clears his throat. "I invited everyone here to bear witness to something that is a long time overdue."

My stomach lurches. *My God, is he going to propose?* My legs feel like jelly, wobbly and unsteady.

Gage takes my trembling hands and turns me so that I'm facing him. My body tingles in anticipation, from my head all the way down to my toes. I nod, silently goading him to say the words.

"Millie Mills, you've dedicated so much of yourself to the hotel, to the staff and your guests."

I frown. It's not exactly the words I'd envisioned him saying, but I'm sure he has a point.

Gage points toward the hotel, and more specifically the sign. Except it no longer reads 'Stanton and Mills Hotel'. In bold champagne-coloured letters with a black emboss it reads 'Mills Hotel'.

I gasp in a breath. "Oh, my God."

My stomach feels like it's turning a million somersaults. Hot tears stream down my face. I don't know what to do, don't know what to say. Hell, I don't even know if I'm breathing. I do the only thing that makes sense, and that is to squeeze my boyfriend in a tight hug.

People come at us from all directions. They congratulate me and clap me on the shoulder, offering kind words of support. But the sheer mass of people closing in on me has me on edge. Island residents and staff are everywhere I look, and suddenly the sea of faces feels like a sea that I'm drowning in.

My heartbeat begins to pick up pace, thumping harder and harder. Not only can I feel it in my chest, but I can hear its beats echo in my ears.

"Gage." I look to my boyfriend as he shakes people's hands. But I don't see him as anything other than a lifejacket in this moment, one that'll keep me afloat.

"This is too much," I choke out. Feeling the need to escape, I take a few steps back toward the door.

The smile Gage wears drops. Then, like my knight in shining armour, he stands in front of me and addresses the crowd. "Can everybody give Millie some space." He motions toward the beach and at the long line of tables filled with trays of food. "Please help yourself to the buffet before the firework display."

People make their way down the concrete steps to the beach. My staff are there in readiness and help people plate up food. Music begins to play from a DJ box that has been set up inside the gazebo. It's quite comical to see some of the elderly residents sway their hips in time to the music.

It takes a while for my anxiety levels to calm and for my breathing to return to normal. When it does, I focus on Gage, who hasn't left my side. What the hell do I say to this man who has given me so much? I'll save all the soppy stuff for later when we're alone. For now, I will keep everything lighthearted.

"You really are pulling out all the stops," I say.

Gage starts the arduous task of picking confetti squares from my hair. "You mentioned there'd be an island party when it reached a thousand residents."

I nod.

"Well, I don't see that happening any time soon, especially as the houses aren't being built. So, I figured we'd give the islanders a long-overdue party while celebrating your new business venture."

Telling Gage I love him just doesn't seem enough right now. They say actions speak louder than words, and I believe in that sentiment. I lean on the tips of my toes and press a kiss to his cheek.

"Thank you," I mutter.

"I don't want you to thank me."

"Then what can I do to show you how much I appreciate all you've done?"

He glides his fingers across his chin. "I want you to make me proud, but more importantly, I want you to make yourself proud."

I can't help wonder what I did so right in this life and the one before to get someone as amazing as Gage.

A bottle of beer swooshes between us as Malachi appears. "One for the road?"

Gage doesn't take the beer, and instead raises his hand. "No, thank you, brother."

Malachi looks at Gage as though he's grown a second head. Since the pregnancy test fiasco, Gage has stopped drinking altogether. It appears he has something to prove, that being that his life isn't defined by the bottle.

Malachi taps on the face of his watch. "Tick-tock, little brother."

I frown. "What's he talking about?"

Gage leans into me. "When I arranged your surprise party, I'd completely forgotten about the annual Pink Ribbon Breast Cancer Charity Gala back home. I didn't want to rearrange your party, so instead we decided to go to both."

"We?"

"Yes, my siblings and I." He motions toward Farrah. She is standing close to the DJ booth. A scarlet dress hugs her curves, with a corseted bodice that pulls her in at the waist. The colour and the cut accentuate her slim physique. She is talking to my brother, Bruce, a cocktail in her hand. She sees me and smiles, and I smile right back. There is something so likeable about Farrah.

I return my attention to Gage. "But how can you be in two places at once?"

He flashes a glance at his watch. "We can't. The helicopter is waiting for us out front. We leave in half an hour. I will be back as soon as I can get away."

I glance around at all the people here tonight, and as much as I love them, each and every one of them, I still can't help the overwhelming feeling creeping into my stomach from the sheer mass of bodies.

"But it's my surprise party, you can't leave me." More specifically, he can't leave me alone with all these people.

Gage's expression softens. He must be able to read my mind, I'm sure of it. He lifts my chin with his finger. "Exactly. This is *your* party. Your time to shine. Your parents and your brothers are here, Hayley's here, I'm sure you'll be fine with them until I get back."

I swallow the burning lump in my throat. "But I want you to stay."

"I'm sorry, Millie, as much as I want to stay this is one event I can't miss." Gage clears his throat, once, twice before nodding toward the bar. "Please, excuse me. It would seem as though I have a frog in my throat."

Gage heads toward the quaint wooden hut that is serving drinks and gets in line. Leaving me with his brother. I smile, though Malachi doesn't return the gesture. With a reggae song playing in the background Malachi silently regards me.

With my anxiety levels already heightened, I find his silence particularly jarring. "Jesus, Malachi, will you speak already? You're making me nervous."

His brows shoot up at my forthrightness. Honestly, I surprised myself too.

Malachi places one hand in the front pocket of his jacket. He has a way about him that always makes him appear superior to everyone else in his company. "I've had nothing but respect for you, Millie," he finally says. "That is until right now."

His words come out of nowhere and hit me like a slap across the face. I open my arms. "I didn't ask him to sign the hotel over to me. In fact I said the opposite."

Malachi takes a step toward me. I hold my ground. "I'm not talking about the hotel, Millie. What my brother chooses to do in business is of very little consequence to me."

I try hard to read the expression on his face. He doesn't look happy, nor does he appear annoyed. Malachi Calloway is a closed book, one that has been shut with a lock and key.

"So, then what?"

"The Pink Ribbon Breast Cancer Charity is very dear to us, due to our mother passing away from the disease. Although it brings us a lot of pleasure to donate to such a worthy cause, you must understand how hard it is for us to attend. I have a female friend meeting me there, Lucian has Chelsea, and Farrah mingles. But Gage, he is going to the event this evening completely alone."

Malachi's words slice through me. "But I didn't know about any of this before tonight." Gage didn't mention the charity gala until now. A charity gala that is being held in London and will be crowded with people. I swallow that thought away. "Besides, I can't leave my own party."

Malachi leans in close. "You're selfish, Millie."

"How am I selfish?" I challenge.

"Gage has given you so much and asked for nothing in return. If you love my brother half as much as you claim you do, then you'll be by his side at the charity gala."

My palms become clammy at the thought. "But there will be crowds of people there."

"There are crowds of people here, and you're managing just fine."

That's where Malachi is wrong. I am not managing at all. I've lived on the island all my life and am simply not used to a lot of people being around me. I don't know when the fear started or why, but it's there and it's real. "It's called masking, not managing."

Malachi studies me for a beat. "It would seem your decision has been made. Enjoy your party."

With those words, Malachi leaves me and heads for Farrah. He stalks up behind her and, with his hand on her shoulder, whispers something in her ear. She nods, and continues her conversation with my brother. My assumption is he's giving her a countdown as to how long she has left before they need to leave. From Farrah, Malachi makes his way toward Dante, who stands not far away.

"Here." Gage places a fluted glass of champagne in my hand. "It's time we get the party started." He brings the rim of his glass to his lips and takes a swig of his sparkling water.

"Are you sure you won't have a glass of champagne?" I ask, feeling bad that I'm drinking in front of him.

He shakes his head. "Nope. I've had my fill of alcohol to last me a lifetime."

I smile. "Okay."

Without everyone crowding around me I feel more at ease to mingle. I opt for familiarity first and head for my family.

"Mum, Dad," I say and wrap my arms around my mother. She looks lovely this evening dressed in a white maxi dress with a pattern of miniature hummingbirds.

"Your great-grandfather would be so proud of you," she says as we break the hug.

"Thanks, Mum."

"Mr Mills," Gage says to my dad, and then extends his hand.

"Now, son, you know I'm not much of a handshaker," Dad says, but reluctantly takes Gage's hand anyway. To my surprise my boyfriend pulls my dad into a hug.

"It's good to see you, Jonathan."

I can't believe what I'm seeing. This is the first time I've seen Gage willingly hug someone who isn't me. I smile to myself as Gage does that awkward-as-hell clap on Father's back before breaking the hug.

"How are you feeling today?" Gage asks.

"Oh, you know, I have my good days and bad."

By 'bad' my father is referring to when he's particularly tired and his speech is more slurred than normal. But as a rule, my father has made an excellent recovery.

After chatting with my parents, we make small talk with a few of the islanders and guests until finally I bump into Travis and Hayley. My brother is wearing a dark navy suit and Hayley a navy maxi dress. It seems that they also are into the whole 'couples matching' thing. Travis has his arm wrapped possessively around her back as they too mingle.

"Hi, Mommy and Daddy," I coo.

"Hi, Auntie Millie," Hayley coos right back.

"How are you feeling?"

Hayley lifts her hand and alternates between thumbs up and thumbs down. "It's pregnancy, you know how it is."

I laugh, because no, I don't know how it is to be pregnant, but decide to humour her anyway.

Our conversation is interrupted by Malachi, who steps between us. "I'm so sorry to cut in, but I'm going to have to steal my brother for a couple of hours." Malachi looks at me expectantly, but when I don't say anything he returns his attention to Gage. "The helicopter is waiting out front."

Malachi doesn't linger, he heads in the direction of the hotel with Farrah and Dante on his heels.

Gage tips his head back and finishes his sparkling water in one. "I'm really sorry, but I need to run. I will do my best to be back in time for the fireworks."

The fireworks are going off at midnight. That's only three hours away. There's no way he'll make it back. Gage leans into me and places a kiss on my forehead before turning his attention to Hayley and Travis. "Will you look after her while I'm gone?"

My brother Travis snorts a laugh. "Look after her? She isn't five."

Hayley shoots a glance at my brother, telling him to shut the hell up, before she wraps an arm around me. "Sure we will."

Gage smiles, seemingly satisfied that I have babysitters. He turns his back on us and heads toward the hotel to where his siblings are no doubt waiting for him.

"Travis, be a darling and go fetch us both a drink. An orange juice for me and a champagne for your lovely sister," Hayley all but demands.

Travis grunts out a sarcastic reply. I don't hear exactly what was said, but I do catch the word 'lapdog'.

"I love you too," Hayley purrs, and waves him off.

With Travis out of the way Hayley leans into me. "Will you

please tell your overbearing brother that my job at the hotel doesn't include heavy lifting? He wants me to quit and move in with him so he can basically do everything. Since when the hell did I need a man to do everything for me?"

Although I listen to Hayley, all I can think about is Gage getting in that helicopter and going to that charity gala alone.

Hayley shakes me. "Are you even listening?"

I shake my head. "No, I mean yes."

"Well, which is it?"

I lean forward and give my best friend a hug. "I have to go. Will you hold the fort for me while I'm gone?"

"Gone?" Hayley frowns, completely oblivious to what is going on, but I don't have time to stand around and explain. I run toward the hotel, through the door covered in tissue paper and into the lobby. I don't stop until I'm out of the front of the hotel.

The helicopter is on the asphalt not far away. The blades slowly rotate, but the landing skids haven't left the ground. The side door is still open, and I can see Gage and Malachi strapping themselves in.

"Gage!" I yell. I wave my arms as I hurry toward the helicopter.

He turns, about to close the door, but stops when he sees me. He leans forward in his seat and says something to the pilot. I have no idea what was said, but the blades slow until they come to a halt.

Out of breath, I make it to the helicopter.

"What are you doing?" Gage asks.

I smile big. "I'm coming with you to the charity gala."

"Millie, no, you'll miss your party."

I shrug. "I don't like fireworks much anyway."

The part about not liking fireworks is a total lie. But I would miss them if it meant being there for Gage.

Malachi, who is sitting beside Gage, unfastens his seat belt and, leaning out of the door, offers me his hand. "Here, let me help you up."

I'm sure I'm seeing things, but the guy actually smiles. Not a cold smile that causes the hairs on the back on my neck to stand up on end. No, this smile is warm and it's genuine.

I take Malachi's hand and he helps me up. He moves aside so I can take his seat, the one beside Gage. The second I sit down I am pulled into my boyfriend's arms.

"I couldn't love you any more than I do in this moment," he says.

I smile up into his crystal-blue eyes. "The feeling is mutual."

EPILOGUE

Millie
Months later

The scent of mulled wine, nutmeg and cinnamon are all around me as I carefully place the angel on top of the tree. "How's that?" I call.

Hayley gets up from her seat in the lobby and waddles a little closer. I can't help but smile at the woolly jumper she is wearing. It is a deep scarlet with tiny embroidered candy canes on the front and back. The words 'all I want for Christmas is you' are displayed on her chest with arrows pointing to her protruding stomach.

"I don't know, it doesn't look central," Hayley says, and makes that weird rectangle shape with her thumbs and pointer fingers, the one I imagine a film director doing.

"A little more to the left?" I ask and reposition the angel.

"No, that's too much. Try a little to the right," Hayley says.

Sighing, I move the angel again, before almost jumping out of my skin and off the ladder when Hayley screeches. "Stop! Don't move her another inch." I stand deadly still as Hayley tilts her head, first to the left, and then the right. "Perfect."

"I don't know about that," I say, scrutinising the porcelain figurine. She still doesn't look central from where I'm standing, but I've left Gage footing the ladders for the past fifteen minutes while I added the decorations to the top of the tree. I think it's about time I give the poor guy a chance to sit down.

I climb down one rung at a time, and as I reach the bottom Gage pulls me into a hug. I hug him right back.

"You've done a great job," he says.

I point between us. "I think you mean *we've* done a great job." He has to take some of the credit after all, as I didn't decorate the tree by myself. I break the hug, and, taking Gage's hand in mine, I step back and take everything in.

Our twenty-foot tree has been beautifully dressed in rose-gold decorations, from large floaty ribbons to floral baubles, tinsel, and Santa Clauses holding scrolls. Each scroll has a staff member's name written on it in beautiful calligraphy-style lettering.

"How are the presents coming along?" I call over to Tanya, who is stood at reception gift-wrapping empty cardboard boxes to put under the tree.

"Slowly," she calls, and cuts a long piece of tape.

"I'm good with that," I say, and mean it. I don't want anything rushed. Everything has to be perfect, which reminds me. My attention is back on the tree and, looking up, I scrunch my nose. "My God, Hayley, the angel looks like she's had too much mulled wine." How Hayley could say the positioning was perfect is absolutely beyond me.

"I've heard that pregnancy can affect your vision, so blame your niece." Hayley returns to her table, where her snowman-themed mug filled with hot chocolate and floating marshmallows waits.

"Will you relax?" Gage's voice finds its way into my ear.

"I can't," I say, rocking back and forth on my heels. "Something is missing. And I don't know what that something is."

"Lucy and Martha are busy Christmasing up the bedrooms as we speak."

By 'Christmasing up the bedrooms' he is referring to the wreaths I want hanging on every door, the sprigs of holly on the nightstands, and the stockings hanging from the newly fitted fireplaces.

"Do you think each room needs a Christmas tree?" I ask.

Gage laughs. "Take a look around. I think you've done enough."

I do just that. Our newly decorated lobby has been kitted out with the most ostentatious decorations ready for when the hotel reopens tomorrow and the first of our guests arrives. Life-sized nutcrackers stand at the foot of the stairs. Tinsel and baubles the size of small pumpkins line our bespoke banister. "I don't know, Gage, something is still missing, and I can't put my finger on what."

"Hey, guys, it's snowing," Tanya calls.

In the night sky I can just about make out tiny specks of white. They float down from the windows surrounding the Christmas tree. It isn't long before those tiny specks become a flurry of white.

I smile up into Gage's eyes. "That's it. That's what was missing."

Gage reaches into his jacket pocket and pulls out some green leaves that have been held together by a red ribbon. He lifts it between us and puckers his lips.

"Wait, is that…"

"Mistletoe, sweetheart. Now stop talking and kiss me."

I lean forward, our lips pressing together in a soft and sensual kiss. His tongue finds my tongue and he deepens the kiss.

"A-hem," a voice calls. Smiling into the kiss, I turn my head to the side.

Tanya stands, her hand on her hip. "It's six o'clock. Should I tell the others we're ready?"

Gage flashes a glance at his watch and nods. "Yes, go rally the troops."

Gage and I make our way toward the hotel restaurant. The scent of turkey, cranberry sauce and mulled wine is all around us as we enter. I stop and look around with pride. This is the first time I've seen the restaurant since the team of decorators came a month ago. They were busy adding the finishing touches this morning, and they certainly haven't disappointed.

The vast space no longer looks like something that fell out of the 1960s, but a classy area where guests can dine. The old tables have been replaced by new, which for this evening have been set in a long line. A fancy white tablecloth runs the full length with a long red runner from top to bottom. The tables are set with scented candles and Christmas-themed centrepieces.

Forty-five places have been set, each with plates, cutlery, and the obligatory Christmas cracker. This evening is an early Christmas celebration and is all about the staff. This is my way of thanking each and every one of them for the hard work and dedication they have put into the Mills Hotel. After dinner we will gather in the lobby and eat roast chestnuts.

Gage makes his way toward the head of the table and pulls out the seat. "My lady."

I chuckle like a damn teenager and make my way over. But I don't sit down, I won't sit until every staff member is here. Voices begin to echo from outside, and heels click on the tiled floor as my staff begin to enter. As requested, they are all wearing Christmas-themed jumpers. There are a range of designs from caricature Santas and snowmen, to jumpers that light up, to the more adult-themed jumpers with randy reindeers and a topless Mrs Clause.

I flash a glance at my own jumper and try not to laugh. I've never really been into the whole Christmas spirit before and have never bought a jumper for the occasion. However, my brother, Travis bought me one a few Christmases ago, depicting old St Nick himself smoking a spliff, with the words 'have a smokin' Christmas' written across my chest. I will need to buy myself a more appropriate jumper for when Christmas is here, but for now it will do.

Chair legs screech as chairs are pulled from beneath the table, but like me, everyone remains standing. The team of caterers Gage hired for the evening do their rounds up and down the table, filling glasses in readiness for the toast. When champagne flutes are filled I lift my glass.

"I'd like to make an announcement before the toast." I look down the tables at faces old and young. At my housekeepers, my team of gardeners and finally the receptionists.

I flash a quick glance at Gage, who nods. I'm actually doing this. I take a deep breath. "I would like to firstly thank everyone for your hard work. I appreciate each and every one of you here today. I don't see us as work colleagues, but an extended family. A family whom I trust with my life and my business." I let out a laugh. "So to get to the point, I am going to take a step back. Gage and I are planning a few holidays in the New Year, and on top of that we will be travelling to London at least once a month so Gage can check in with his own hotels. My visits will range from a few days to a few weeks. I know I'm leaving my hotel in good hands, but what I really need is a manager to oversee everything in my absence. The job includes a substantial pay rise. Application forms will be available at reception from Monday. I encourage everyone to apply."

Hushed whispers echo around the rooms as people talk amongst themselves. I smile at Gage and can't help feel as though this is where our adventure truly begins.

It took several trips to London for me to finally get control of my anxiety. It wasn't easy, and knowing that, we started small—a few hours here, an evening there, and very soon we were spending full weekends in different Calloway hotels. I can't say that I'm altogether comfortable with big crowds, but it's getting easier to cope.

Gage clears his throat. "Now, about that toast."

"Yes, the toast." I raise my glass. "To us, Team Mills Hotel."

Glasses are raised. "Mills Hotel!"

We all take a sip of champagne—that is, all of us with the exception of Hayley and Gage, whose glasses are filled with orange juice. One by one we take our seats.

I sit quietly and watch as staff make merry and get into the Christmas spirit. Crackers bang and it isn't long before everyone at the table is wearing paper crowns and reading cheesy jokes that came from the crackers.

Between frivolities the catering staff begin handing out starters, a mixture of prawn cocktails, bruschetta and stuffed mushrooms. I raise a brow at the waitress as she hands me a prawn cocktail. She clearly didn't get the memo that I hate fish.

"I'll take that," Gage says, and switches my bowl for his plate.

"Much better." I press the prong of my fork into the mushroom.

When everyone has eaten our plates are taken away and replaced by our main courses, from nut roasts and vegan wellingtons to finally the traditional dish of roast turkey with all the trimmings.

I can't help but grin like the Cheshire Cat as I watch everyone dig in. I am bursting with pride. Pride at how beautiful the hotel looks. Pride at the stunning spa Gage insisted on paying for. Pride at how amazing my staff are. I'm proud as hell that with the help of Gage, we have transformed a modest hotel into something of pure luxury. As beautiful as the hotel is, we have managed to keep a very important element, which is its home-away-from-home feel.

We finish our mains and desserts, and honestly, I don't think I can move from my seat. At least not for half an hour.

"Please, pass on my compliments to the chef," I say to Gage, and tap my rather full stomach.

"Why don't you thank him yourself?" Gage clicks his fingers at one of the waitresses, who hurries toward the kitchen. My eyes go wide as she re-emerges moments later with Daniel. He is dressed in the typical chef ensemble, complete with the signature hat.

"Oh, my God, Daniel!" I jump from my seat and run over to hug him. I haven't seen my best friend in person for what seems like a lifetime. "How are you?" I say, squeezing him tightly.

"I'm great. I've been working as head chef in the Calloway Hotel in Birmingham for the last few months."

"So I've heard. How's it going?"

Daniel wipes his brow with the back of his hand. "Amazing. I'm getting fantastic feedback."

"That's fantastic." I am so happy for Daniel and how far he has come from the guy who practised cooking in his mum's kitchen. "And what about your plans of opening your own restaurant?"

Daniel looks at Gage with a question in his gaze. I look between them for a beat. Gage finally nods.

Daniel leans in close. "It isn't common knowledge yet, but Gage is funding me."

"Funding you?" I question. "I don't understand."

"Gage is buying me a restaurant. All I have to do in return is to give him twenty-five percent of the profits for the first five years, and five percent for any years that follow."

I'm lost for words. "And my uncle? I don't suppose Gage has given him a hotel?"

Daniel laughs. "No. But actually, Malcolm is doing so amazingly running the Birmingham hotel that Gage may promote him to regional manager."

I genuinely am lost for words. I won't deny that my uncle was fantastic at running Stanton and Mills. And I guess he won't be as tight with money when it comes to the Calloway hotels, seeing as it's not coming directly from his pocket.

"It would seem you've both landed on your feet," I say.

Daniel nods toward the kitchen. "I need to get back, but I'm staying with my mum over the weekend. We must catch up."

I nudge his arm playfully. "Yes, it's only months overdue."

I retake my seat beside Gage and, leaning into him, say, "I can't thank you enough for what you have done for Daniel and my uncle. You didn't have to."

Gage shakes his head. "I'm not a philanthropist, Millie. I saw a lot of promise in Daniel. Promise I will see a great return on over the coming years. And as for your uncle, he has gone from strength to strength."

We remain seated around the table drinking wine, sharing jokes and stories. When conversations start to die down I sense it's time to move the evening along.

I get to my feet. "How about we take the party to the lobby, where there'll be music and roasted chestnuts?"

The older members of the party retire for the evening and we say our goodbyes. Jeffrey, my head gardener, carried on ahead and is already in the lobby when we arrive. He holds a large pan filled with chestnuts and heads toward the fireplace. Part of me is anxious that he'll set the place on fire, but he has assured me he has done this plenty of times before and knows what he's doing.

"Alexa, play Christmas songs," Tanya calls. "Alexa, dim the lights."

Hayley is the first to get to her feet and start to dance, followed by Tanya and Nadia. Gage helps the garden staff push the tables aside so the empty space can be used as a dance floor. A dance floor that is filled with bodies. Gage makes his way toward my chair and holds out his hand.

I shake my head. "You know as well as I do that I have two left feet."

"Well, it's a good job I'm not asking you to dance."

I frown. "Then what?"

"Come with me. A taxi is waiting outside."

"Taxi?" He isn't seriously suggesting we leave the hotel. I shoot a glance at Jeffrey, who is stoking the fire. My body stiffens. "Gage, I can't…"

Gage pulls me to my feet. "Relax. There are plenty of fire extinguishers around the place. And if that fails then the hotel has insurance."

"Are you trying to make me laugh or feel better? Because neither of those things are happening right now."

I'm sure my words fall on deaf ears as Gage continues on and guides me toward the door to leave.

"I'm serious," I say and attempt to pull my arm free.

"Jeffrey has everything under control," Gage says.

"I really, really don't think this is a good idea."

My words do little to perturb Gage. If anything he only walks quicker. He grabs my coat that is strewn over the reception desk as we pass and drapes it around my shoulders.

"Will you tell me what's so important that we have to leave this second?" This time when I pull my arm free, Gage releases me.

Gage's shoulders drop. "I guess we can rejoin the party if you don't want me to show you our home."

"Oh, my God, really?" I push my arms into the sleeves of my coat and fasten the buttons. "Let's go."

Gage walks ahead and opens the door that leads out of the hotel. "After you."

As much as I want to see our new home, I can't leave without doing one thing. "Jeffrey, no more roasting chestnuts till we return."

"You got it." Jeffrey gives me a two-fingered salute and places the pan on the hearth.

I'm overcome by a whirlwind of excitement as we head outside. We are surrounded by a flurry of white as snowflakes fall heavily around us. Our shoes crunch on the snow that has settled on the ground as we make our way toward the taxi.

Gage hurries in front so he can open the door. Without hesitation I slide in. True to my word, I stayed away from the plot of land where our new house was being built. Though I can't lie, I was tempted on more than one occasion to sneak over and take a look.

We pass through the town toward the cliffs. It isn't long before we pass the Snow Hub, a new leisure complex Gage has had built for the islanders. The leisure complex is complete with a fifty-metre pool, ice rink, and slopes for skiing and tobogganing. The Snow Hub isn't open yet, due to works still being carried out, but the builders are hopeful that they'll be finished early next year.

The taxi continues on down a narrow road lit by old-fashioned lanterns. It looks so quaint and idyllic, and I love it. A brand-new house comes into view, an adorable thatched cottage with the most breathtaking view of the sea. Light from inside seeps out from gaps in the thick curtains. I frown, and, looking up, notice smoke billowing up from the chimney. If I'm not mistaken, it would seem as though someone is already living here. But that can't be the case. Gage has obviously had someone sneak back and get the place set up in readiness for us.

I have my fingers poised on the buckle of my seat belt, ready to unfasten it and get out of the car. Except the car doesn't stop, it continues on up toward the cliffs.

"Erm, Gage?" I laugh and point behind us toward the cottage. "Our house?"

"That isn't our house," Gage says matter-of-factly.

"If not ours, then whose?"

Gage deadpans, "The Walkers', of course."

"As in Patricia and Rodney? I don't understand. They live in the bungalow attached to the lighthouse."

"They did. But as you know, they've been struggling with

mobility recently. It made sense for them to live closer to the town."

We're quiet as the car continues its journey up the cliff. The beacon from the lighthouse sporadically illuminates our way as it completes its three-hundred-and-sixty-degree rotation over the ocean. I can't help wonder if Gage has a demolition order on the building, seeing as no one is there to tend to it. But Gage knows what it means to me. Surely he wouldn't?

The thought has me shuffling in my seat. "If the Walkers are living in the cottage, then who is going to tend to the lighthouse?"

My question is answered when the lighthouse comes into view. The small bungalow that adjoined the structure before is gone and in its place is a contemporary white two-storey building.

Gage squeezes my hand. "We're here, sweetheart. Welcome home."

"No way," I say, completely dumbfounded. It is more than I could have ever imagined. "How the hell did you manage to keep this a secret for so long?" Surely someone knew the Walkers had moved out, and it only takes one person knowing for news to travel like wildfire.

"It wasn't a secret. I discussed my plans at a town meeting, and with everyone in agreement, I swore them to secrecy."

The taxi pulls up outside, and with shaky hands I unfasten my seat belt. Gage is first to get out of the car, and, rounding the vehicle, he opens my door. It doesn't feel as though I'm walking, but instead floating next to Gage.

We are bathed in light one minute and complete darkness the next from the rotating light above. My heart is pounding as we make it to the shelter of the wraparound porch and the front door. A front door that has been decorated with the most beautiful rose-gold Christmas wreath.

"My God, Gage, tell me I'm not dreaming," are the only words I can manage.

Gage laughs. "Perhaps, but you never have to wake up."

He reaches in his pocket. I expect him to pull out the key for the door. But instead he pulls out something else. It only becomes clear what that something is when the light is overhead. I stare down at a small red box. I look back to Gage, whose expression sobers. Without a word he crouches on one knee.

"What are you doing?" I stupidly ask.

Gage takes my hand in his. "You said a long time ago that the lighthouse represented home to you. Well, I've never associated home with a building or a location. Home to me is a person, and that person is you. You are my home, Millie, and this right here is our forever. The place I want us to grow our family. But I would really like it if you stepped through that door not as Millie Mills, but the future Mrs Calloway."

It's now I notice the wall plaque secured on the side of the building. A plaque that reads *The Calloways*.

Gage releases my hand and opens a small box, displaying a beautiful ring with a stunning diamond solitaire. "Would you do me the honour of becoming my wife?"

I gasp, and, bringing my palm toward my mouth, begin to nod and cry simultaneously. "Yes, I will, I do!"

Gage takes the ring from the cushioned pillow and glides it up my finger. Then, getting to his feet, he lifts me from the floor honeymoon-style and walks us inside our new home.

Closing the door behind us.

The end

Thank you for reading *A Billionaire's Promise*.

I hope you loved Millie and Gage's story.
If you'd be so kind, please leave a review.

Watch out for Malachi's story from the Calloway series. For updates about the release of his book, make sure you join my newsletter.

BOOKS BY LAURA RILEY

British billionaire romance

Charmed (co-written with April Wilson)
Captivated (co-written with April Wilson)

Stepping Stones series
Finding Our Forever
Yours to Keep
Falling Into Us

The Calloways
A Billionaire's Vow
A Billionaire's Promise
A Billionaire's Baby (coming soon)

ACKNOWLEDGEMENTS

I'd like to thank Louise Hallett and April Wilson for being amazing beta readers, for reading my first draft version right the way through to the finished project. RJ Locksley, my amazing editor. Wander Aguiar and his team for my cover image, Maria from Steamy Designs for my cover and Stacey from Champagne Book Design for my stunning formatting. Lastly a shout-out to blogger and special friend Nyla.

CONTACT ME

Join Laura Riley's mailing list at
http://eepurl.com/ds_fXj
for news and exclusive material.

Reading group
www.facebook.com/groups/1116820285338874

Facebook
www.facebook.com/authorlaurariley

Website
www.authorlaurariley.com

Instagram
www.instagram.com/author_laura_riley

TikTok
www.tiktok.com/@author_laura_riley

Printed in Great Britain
by Amazon